ASTRA AND FLONDRIX

SEAMUS CULLEN

ASTRA
AND
FLONDRIX

PANTHEON BOOKS

NEW YORK

First American Edition

Copyright © 1976 by Seamus Cullen

Library of Congress Cataloging in Publication Data

Cullen, Seamus, 1927 —
Astra and Flondrix.

I. Title.
PZ4.C9627As3   [PS 3553.U3]   813'.5'4   76-53815
ISBN 0-394-73339-8

Manufactured in the United States of America

To Herbie Brennan,
magus-friend, without whose advice, encouragement
and unshakable faith this work might never have
seen the light.

TABLE OF CONTENTS

THE WORLD OF MEN

Igorin (who becomes Flondrix of the Elvan World)
King Barlocks (The Dark King)
Ungar, a Shepherdess and Igorin's Foster Mother
Gonzola, the Dark King's Magician
   (also known as Dr Roland Warner)
Sordo, Magician to the Dwarfs
Bumbree, the Horrible Witch of the Creepy
   Cottage
Lord Rodney de Minge,
   Baron of the Enderlands and the King's Commander

THE ELVAN WORLD OF THE SACRED GLADE

Glortan The Great, King of the Elves
Aureen, Queen of the Elves
Glortina, Elvan Princess and Glortan's Sister
Astra, Daughter to Glortan and Aureen
   (also known as Barletta)
Sylvor, an Archer

VISITORS FROM ELVANHOME

Elvanlord
Yana (also known as David Queensway)
Themur (also known as Ian Reine)

VISITOR FROM BENEATH

Daemon—Baalim (also known as The Beast Beneath)

THE WORLD OF DWARFS

King Schtoonk, King of the Dwarfs
Queen Schtenkah, Queen of the Dwarfs
Prince Schtark, Their Son
Princess Schrink, Their Daughter
Dimbek, Hogbek, Dogbek, and Rimbek,
    Four Brothers
Knarbo, Kniput, Knukah, Kneko,
    Brides of the Four Brothers
Farful and Fertig, Sordo's Apprentices
Boff, King of Mice
Binny, Queen of Mice
Tup, Captain to King Boff

WORLD OF THE UNDER PEOPLE

The President and Commander-in-chief
Kranz, The Magician

ASTRA AND FLONDRIX

I

The Enchanted Prince

❀❀❀❀❀❀❀❀

Once upon a time, many long years hence, there was an enchanted forest which stood at the very border of the Dark King's Realm. King Barlocks was his name, but his dark, glowering face, his raven beard and brows had earned him this sobriquet. The black eyes that glowed murkily and the black velvet costumes he wore constantly enhanced the impression of total darkness that seemed to move everywhere with him.

The enchanted forest was at the very edge of the kingdom, and few living men could say for sure what lay beyond; those who could, never spoke of it. There were many wild tales, of course.

Travellers passed along the roads from time to time in those days and it was the custom of the simple people to gather at one of the inns where a stranger tarried so they could listen to his talk. Many boasted of having travelled through and beyond the forest, but none ever told a convincing tale. The good people of the realm seldom went into the forest. Few, at least, who ever came back to tell about it. They said there was a magic range of mountains in the centre where Schtoonk, the Dwarf King, reigned. The horde of gold and jewels amassed by the dwarfs would surpass even King

Barlocks's wildest dreams, they declared. But if there really was such a mountain range, they could not be sure. Even on a very clear day it could not be seen. Not even from the tallest tower of the king's castle. The king himself, ever since he had been a small boy, dreamed of those mountains and the treasures stored beneath. Every clear day he navigated the difficult stone steps circling the tower, but he had never once glimpsed a shadow of the mountains. Privately, he believed they were bewitched so that no mortal man might ever catch sight of them.

The villagers said that deep in the forest lived the Elves, with their ruler Glortan The Great, whose secret powers no equal knew. Glortan was described as incredibly tall and slender with hair that shone like gold. Although his face was wondrously beautiful, his eyes were so strange and uncanny that no mortal man might safely gaze into them. They sparkled like the first evening stars in the deepening vaults of heaven and when he became vexed, one stern look was enough to turn a man into stone. His regal head was held high by a long and aristocratic neck that arched like a thoroughbred steed's. The people whispered that Glortan had a sister, Glortina by name, who was even fairer than he. Her beauty was so overwhelming that the beasts of the field and forest fell to the earth in a swoon when she passed by in her golden dress and tiny golden slippers. The wind stopped rustling the leaves and even the trees themselves bent their branches low at her passing.

It was also said that a particularly fearsome witch lived not too far from the edge of the forest, but still not too near the realms of the Elvan King and the Dwarf King. Steeped as she was in her own muddied form of Dark Magic, she had every reason to fear the High Magic Knowledge of the Elves and the lesser though practical Crafts of the Dwarfs. Her name was Bumbree, and many were the stories of the spells and enchantments she had cast on hapless men and beasts alike. Bumbree had very strange ways and the superstitious villagers believed that all too many careless travellers, wandering too close to her Creepy Cottage, had been turned into wild and unheard of beasts for Bumbree's unwholesome purposes. None of the good folk who lived near the castle claimed ever to have seen her. At the very mention of her name, the most fearful among them would make strange signs on their chests and faces with their fingers or trace the X sign on the ground in front of them to ward off all evil.

Woodcutters walked miles each day to a smaller forest at the eastern end of the kingdom, and none would go near the enchanted forest, no less aim an axe at one of its trees. One person alone seemed unafraid. Her name was Ungar and she lived at the northern edge of the forest, many miles' walk from the village. Her cottage and small outbuildings were under the very shadow of the great trees, hemmed into a narrow, protected vale between the forest and the tall hills that rose abruptly to the north. All the farmers in the lowlands kept cows and pigs, but Ungar was the only shepherdess in the realm. Her sheep roamed the northern hills and mountains and all the wool and mutton in the kingdom came from Ungar's flocks.

Ungar had lived alone in her far-off cottage longer than most villagers could remember. Her father and husband had been shepherds, but they had both died a long time ago. Some years after, Ungar had reached an indeterminate age; her body and limbs, very strong and healthy, had thickened slightly and her bright, sandy locks added a few strands of silver. There it all stopped and she stayed that way, looking strangely ageless and aloof in her dour way. Yet she always seemed to know and understand a lot more than she was willing to communicate.

Late at night in the inns, men would whisper about her. They said she could lift a full-grown ram with one arm and carry him into the house. 'Aye, and what does she with him there?' sniggered a drinker. All the men would laugh to indicate no answer was required. Another would suggest that she suckled new-born lambs at her own breast in the freezing early spring. A round of suggestive laughter would draw another comment: 'What be so strange in that? Is it not the natural way of all mothers?' Wicked chuckles would ring through the smoke-filled ale room and the candle flames would dance and flicker.

One thing they could never explain was the strange, darkling lad they called Stupid Igor. Ungar said she had found him, a wee infant, lying on a heap of straw in one of the sheds, the ewes gathered tightly about him to give their warmth, their patient eyes staring into space. If any man scoffed or jeered at this in her earshot, he would go limping home, howling for his trouble.

This lad was unbelievably handsome even as a small boy. His head was ringed with coal-black curls and his easy smile could light up a room; his white even teeth actually flashed in the dark. His eyes were deep luminous violet and almost as large as a deer's. As he grew, he became ever more agile and strong. He spent every waking hour with the sheep and there was no dog who could outrun him, nor a goat so nimble he could leap from crag to mountain crag as swiftly as the boy.

Ungar had called him Igorin, after her father. But since he was shy of strangers and would run off startled as a hare if anyone but Ungar approached him, it was thought he was witless in the village. As he never answered when the villagers called to him, they assumed he was mute. But Ungar knew otherwise. He would answer her readily enough, though he seldom said more than a few words to her at a time. Only once had she been lucky enough to hear him telling stories to his sheep. How the words had come tumbling from his lips then, like velvet water cascading from rock to rock. When he heard Ungar's unwary footstep, the silence was as sudden as a rivulet of rain evaporating in the bright sunshine.

Since then, no matter how quietly she approached, he always heard her. His ears were as keen as those of a wild animal. So were his eyes; no bird, not even the smallest insect could evade his quick glance. In the thickest fog or blackest moonless night, he could find each missing lamb with those eyes and ears, plus the unerring acuteness of his nose.

Igorin grew up in the natural simplicity of the animals around him. He knew their world better than the world of the villagers he distrusted so intensely. They penned themselves up in reeking, smoky houses and smelled nowhere so sweet as the cows and sheep who lived in the open.

Ungar could not persuade the boy to don the short sheepskin trousers and jerkin she made for him each year until the winter snows were upon them. No sooner had the snows begun to melt than Ungar would see him like a tiny dot far up in the hills. Off would come jerkin and trousers and he would roam naked over the hills throughout the entire long summer.

One question Ungar could never answer was where the child had come from originally. Some villagers ventured he had been put there by the Elves because he was so shy and had so many of the natural Elvan graces and easy physical powers. But only two mortals knew the true story: King Barlocks himself and the adviser he trusted most, the famous magician Gonzola.

Gonzola had been all through the enchanted forest. He had even visited the fabled halls of the Dwarf King and, on more than one occasion, had been the guest of the Elvan King, Glortan the Great. He had fought mighty battles of magic with the gruesome witch, Bumbree, who had tried to snare the powerful magician with her spells. King Barlocks suspected some of this, but there was much in Gonzola's history even the Dark King was unaware of. As magical leader of the Order Most High, Gonzola had detected a black plot against the kingdoms of men and Elves by his brother magician, Kranz. Glortan had banished Kranz to the world of the Under People, a dreadful time trap, a place where time stood still and the unfortunate mortals lived through the last day of the destruction of their world, a destruction repeated each day through eternity. Kranz's accomplice, the phantasmagoria Daemon-Baalim, had been imprisoned below and became known as The Beast Beneath. In all of this, the enigmatic magician Gonzola had played a leading part.

Since then, he had remained in the Dark Kingdom throughout the reigns of Barlocks's grandfather and father and had served each of them very well indeed. However, the Dark King had begun to wonder in earnest about the magician's mysterious past ever since he had fallen under a frightful Elvish spell himself.

It so happened, about seventeen years ago, before Igorin the young shepherd was born, that King Barlocks had gone hunting with a few of his retainers. They had put up a magnificent stag near the enchanted forest and, in the heat of the hunt, the king had passed into the trees before he was even aware of it. His retainers shouted after him, pleading and wringing their hands, but their cries fell on deaf ears as Barlocks leaned over the neck of his huge horse, the lance held out in front of him, ready to strike. When he was almost on the now tiring stag, the animal disappeared in a blinding flash and, a few paces beyond, leaning naked against a tree, stood the most beautiful woman he had ever seen. She was tall and slender and her body glowed with a golden fire. Great ringlets of silver hair fell tumbling over her shoulders and spilled nearly to her hips. The lance shattered in Barlocks's hand and the horse stopped as though he had struck an invisible wall. Thrown to the ground, sprawling ignobly on his stomach, Barlocks's eyes never flickered once from the incredible vision before him.

The king's eyes roamed over the cascading hair, down over the glowing body and his breath caught in his throat when he realized the swelling breasts were mounted with vermilion nipples that flashed and twinkled in the murky forest shade. Then at last his eyes alighted on the very small triangle of silver hair tipped in reddish golden flames. Overwhelmed, he wept with intense emotion, begging the lovely one to step closer. He swore he would love no other as long as he lived and would give her anything, everything within his power, if she would only be his. For ever.

The radiant beauty smiled suddenly and shook her head, the long tresses trembling with the movement, sending tiny sparks floating down to the dry leaves gathered about her feet. She shook her head once more and vanished. In that last instant, piercing the intense love he felt, something in those fabulous eyes sent a chilling premonition through his heart.

Grim-faced, Barlocks left the wood leading his horse, the shattered lance abandoned on the ground behind him. He said not a word to his retainers, but remounted his frightened steed and galloped back to the castle as fast as the animal's long legs could carry him.

When Barlocks finished this tale of his enchanted encounter, a tale he would entrust to no other person save Gonzola, the ancient magician nodded sagely as he paced up and down the king's private chamber. Then he stopped in the middle of the room, scratching carefully inside his thick silvery beard, while his deeply sunken eyes peered out from beneath the dense white brows.

'Sire,' he said ominously, 'there can be no mistake. Your calamity could not be worse. You have been bewitched and fallen in love with none other than Glortina, sister to the Elvan King himself. And by the High Elvan Law,' he added, 'your love is *forbidden*.' The words rumbled through the chamber like heavy wooden bowls in the hollow mountain caverns of the dwarfs.

Gonzola spent more than an hour patiently explaining the facts of Elvan life to the king. He drew pictures and told the king as much as he dared concerning the differences between Elvan and mortal systems of reproduction. But the king's eyes, ears and mind were closed to all else save Glortina's beauty. If the magician would not use his mightiest powers to win Glortina, the old man would be drawn and quartered, then burned at the stake.

'I understand, I understand,' the ancient sage reassured Barlocks calmly, ignoring the hysterical threats, 'for the enchantment is of the highest order. This was done to you deliberately. But why? There is something very dark and murky here, something that perturbs me deeply, yet I cannot say why. Glortina knows you will send me to entreat for you. I assure you, Glortan will be furious. But of one thing I am sure, my liege. If they were to say yes, you could never live up to the terms they would impose.'

After many more hours of threats, arguments and promises of reward, Gonzola took his leave, assuring the king he would do his best. He left with great foreboding in his heart and, in less than a week, was back at the castle, his face more haggard than usual, his awesome black steed looking emaciated and on the verge of collapse.

'It is just as I suspected, sire,' the old magician said wearily, 'Glortina may come to you for eleven months and twenty-nine days; were she to stay longer, she would lose her immortality and great Elvan powers in the halls of men. And she may come only on the strictest conditions imaginable . . .'

She would be at the king's side night and day to entertain him with wondrous Elvan stories and to sing to him or play music on the harp. However, the king must never think to touch her in the fashion mortal men touch mortal women, he must never attempt to do with her the things mortal men do with mortal women. He must swear a sacred oath on this and, should he ever break it, an Elvan curse would come down upon his head that would make any horror story he had ever heard seem like a mere fairy tale. One wrong move and Glortina would be gone for ever. But the curse would be on his house to the end of time.

'Now what is your answer, sire, for I must wing it back to them immediately. I don't mind telling you, I nearly forfeited my own life making this appalling bargain.'

'Yes!' the king jumped up, embracing the magician. 'A thousand times yes. I promise. I swear on the head of my father. Anything! Anything for the beautiful Glortina.'

*

The following morning the king awoke to find the Elvan Princess stretched out beside him on the great white bearskin robe, her glittering silver hair surrounding her like wreaths of soft flame. Impulsively, with a wanton will of its own, his hand glided towards her, towards the glowing golden skin and the little tuft of silvery hair tipped in gold. She opened her eyes suddenly and his arm was struck numb. And it stayed so for the entire day, suspended at an awkward angle. Startled and chagrined, he pleaded with Glortina to have mercy on him but she answered off-handedly that there was nothing to be done, he would simply have to wait until the next morning. After all, she pointed out, magic was always much easier to turn on than off.

Disgruntled and somewhat swollen with the pressures of passion, the king slipped out of bed and sat down on the royal chamber pot. He looked dumbly at the stiff arm, cocked out ridiculously from his shoulder, and bit his lip. Glortina raised herself up on her elbow and peeped over the side of the bed. When she asked, with a puzzled expression, just what he was doing, he explained that there was another chamber pot on her side of the bed if she so desired. As her eyes still seemed puzzled, he raised himself up a little so she could see the yellow liquid pouring from his penis. Shocked, she drew back sharply, wrapping the great bearskin around her. Her face hardened into a fastidious and disapproving expression.

'What disturbs you so?' he asked. 'Is it Elvan custom to do this in private? Not so with us,' he assured her, 'for we find it the most natural thing in the world. Like eating or breathing.'

'Natural?' she scoffed disdainfully. 'Just like that disgusting thought you had on your mind a few moments ago? Mortals may do these things . . . Elves don't!'

The days passed and the king was enchanted with the lovely songs, the harp music and the wondrous stories Glortina told. But underneath it all, he continued to fuss, fume and smoulder. Each morning the lovely creature rose naked from the bed and poured the contents of a small phial over her body until the delightful, maddening scent filled the room. She would reach up to the peg where she had hung her dress the night before and lo! it was a new dress. Shimmering down over her body, the gossamer cloth would gather and cling to her until the poor king could not be certain if she was more beautiful with the dress or without it.

Once more he went to Gonzola, beseeching and spilling out the imprisoned miseries in his heart. The magician was shocked and reminded him sternly of his great oath. That angered the king for he did not like to be reminded of his honour and obligations. When Gonzola broached the handsome reward the king had promised him, the king's face went purple with fury.

'Sire, I do not remind you of these things for my own sake,' Gonzola spoke consolingly, 'but to make you see the catastrophe you would bring down on yourself and this house. You are still not fully aware of High Elvish Power. Yet you court disaster openly. As to my reward, how can I in good conscience benefit from sorrow or folly? You did accept the terms and now you would throw all caution to the winds. Your majesty, what am I to do with you?'

The determined and desperate king went on until Gonzola finally relented. Yes, there was a way. Did the king not notice that Glortina never touched mortal wines, ales or mead? She always came to table with a tiny flacon filled with a special nectar essence consumed by the Elves. Should one drop of mortal wine touch her lips, she would sink into a deep and helpless swoon for fully twenty-four hours. Gonzola assured the king that nothing so unsubtle as pouring wine in her goblet would work, but that he must let the magician handle this. That night, at the dinner table, a deception so

23

clever as to evade Glortina's scrutiny would take place. The king went skipping off like a boy on the last day of school. But the unhappy Gonzola sat there sadly shaking his head as he felt the fateful skeins winding tighter.

'Wait till he discovers what he's going to discover,' the aged seer whispered to himself. 'Well, the weather may not be pleasant now, but it might be the best time to take my annual leave all the same. Even if it means nothing more stimulating than a magic wrestling match with Old Bumbree of the Triple Dugs.'

*

Barlocks excused himself from table soon after he had been seated. As he walked to the door, he glanced back at Glortina and the ring of nobles sitting around her, their adoring faces devouring her every look and word. He watched her pour the few drops she took every evening from the delicate magic flacon. Then he sped straight to the kitchen. When the cook was engaged with his back turned, the king lifted a bowl filled with soft butter from the ponderous wooden table and sneaked out. He sped up the stairs to his sleeping chamber and secreted the bowl under his bed.

By the time he got back to the banqueting hall, there were already loud shouts of dismay. Glortina was slumped over the table, deep in a deathlike trance. The king shouldered the troubled retainers aside and lifted the Elvan Princess in his arms. He was amazed at how light she was, no heavier than a small child. At the top of the stairs he turned to confront the sea of anxious faces. He ordered his nobles and retainers to return to the banqueting, assuring them that their adored princess would recover by morning.

King Barlocks stretched the still Elvan form out on the bed and slid the dress over her head, the golden slippers from her feet. He stood trembling, looking down for the thousandth time on the vision of loveliness that never dimmed in his eyes or heart. He tore himself away and quickly pulled the chains and decorations over his head, the tunic and hose following, all jumbled in a heap on the floor as he leapt upon the bed. He stared at Glortina, and felt his engorged penis slam into his abdomen as though he were a rutting horse. Kneeling close beside her, he slowly drew his face and short black beard upwards from her petite toes to her knees and thighs, drinking in the delicious scent of her glowing skin. His lips coursed over her hips, for the moment avoiding the cup of joy, to thrill at the splendour of the small but fully upthrust breasts. He hungrily gathered the nearest sparkling vermilion nipple into his mouth and a shock ran up and down his spine, turning his blood into a torrent of flaming molten metal. A strange and delirious liquid filled his mouth, affecting every nerve and cell in his body. His penis crackled like a charge of lightning and later he swore to himself that a burst of flame had shot from his anus. His senses reeling, he moved his head away from the nectar-filled mound, brushing his lips over the firm abdomen, down and down until the golden tipped triangle of soft, silvery maidenhair crackled in his beard.

Hands shaking like a palsied old man's, he opened the yielding thighs, hesitated one brief moment, then thrust his greedy tongue in as deeply as he could. The tongue bounced off unyielding skin. Jaw muscles aching, he tried harder, thrusting and bunching his cheeks, ramming his tongue at the spot with all his might. Nothing gave way. Gasping in desperation, he yanked the thighs wider apart and ran his tongue up and down hysterically, searching everywhere. Sobbing, he rose painfully and reached over to the candlestick on the bedside table.

There was nothing! He lowered his head and thrust the flame as close as he dared. The silver hair with the glittering golden tips ended at the lowest point of the triangle. Below that . . . nothing but unbroken skin. He reached under her roughly and probed between her buttocks. Nothing but unbroken skin. Smooth . . . not a crease, not a furrow, not a hint. He returned the candle to the table and sat back on his heels, sobbing uncontrollably.

In her deep sleep, Glortina sighed one long peaceful sigh and stirred slightly. The king gazed at her maddening beauty in the soft light and sighed brokenly in turn. Suddenly he noted her lips were parted and her neck arched invitingly. With choking frustration welling up in his throat, he bent sideways and reached under the bed. Barlocks touched both those lovely lips with butter and laughed softly with bitter cynicism. Inching his hips up to the pillows, he thrust his enraged penis at her half-opened mouth. When he felt his testicles firmly pressed against her chin, the explosion came as it had never come before. It seemed to him that gallons upon gallons of thick liquid poured out of him and down that long, lovely throat.

Shrivelled and cowering, the haughty king of a few moments ago whimpered like a frightened child and burrowed under the heavy bearskin robe.

*

It was not until many hours later that Barlocks discovered his bed chamber was under a magic spell. It lasted for a full twenty-four hours, but he knew nothing of this since that was how long his enchanted sleep lasted. The king's retainers could approach within ten feet of the door and there they were stopped by an invisible wall. Not even Gonzola could approach the door and he told the captain of the guards if he and his men attempted to scale the wall outside the window, they would find a similar magical barrier awaiting them there. The room was sealed by the spell and there was nothing to be done until dinner time that night. Without explaining this prediction, he warned them that although the invisible wall would disappear then, only the magician should enter the chamber until the place could be purged of all lingering affliction. That warning was all they needed to speed them down the stairs.

At dinner time that night, Gonzola casually opened the king's chamber door and strode halfway across the room, his eyes not yet accustomed to the gloom. When he thrust the candle in front of him, a strange sight met his eyes. The king was naked and sleeping peacefully on his back. On the pillow next to him was a new-born baby, also totally naked. The infant remained motionless and silent, despite the chill in the unheated chamber. Glortina was nowhere to be seen, nor was there anything in the room to suggest she had ever been there. That is, except for the ghostly Elvish characters which glowed eerily on the wall over the bed.

'Wicked king, you betrayed our trust and broke your mighty oath,' Gonzola translated the Elvish writing slowly, for it had been years since he'd had occasion to read the tongue, 'and so upon you shall befall the ruin you have courted. Here is your seed, improperly placed in defiance of your oath. And in it is the seed of your own destruction and that of your proud and mighty house. When the time comes, you shall reap our vengeance, for no mortal may despoil and pollute that which is Elvish without paying a terrible penalty.' As he read the last words, recognizing Glortan's seal, the writing faded and was gone.

On tiptoe, Gonzola walked to the bedside and stared down at the infant. Its eyes were wide open, unlike most human babies, and it regarded the magician with intelligent scrutiny. The baby's head was covered with thick ringlets of hair as jet black as the king's. As Gonzola bent forward to get a better look, the king sat bolt upright, nearly knocking the tranquil child off the pillow.

'Careful,' rumbled Gonzola, 'you'll upset the baby.'

The king bounced clear of the bed, his feet landing with a thud on the hard stone floor.

'Wh-what?' gasped Barlocks, looking down at the infant.

'Your son,' explained the magician sarcastically. 'Also, your undoing, I might add.'

'My son? This is *my* son? How do you even know it's a boy? Look at that. No whango, no cobblers . . . nothing!'

'I know you are upset, sire,' Gonzola mumbled from behind his beard, 'but that is no reason for such crudeness of speech. Take my word for it, it is a boy. And *your* son. I tried to explain all this to you, but in your great passion you would hear none of it. I imagine you discovered some of those startling things on your own last night, did you not?'

'Did you know about *that* all along?' demanded the king menacingly.

'Now, now, my lord,' the magician rebuked him softly, 'don't try to make me responsible for any part of this misfortune. I did your bidding with the greatest reluctance and all the time warned you about the dire consequences.'

The king shook with ill-concealed rage. 'Why didn't you tell me she didn't have a — a — you know what?'

'Had I done so, my liege, you would have had me thrown in the dungeon. I would have had an unnecessary dark, damp and dreary twenty-four hours. The result is the same,' Gonzola pointed out flatly.

'But how – how do they do – I mean . . . I just don't understand,' stammered the king. 'She is the most beautiful creature who ever . . . it's unfair, it's inhuman!'

'Inhuman it may be, but it is definitely Elvish,' retorted the magician. 'However, we can talk about all that later, when you've calmed down and come to your senses. This child must be spirited away immediately, before anyone suspects a thing, before there is one hungry cry from him.'

'Wait, drat it,' bawled the king. 'How can you say this is my child? How on earth can it be? She was here less than a month . . . you saw her. I mean, you know she wasn't with child. Aha!' the king exclaimed cunningly, 'you're trying to fox me, are you not? You know this is impossible, she has no – no – you know what I mean.'

'Nor does she have a navel,' the magician reminded him. 'Neither does that infant. Would you care to tell me what you did after you made your discoveries concerning Elvan anatomy last night? No need, I *know*. For *that* is how it works for Elves. But only when an Elvan woman wills it or is drugged. Furthermore, it takes them nine hours, not nine months.'

'Are you sure?' the king asked weakly, sitting carefully on the edge of the bed.

'Absolutely,' Gonzola answered gruffly. 'Look at the child carefully. Your eyes, save for the violet colour. Your hair. Even the skin is much darker than the normal Elvan shade. Come, we have no time to lose.'

'But – but . . .' sputtered the king.

'No "buts",' Gonzola scowled, 'can't you remember the curse over your head? To have an Elvan child here is like courting the worst disaster. The things he would learn here? No, he must be hidden so none can

29

find him. He must grow up in absolute innocence or your life won't be worth living.'

'But how?' moaned the miserable monarch.

'Leave that to me,' Gonzola advised, 'my line of country, as it were.' He scooped up the child and wrapped it well in the voluminous folds of his cape. He leapt nimbly to the window ledge and stood there silently invoking a spell. A moment later he was floating down to earth on the far side of the moat.

On his return an hour or so later, the tired magician had to answer endless questions from the king, whose tongue by then had untied itself thoroughly. No, the child would not starve. Elvan children can find nourishment in the paps of an old ewe or an old woman. Glortina was back in her brother's realm. How? The Elves call them the Other Paths. In less than a second from the time she disappeared. No, it was highly unlikely Barlocks would ever see her again. As for the child's glaring lack in the lower regions, that had to do with the highest Elvish Lore.

What Gonzola, the all-knowing, did *not* know concerned an even more secret event of the past evening. At the exact moment Glortina had produced a son for the king, as a result of his treachery, her brother Glortan's wife, Aureen, had produced a daughter. She was named Astra and she was the fairest of them all, outshining even her Aunt Glortina and her mother, Aureen. Her eyes were the greatest wonder of all, sparkling like emeralds in a pale sky.

II

Ungar's
Simple Rustic Cottage

◉◉◉◉◉◉◉◉

Igorin lay stretched out warm and comfortable in the large bed made of fresh straw and covered lavishly with sheepskins. His mind was untroubled and his dreams were pleasant. In fact, Ungar had made a delicious leek pie for his supper, telling him it was to celebrate his seventeenth summer. He had counted that out on his fingers and toes when she told him and he had laughed and laughed, thumping his small, slender feet on the hard-packed earthen floor near the hearth. When she asked him what amused him so, he told her he had only three summers left, obviously, for there were but three more toes to go. Ungar did not laugh often, but this time she laughed till she cried, hugging and kissing the dear boy for all the happiness and joy he had brought into her lonely life.

As Igorin slept peacefully, King Barlocks stood alone leaning over the parapet of his high tower, gazing intently to the west where the moon was setting. Seventeen long and lonely years had pinched his face and shot streaks of silver through his hair and beard. His eyes smouldered in the bright light of the westering moon as he searched in vain for the elusive enchanted mountains of the dwarfs. Then his eyes shifted towards the nearer edge of the forest, hoping that this night, as he had hoped every night for seventeen years, Glortina might emerge and beckon to him in forgiveness.

His unrequited love for Glortina had made all women unattractive to him. There was another reason, of course, but this problem was one which he confided only to his trusted magician, Gonzola. Within an hour of the baby's departure with the magician on that fateful night, the Dark King's penis and testicles had begun to shrink. Gradually, hair had begun to fall from his body, first from the pubic area, then from beneath his arms. Exactly eleven months and twenty-nine days from the day Glortina had arrived by magic on his bed, he had not one hair left on his body, and his penis and testicles had shrunk to the size one would expect to find on the body of a new-born infant.

All of Gonzola's spells and incantations had proved powerless over the Elvish curse. The curse did not stop at size alone, but caught the poor king up in all the usual embarrassing features of an infant's structure and containments. For sixteen years and a day, he had been forced to wear nappies both day and night. In the middle of an important State Reception, of which there were many, the king would feel the familiar warmth creeping over his thighs and bottom and would have to excuse himself abruptly to run and change his nappies. The long string of them hanging each day from the clothesline behind the kitchen was a humiliating and demoralizing sight the king avoided like the plague.

Still, that was not the worst. Although he would never reveal the afflicted parts to anyone, not even Gonzola, each night he lay exposed in his dreams to legions of laughing, derisive women, their faces contorted in cruel glee and their fingers pointing accusingly at his infantile equipment. He also suffered the perversely persistent urges of a nappy-irritated baby. Where in the happy past he would perhaps once or twice a day manipulate his prideful penis with the whole of one hand and flatter himself on its equine beauty and fearsome virility, he was now forced to do the same thing ten or more times a day, using two fingers very carefully lest he lose his grip. It took no time at all, but the dry, faint climax gave him no pleasure.

As he stood watching the edge of the forest, his fingers began to move inside the tops of his long hose, searching out the large nappy pin. The moon sank, the tiny penis throbbed but Glortina never appeared. His eyes shifted momentarily and indifferently to the hills north of the castle bordering the forest. Gonzola had decided the king should never know what had become of the baby for his own good, and the king had been sunk too deeply in his own sorrow to ask or argue. The unfortunate Barlocks had experienced merely the first hints of a dire and dreadful curse; he had yet to learn how relentless and enduring is the stern justice of a wronged Elvan King . . . and his defiled sister.

*

Igorin stirred in his sleep when he felt Ungar's large body begin to twitch and shudder in the bed. His brow furrowed for a moment, an unusual sight on that normally bright and sunny face. With a low moan vibrating in the night, the woman's bulk thrashed about and she awoke fully, trembling for a moment before heaving herself off the soft, warm bed. With one eye, the disturbed Igorin watched the large naked form plough through the shadows and pass the glowing embers of the hearth as Ungar made her way towards the back door. A few seconds later, he heard the heavy plank that covered the deep narrow trench being moved by her strong hands. Then there was a loud swishing and splashing that went on for a long time, eventually petering out in three short bursts and a dribble. He waited, his ear cocked, to learn if there would be more, if she would do the other strange thing now. He heard her groan in a strangled way and a wet plop sounded in the trench, followed by another and yet another, finally ending in a loud roar that diminished to a fluttering noise like the ones he made when he blew air through his puckered lips. A faint, unpleasant aroma reached his uncannily sensitive nostrils and he pinched them closed.

Why did she do it? He never could understand, no matter how many times she tried to explain it in her dull, simple way. He had seen the holes in her body where the water and the dung dropped from, but why was it necessary? She said all the animals did these things and he had to agree. All his life he had been walking barefoot across the wettings and the dung-covered ground. He had never questioned that . . . but she was not an animal. So many times he had asked her why he had no such holes in his body. After all, he ate food, the same food she did. And much of it was green like the grass the sheep devoured from the beginning to the end of every day. She would explain helplessly that he was not a girl, only girls had two holes. Then why didn't he have one hole? The rams had one hole. If he was not a girl, was he a boy? Were not the rams boys? Why did he not have one of those big things the rams had, those things that excited her so much when they went up into one of her holes, the bigger one in the centre with all the hair around it. He had hair there now too, strange golden hair with silver tips, but no thing like a ram. With great embarrassment, she chided him about patience. He would have to wait, perhaps some day soon . . . and then she would wander off, suddenly finding something very important to do.

He heard Ungar uprooting the long grass near the trench and knew she was finished with this odd duty of hers. He wondered if it had irritated her and made her restless as it so often did. Would she carry one of the rams back with her? He listened to her diminishing footsteps as she headed towards the sheds. His mouth formed a small pout; he did not like the big rams with their muddy hooves bucking and bleating in the bed, shedding fleas all over. He never told Ungar this because he loved her dearly and in some unconscious way understood her need. But rams's hooves are sharp and they have a strong, musky smell. When it was all over and the ram safely back in its pen, it took some time to clear all the smells from his nostrils and get back to sleep.

Ungar's figure filled the small doorway and the ram's rampant hooves clattered loudly against the wooden frame. With her free hand, she gave the beast a sharp wallop on the side of the head and it stopped fighting.

Elbow crooked, Igorin cocked his head on his hand and watched her settle the big ram on the bed. She stood there holding his throat in one hand as the other reached under the beast to stroke the sheath that protruded from his belly. Soon the long thing came out and began jerking spasmodically in her strong hand; the ram began bucking and kicking out his hind legs.

Quickly, Ungar climbed on the bed, still holding the ram's throat as she moved herself on her knees until her bottom was under the ram's nose. He leaped up on her and began thrusting. But the long quivering thing went wide of the mark. The beast, not knowing any better, made a thrust at the smaller hole higher up, the one that made the dung come out. Igorin giggled uncontrollably as Ungar let out a loud yelp, half startled, half in pain. She looked at the boy ruefully and he relented. He got up on his knees and pulled the beast higher on her back, reaching his free hand under its body to steady the flailing thing. Gently he guided it into the proper hole and a sigh of bliss broke from Ungar's panting lips. Laughing happily, Igorin tickled the animal's huge testicles until the thrusting thing was buried all the way inside the woman's body. A minute later, she collapsed on the bed with a cry of delight. The poor ram was left butting away at thin air, his forelegs sprawled out. Out of pity for the animal's evident pain, the boy reached under him again and stroked the swollen thing until the ram bleated and spurted a thick white fluid on the backs of the woman's sprawled legs.

Nimbly, the lad leaped over animal and woman, landing lightly on the earthen floor. He picked up the ram as though it were a kitten and ran out to the shed to put the beast back in its pen. When he returned, he covered the inert form of Ungar with sheepskins and crawled in beside her, cuddling up to her warmth. Half asleep, she folded the boy in her big arms and threw one mighty thigh over him. He nestled closely, pillowing himself on her generous breasts. He breathed that warm smell and tried not to notice the musky odour that still lurked everywhere. She thanked him sleepily, as she always did, for taking the ram back. He nodded his head sleepily in response.

As he brushed an inquisitive flea away from the silver-tipped hair beneath his belly, he noticed for the first time a painful, throbbing swelling under the skin. It seemed as if something were trying to burst forth. Ungar's heavy thigh was pressing on the spot and he felt as though he would faint from the excruciating sense of something inside his body trying to tear itself loose. The ache throbbed down to a place where a back hole would be if he had one. Fortunately, sleep caught up with him before he could agonize further about this strange new sensation.

Miles away, in the Dark King's castle, the king fell out of bed clutching his groin and gasping. His tiny penis was swollen and had turned a fiery red. As Igorin fell into a deep sleep, the king fainted with the pain and remained all night, stupefied, on the cold stone floor.

III

Innocent Days
of
Hill and Dale

◉◉◉◉◉◉◉

The following day Igorin stood on the highest stony rampart of the northern hills, his sheep gathered in a small vale of lush grass under his watchful eye. Rising tall in his splendid nakedness, his toes clutching the rock securely, he shielded his eyes and scanned the south-west, far over the enchanted forest to where the sun sparkled on the fascinating White Mountains in the distance. He was looking longingly at the very mountains which had evaded his father's vision for nearly half a century. He had mentioned them only once to Ungar and she had smiled knowingly, thinking the boy had heard one of the village tales. She did not know that it took an Elvish quality of sight to see them.

It was the eve of Midsummer and the sun beat down on hill and dale alike, igniting a memory inside the boy of the strange feelings he had known the night before. Unconsciously, he stroked his flanks with warm palms; as he did so, a movement near the base of the mountain caught his eye. At the edge of the enchanted forest, a large fallow doe stepped out from behind the trees and stopped, looking up at what must have appeared as a dot of a figure, silhouetted like a mountain goat on a sharp pinnacle against the sky. But this was no ordinary doe. She not only saw the figure clearly, but identified it correctly with no trouble at all. With great leaps she left the trees and the lower rock croppings, bounding gracefully ever higher and higher.

Something about the deer's size and purposeful movements riveted the boy's attention. He never took his eyes off the creature as he slipped sure-footedly down from crag to crag, moving as nimbly as the doe. He halted on a protected ledge covered in soft, dry moss, some fifty or sixty yards above the vale over which his sheep were grazing.

The deer disappeared as she neared the upper rock outcroppings. Then she appeared just as suddenly, walking lightly and swaying slightly among the sheep below. The boy gazed in wonder for the sheep never raised their heads nor stopped their ceaseless cropping of grass. As the doe moved, she brushed against one of the sheep, then another, but they took no notice. At last she was standing directly below the ledge, looking up at Igorin.

The two stood transfixed, staring at each other for long minutes on end, large velvet violet eyes unblinking above, larger eyes, velvety too and almost as violet gazing up steadily from below.

Without seeming to move, the doe inched her hind legs apart and began pouring fluid from within her body on to the sun-parched ground. Great clouds of steam rose until the boy was enclosed in a sound-proof vapour that filled his nostrils with the most haunting scent he had ever known. Through it was blended hints of lavender, sage and attar of roses, a thousand more exotic things he could not even imagine. His senses were overcome and his head began spinning wildly, strange yearnings and desires boiling through his blood so fast his feet no longer seemed attached to the ledge. The overpowering scent came closer and closer until he thought he was deep in an exquisite garden and fast asleep. Indeed, his eyes did close and he never felt his feet move. He did not feel the air moving over his body as he gently wafted down the nearly sixty yards between the ledge and the vale below. When he opened his eyes, the beautiful creature was standing in front of him, her wet nose nuzzling the soft silvery hair which grew to a point just where his thighs began. Her long tongue flicked out and, smooth as ferns in the rain, moved between his thighs, up along the crease between his buttocks, pressing excitedly and insistently. The boy shuddered and he thought his feet were leaving the ground again.

Abruptly, she turned around and rubbed her tail across his abdomen. When she raised the tail, he looked down at the shining pink skin that formed a swollen crevasse. A fluid like molten pearls welled out of the opening and the scent of flowers struck him once more. He reached down and touched the spot, feeling the doe quiver intensely as he did. In the natural way of a child, unthinkingly, he raised the fingers to his lips. The scent nearly put him in a swoon and the taste on his tongue surpassed the delicious flavour of wild honey scooped from hollow trees.

He touched the spot again and brought more to his lips. All at once he could hear bird song for many miles around, farther than the sounds had ever carried before. More amazing still, he could understand the meanings of the notes like a language. Then he heard one of the sheep saying to another: 'I wonder where Igorin has gone off to? He's not on top of that crag any longer.' 'He'll be here soon, not to worry,' answered the other.

All this passed through his startled mind in a fraction

of a second. Impulsively, he bent forward and pressed his lips fully to the delicious spot. The more he drank, the more deeply he inserted his tongue, the more violently shook the doe. A small, throaty scream broke from her throat and she turned her head to stare at him.

'Enter into me now,' she pleaded, her voice breaking.

'What?' he asked, surprised by her voice, but more amazed still by the words themselves.

'Your beautiful twin-tipped spires,' she answered, panting. 'Press the spot and make them come out so they can go into me. Quickly, or I shall die.'

Standing up straight, almost understanding, he looked down at the emptiness below his trunk and began to cry bitter tears.

'What is the matter, dear sweet boy?' asked the doe, close to tears herself. She watched the large drops splashing down his chest and running into the silvery tuft of hair.

'I haven't any,' he cried piteously. 'I never have. I don't know why.'

'You poor ninny,' she scolded, 'of course you have. Have you no born Elvan Lore? Did you never look for the secret spot?'

He shook his head sadly, not understanding half her meanings. The doe trotted purposefully behind the boy and when he started turning too, she told him to stand still. He jumped when he felt her warm, moist muzzle thrust itself between his buttocks. She ignored his agitation and pressed on, searching carefully with her nose. She found the exact spot she was looking for and pressed hard.

A strange sensation, half pain, half pleasure shot across his groin and then he felt something like a white hot wire going through his insides and coming out the front. When he looked down, he saw the flesh beneath the silver-tipped hair opening wider and wider. Out slid an enormous sheath, thicker than a human foreskin yet not quite so dense as the tubular covering of an animal's penis. As the lovely doe pressed with greater urgency and determination, the sheath, which was growing out of his own pubic flesh, extended further and further, not stopping until it dangled just short of his knees.

The boy's breath came in short gasps as though he had been racing up a mountain. And a panic he could not explain soon had his heart beating at triple speed; eyes dilated to the size of small saucers, he watched the ponderous sheath throb in the clear light. It quivered erratically, glistening with a pearly tumescence that flashed in the sun's rays each time it jerked up and down. But inside the panic at such a sight dwelt a growing, swelling thrill of surprise and delight. He had to steady himself on his small, elegant feet in order not to fall forward as a result of the sudden weight thrust out before him, to say nothing of the giddy sensations which brought him to the brink of unconsciousness.

When the doe found her voice, it quavered melodiously in her throat. 'Pull back the sheath with your hands,' she gasped, her head pressed against his hip.

Reaching out with both hands obediently, he pulled the sheath back easily, hand over hand. In the brilliant sunlight, his amazed eyes watched not one entasis, but two turgid, glistening columns appear, one directly beneath the other. The uppermost shaft was as brilliantly white as a bowl of fresh milk, tipped with a swollen, pulsating tip of pale vermilion that sparkled in the midday sun. Directly beneath this pillar was another of a deeper hue, a blend of bronze and gold, the tip glittering with the pureness of the finest silver. Both new limbs were so extraordinarily beautiful and delicate in their fashioning, for all their size, they seemed the work of a magical sculptor.

The doe tore her gaze from the overwhelming sight, her own limbs having gone weak and watery, scarcely able to carry her out in front of the boy. She stood there shivering, looking hesitantly behind her as though frightened now of the terrifying manifestation she had wrought. Calling upon her courage, she backed gently towards Igorin, her tail held as high as it would go.

'Hold them together, my own dear love, and press their precious tips into that swollen well whose nectar you so enjoyed,' she whispered hoarsely.

'Will they not pain you?' he asked, his voice full of concern.

'Not near so much as one more moment apart from you,' she reassured him.

Firming up his resolve, he did as he was bidden, hunching his shoulders forward, his arms extended to press the silver and vermilion tips together. Touching them to her quivering pink flesh, he watched fascinated as the pearly liquid poured from her body and splashed on the ground.

No sooner than the contact had been made, flashes of fire coursed up and down the insides of his legs, making his knees clatter together. Through half-closed eyes, he saw the same thing happening to her. With a supreme effort of will, she started to back up, taking one slow, delicate step after the other. Eyes swimming, trying to beat through the mounting waves of oblivion, dimly he saw the twin shafts disappearing inch by inch into the sweet opening that stretched and stretched to receive him.

Only faintly did he hear cries, some deep and disturbed as the very throbbing of the earth, others shrill as the frenzied call of birds on the wing and then sinking back again through ever deeper warbles. He did not know how many of those sounds came from his own throat. Nor did he know that this magic union, obeying no laws of man, went on and on as though the sun had stopped in mid-heaven, bowing its head in homage to the divine bliss it witnessed below.

At one moment Igorin was aware they were no longer standing, that her legs had slowly given way and that his knees were splayed to either side of her lowered haunches. He saw his hands for a moment, first stroking her flanks and then busy fingers moving around the edges of her orifice, coaxing still more of the glorious fluids from her. He found himself lying on top of her, as she had somehow managed to turn over on her back. He felt her hind legs locking his thighs to her, his face and head held close to her pulsating throat.

She whispered a beautiful word to him in a musical language he had never heard before. He did not know what it meant, yet it seemed to say that he should come with her, come with her to a world beyond worlds, a fabled place filled with nothing but bliss where the firmament shook and heaved, where the heavens undulated and split asunder, spewing out flames and lightning and the sun changed colour a thousand times in the blink of an eye while silky clouds of gold poured warm nectar over everything.

When he awoke, the sun was beginning to sink towards the western horizon, causing darkly burnished glintings over the roof of the enchanted forest. His eyes opened to see the sheep moving steadily to the far side of the vale, working their way through newer grass along the path towards home. He saw the westering light of the sun creating violet shadows along the over-hanging crags and precipices of the mountain, the stone glinting with reds and yellows along the higher peaks.

His head was nestled into warmth and delicious fragrance. His hand moved out tentatively, exploring a warm flank. A deep moan sounded near him and memory flooded back. He sat up startled and looked

44

down. Beneath the now darkly matted tuft of silver-tipped golden hair there was . . . nothing.

A sob broke from his gaping mouth and the doe turned quickly, circling his body with her own, nuzzling his cheek and making soft, comforting noises, like a mother cooing to a disturbed child. Her head moved down and the silken tongue licked the hair at the bottom of his torso until it sparkled brightly again.

'Where did it go?' he asked miserably. Then words tumbled out swiftly, one question following the last in such a jumble and profusion that she had to blow in his ear, making a loud whistling noise until he stopped asking so many questions.

She told him it was not yet the time for him to know her true identity, though obviously he had guessed that she was not what she seemed. She would tell him about himself, but only as much as it was safe for him to know for the time being. She promised to teach him many splendid things, things for which he had the natural born power. But he would have to swear great oaths of secrecy, for if he misused these great powers, if he were ever careless or stupid in their use, he could cause harm to himself and to her, harm beyond measure or repair.

His eyes narrowed and he looked at her suspiciously. It was a look that had never crossed his face before, a look for which he hardly could find a word to describe the feeling. The best word might be jealousy.

'You must have done that many times before,' he stated accusingly.

'Done what?' she asked irritably, interrupted in planning the first stage of his education.

'Ummh — "that" —' he said. 'I don't know what you call it.'

'I suppose I shall have to make a few things terribly clear,' she sighed with a touch of vexation. 'You and I are of one blood — on your mother's side, that is. Of course, you do not know your mother ...'

'I do know my mother,' he interrupted. 'She lives right down there.' He pointed in the direction of the cottage, hidden in the valley below.

Patiently, she explained to him that Ungar was merely his foster mother, that he had been found in the hay among the sheep. Ungar's husband had died long before the boy was born. She also told him vehemently that she had never done 'that', as he had called it, for she could not, not until he had reached seventeen. There was no other mate for her in this world or among all the planets and stars. He was the only one and she had waited gladly for him. He would understand all about that one day soon, just as he would understand many things. He would have to accept what she told him, just as he had to accept the form he saw before him. He would understand all soon enough, but everything in its time and place.

Afraid to interrupt once more, the unhappy boy pointed again to his bereft groin.

With a tolerant smile, she reminded him that there was a precise spot between his buttocks which, when pressed in firmly, activated the shining twin spires. However, she warned him seriously, once they were activated, they could not retract and disappear again until he had experienced the bliss of the world beyond worlds. It would not take a great amount of imagination to realize what a terrible predicament that would be.

'Never, never, never do that unless I am here to guide and relieve you. Do you promise solemnly?' she demanded.

'But what if it should just happen?' he asked, the dawn of cunning twinkling behind the clear innocence of his eyes.

Nuzzling Igorin's ear affectionately, she assured him she would teach him how to call her to his side when the need became overpowering. She would hear his call, no matter where she was, and come to him more swiftly than bee or bird could fly.

'But what if it isn't that?' he asked, still perturbed. 'What if I should fall, or just sit down hard without thinking and it gets pressed there?'

'Very well,' she relented, 'there is one other course. But it is for extreme emergencies only. You place one hand near the tip of each spire and you stroke them back and forth vigorously. All the time you do, you will be thinking of me and longing for me with all your heart. Thus, I will know your plight and I will send you the bliss you need.'

Her head rose sharply and she stared deeply into his guileless young eyes. 'Remember, this is for dire emergencies only. You do not want your eyes to dim and your wits to become addled, do you? You do not want those beautiful shafts with their splendid tips to become dull and lose their colour, do you? Or find unsightly pimples on your face? You might even start ugly warts growing all over the palms of your hands. You would not like that, would you?'

He shook his head violently and shuddered at the thought.

Smiling and pleased, she told him to cross his legs and sit very straight with his hands laced behind his head, his eyes closed and turned back as far as they would go. He was to breathe deeply and steadily and form a picture in his mind of the exact spot on his spine where the point of her hoof rested. In the most simple terms she could find, she explained to him that this was the source of the magic essence of his people. He was to peer into that spot in his mind and summon the force, urging it up and up until it reached a level inside his

47

spine just behind his throat. At this exact point, all the Elvan people had what were known as the 'singing rings'. Their necks were long and elegant not only to contain the rings, but to give their sound resonance.

She watched him intently as he strained, guiding the force as she had told him. At this point, she added her own efforts to help him along, sending messages of encouragement as the force rose. Much of her consciousness was already inside his mind, listening carefully for a singing vibration that was far above the range of human hearing.

When the singing began, faintly at first, she told him that this wondrous force, when built to its peak, can influence all matter and energy, making every atom do its bidding, even exerting a powerful influence over time and space.

'Let us test it now,' she urged softly. 'Tell the singing rings to lift your body a few inches off the ground.'

She watched his face and was delighted with the deep powers of concentration she saw there. A second or two later, his hands still clasped behind his head and his legs crossed, his body rose six inches off the ground and stayed suspended there. The boy smiled and seemed not the least bit troubled by the strange experience.

Next, she directed him to concentrate the energy condensed in the singing rings and aim it at a point just between and behind his closed eyes. He was then to tell the force to turn him upside down and settle him, lightly as a feather, on the top of his head. Almost immediately, his body turned in the air and came to rest on the top of his head.

'You've done it perfectly,' she cried. 'Now, with careful attention, you can rearrange matters to your own desire. But let us not be too ambitious until you have mastered the art fully.'

The doe described a faun to young Igorin, giving him all the details of its shape, outlining the pointed ears, the tiny horns, the goat's legs and the large priapus which stayed erect almost permanently. When he had the picture clearly in his mind, she urged him to concentrate on it with all his might, telling the great force to rearrange every particle of his body to conform with the image. As a humorous afterthought, she directed him to see the shape behind his eyes sitting right side up.

A bluish light began surrounding the upside-down boy and rings of a more fiery light began forming inside the blue aura. In this dazzling display, his form became indistinct by degrees until it disappeared completely in the whirling and dancing of the subtle, chameleon flames. There was a sudden Poof! and a few wisps of smoke and a young, grinning satyr was sitting on the grass, a long pointed phallus waving jauntily in front of him. Quick as a flash, flecks of foam covering his lecherous mouth, he leaped upon the prostrate doe and sank the rigid priapus into her wound as deeply as it would go.

The doe received the battering with good grace, wishing she had suggested a less rambunctious form for him. It was over quickly and Igorin felt very foolish, not at all understanding what had swept over him. His impolite behaviour embarrassed him as he looked down at the only slightly slackened priapus. The liquids still issuing from it reminded him of the strong smell of rams, yet they excited him immensely in his new guise. The doe was stretched out where he had abandoned her, licking her rather sore and offended orifice; not, however, without a certain smile of new contentment.

She looked over at the bewildered faun, the smile still fixed. 'The forces you have summoned are still concentrated. Now, close your eyes and hold your breath while you concentrate behind your eyes on your true form.'

He did as he was told and a few seconds later there was a brief blue and yellow flash, a puff of fine white smoke and the real Igorin, as beautiful as ever, was sitting beside the doe. He opened his mouth in surprise then smiled happily.

She warned him that he must be extremely careful in the use of such awesome forces. It took time to become so adept that there was no chance of mishap. For this reason, he must give his oath not to tamper with his shape unless she was there to guide him. That he might lose himself beyond recall was the dreadful possibility if he became foolish and impetuous. There were realms where even she could not reach him.

Igorin promised faithfully that he would obey her instructions. He was still trembling with the strangeness of his recent experience.

'Listen carefully, Flondrix my love, for now you must commit many things to memory,' the doe instructed.

'Why do you call me Flondrix?' he asked. 'My name is Igorin.'

'Your name is Flondrix,' she corrected him. 'That is your true name among our people. Prince Flondrix, in fact. Ask no more questions, you will know your true identity when the appropriate time comes. For the time being, you will not be able to hear that name from any lips but mine.' She closed her eyes for a moment and when she opened them, she told him to shout the new name aloud. He did, but he could not hear a sound.

He listened intently as she described the great Elvan festival of Midsummer. It would start this night as the moon rose. Each year, many snoops and spies hoped to catch sight of the festivities in order to ferret out the secrets of Elvan Lore. Witches and mortal magicians were easily foiled, but the dwarfs could be uncommonly canny; they had their own ways of creating the impression of invisibility. For these reasons, the Elves wore the disguises of the animals of wood and field. Cavorting in these forms, no outsider could determine the true and innermost natures of the Elves. To have these known would be the undoing of their great power and a threat to all the known worlds.

The doe excused herself then and walked behind a large rock a few yards away. He heard the splashings on the ground as she emptied herself of fluids. When she returned, he looked puzzled and asked her why she had to do that; he never did, he didn't even have the places to do it with. Suddenly, he smelled the glorious aroma wafting towards him. The doe licked his brow until the worried frown disappeared.

'When we take the guise of an animal, to some extent we must obey their physical needs. Had you been a faun a bit longer, you would have done so too. And without going behind a rock, I assure you. As for the smell, well, all you have to do is concentrate your new powers. You can make any smell you wish. So why not choose an exotic garden?'

Before he could ask any more questions, she reminded him it was getting very late and that she would have to depart soon. They had been talking about Midsummer and it was important that he remember every detail of her instructions. He was to come to her tonight, to the Sacred Glade of her people.

'Flondrix, I have waited all these years, longing to be with you. I could not bear one more Midsummer festival without you at my side. Now, listen to my plan.'

As soon as Ungar was asleep, he was to climb naked to the top of the cottage and wait for the moon to rise.

He would sit as she had instructed him, and concentrate his forces, imagining the form of a great eagle. He was to keep the words 'Sacred Glade' in his mind and his wings would carry him there unerringly. There, he would land at the edge of the glade, alighting on a low, stout branch of a tree she would choose, and change immediately to the guise of the faun. He would find his doe waiting for him there, at the base of the tree. He was to fear nothing, for she would protect him from all harm. And ere the morning light, he would be winging back home again, filled with greater strength, power and knowledge than he had ever dreamed possible.

'Before you think of any more things to ask me,' she admonished, 'there is one lovely rite we must perform before the sun sets and I must leave. This rite will make our union complete, perfect and endless. It will also bestow upon you your full Elvanhood. But you must volunteer to give me your sight and not ask it back until I am ready to return it to you.'

'Why must I do this?' he asked, hesitating.

'You will experience the ultimate bliss of the world beyond worlds,' she answered. 'But to witness this with your eyes would so astound you that you might become confused and frightened, thus jeopardizing us both. We could become lost . . . out there.' She pointed to the sky over his head.

He hesitated only a moment longer, feeling a great heat building up inside himself.

'I do gladly relinquish my sight to you and I will wait until you return it,' he said with determination.

As soon as the words were out of his mouth, he could see nothing about him; all his vision was filled with beautiful floating clouds from which cascaded jewels of fiery hues.

At the very same instant, the doe disappeared and in

her place stood . . . Astra. Astra, the gemstone of the Elves, prized by Glortan The Great above all his powers and possessions. Many wondrous things had he taught this angel-child of his, but even he did not reckon on how subtly she had progressed and developed her magical abilities. By hard work and concentration, she had discovered things that enabled her to move beyond his control and keeping. Even as she stood there in the vale outside the enchanted forest, Glortan believed he saw her moving through the Sacred Glade near his palatial tree house, so clever were the spells she could work. Not that these spells were beyond his great powers, but as Astra was above suspicion, he was content that all was as it seemed and his attentions were focused elsewhere.

Astra's neck arched magnificently and the silver and spun gold of her hair, the radiance of her body, the magical lights twinkling in her maidenhair, the flashes of her vermilion nipples made the setting sun look pale and watery, rather than the deep, fiery orange it actually was.

As she stood looking down adoringly at the temporarily sightless boy, she reached between her delicate buttocks and pressed one tiny spot firmly. The flaming silver tips of her golden maidenhair began to part as the skin beneath opened. Suddenly, two perfect, full, luscious vulvas formed, the two clitorii blending and overlapping at the centre, the vaginal passages at the extremes. The scent that issued from these gold and rose hallowed places exceeded even the perfume the boy had reeled with earlier.

Blindly, his twitching lips sought the precious spots and she held his head gently between her hands, allowing him to seek and explore, inside and out, until her own great emerald eyes began to cloud over and dim with emotion.

53

'Quickly,' she breathed, 'press where you know to press and then lie flat on your back.'

Tearing his mouth away from the two delicate mouths that had been kissing him as passionately as he had been kissing them, he reached a finger behind himself, clumsily and impatiently searching and probing between his buttocks for the secret spot. At last he found it and pushed so hard the pain overwhelmed him as he fell back, not able to see the power and majesty of the great sheath swelling out from his opening body.

Igorin stretched out, pressing his hands to the ground in order to maintain his balance as the weight of his great protrusion swayed from side to side, twitching and quivering. Her eyes half-closed with joy, Astra reached out and slid the great sheath all the way down, tears dotting her cheeks as the beauty of the two great shafts was revealed, glinting like fire and ice in the last rays of the sun.

She put one tiny foot on either side of his hips and raised herself up on the tips of her toes; she just managed to place the two magnificent tips inside her entrances from that height. She held herself high for a few seconds, feeling her whole body shudder as his hips bucked and elevated, sending the shafts into her. Her knees weakened and bent, little by little impaling her further, while time stopped once more.

As he entered more deeply, her entire body began to reform and organize itself to accommodate him, the shafts sliding higher and higher inside her. At last she felt the two splendid tips probing into the lower reaches of her throat. It was essential to his full Elvanhood and their future safety that those globes should be fully imbedded in her singing rings at the moment when the ultimate bliss began.

Down and down she pressed, trying to get the last fraction of him inside her. She reached under his buttocks and pulled him up with all her strength. The silver and vermilion tips touched the edges of the rings, but they could not reach high enough to enter fully. Feeling the first breath of panic, she realized that his attainment was not perfected yet, undoubtedly due to the mortal blood in his veins.

Her panic rising, she felt the huge tidal wave of world beyond worlds forces gathering in his body; that urgency lent new strength to her passion-weakened body and she rose, drawing herself up as quickly as she could, freeing great expanses of him with each upward thrust. His shocked, pained cries reached her and she soothed him with her voice, begging him to hold on, to trust her, to concentrate every ounce of his great force on holding back until she was ready. She knew now that there was only one way to get his precious tips inside her singing rings in time.

Igorin obeyed her words, but unwittingly and unintentionally, as he concentrated, the vision in the magic inner eye broadened and suddenly, beyond the colourful clouds of the sightlessness of his eyes, he viewed the awesome and irresistible beauty of Astra. His shocked gasp gave her warning, but there was no time to exert a blinding spell on his inner eye.

She saw the pulses of his entire body quicken and the muscles tighten and thrash him about as the climax beyond all understanding reached for him. For one second she felt sorry for the boundless journey she had embarked him on and then, throwing all thoughts aside, she commanded her body to rise up in the air until she was suspended head down over his thrashing twin spires. Stretching her neck to the very last fraction it could go, she opened her mouth to receive them.

Down and down she plummetted, the spires rising inside her throat until she felt her face nearing his tuft of silvery hair. She increased her downward pressure

55

until the shock of the twin tips forced the 'singing rings' open. She quivered in the air and forced her face down once more and the great globes were deeply imbedded in the rings. With one final effort, she focused the forces in the rings until they were singing higher than they ever had before.

As the shock waves began to strike, the earth rumbled beneath them and she knew the climax like no other was about to engulf her. The ground shuddered again and the sheep, unseeing but frightened, all huddled at the far side of the vale. The rock near the two lovers split into a thousand pieces and at the last moment, both their bodies rose at a fantastic rate and were exploded out of view, rocketing up into the sky, racing along paths even beyond the ones ordinarily known to the Elves as the Other Paths. Swifter and higher they went, an invisible blaze, shedding colours beyond the mortal spectrum until they circled the evening star and started the downward journey . . .

*

A boy and a doe lay sprawled on the highest pinnacle of the mountain range above the vale.

'See again, my most precious beloved,' the doe whispered hoarsely, helping him to rise.

His eyes unclouded and he looked around, his whole physical presence expanding as he did. Where an innocent shepherd had once stood, a taller, statelier Elvan Prince gazed calmly down at the distant vale, nearly three thousand feet below. While his eyes looked outward, in truth he concentrated another vision inward. He had discovered the whole Cosmos was inside himself.

Astra had conferred upon him full Elvan Being. The risk she took was enormous for only her father Glortan had the authority to permit such rites. Had their climax arrived before he had fully entered her 'singing rings', the disturbance it would have caused in the balance of greater Cosmic Forces would have been so immense Glortan would have known immediately. The penalty, had she failed, was immediate banishment in human form. Gone would be her Elvan Powers and her immortality. Such a risk she had taken for this was the measure of her love for the shepherd she knew to be Prince Flondrix, the lover ordained for her by the stars.

'It is pointless to ask you how one can go beyond the infinite,' he said dreamily, 'but since I have now seen you, though not with these eyes and not with cunning intent, is there any further purpose in hiding your true identity from me?'

'I am Astra, daughter of King Glortan.' The doe dissolved slowly and the incredible Astra stood beside him. He pulled her close and felt his lips sparkle with a strange energy force as they brushed her hair aside. Joyfully, he placed his mouth over hers.

Even Astra was surprised as he calmly gathered her in his arms and stepped away from the pinnacle. They did not plunge down three thousand feet to the hidden vale below; gently they floated, landing next to the rock which had been splintered and pulverized by a force beyond reckoning.

When the sun touched the horizon, Astra moved reluctantly from his strong embrace. He watched her disappear as the doe's form took her place.

'Flondrix, my beloved, kiss once more that now tender spot. In so doing, I shall give you back your shepherd's stature and innocence of manner. Thus Ungar or any stranger you might chance to meet will find nothing amiss. But buried in your heart and mind will remain all your new and astounding knowledge, waiting to surface as the moon rises tonight. Then, I must rush with the wind lest I be late.'

Flondrix knelt behind her trembling form and kissed her deeply with all the love in his bursting heart. Then he rose lightly, smiling blissfully as Igorin once more.

'Just before you go, sweet doe,' he pleaded, 'tell me what it is called, that wonderful, wonderful thing we did that shakes the earth and splits open the skies. Does it have a name?'

'We seldom mention it,' she answered seriously, 'for it is understood without speaking. In our language, which you shall learn tonight, the name of the poem which describes it is used. The poem is called "Chandrala" in Elvish, and it starts something like this in the speech of men:

'Twin spires reaching to fill twin fountains,
Valleys aspiring to absorb the mountains,
The verge of bliss is four into two,
Two for me and two for you,
But ultimate bliss is finally won,
When we two at last are one.'

She turned and nuzzled his sparkling tuft, touching him tenderly with the very tip of her tongue. 'I must go now,' she whispered. 'Watch for the rising of the moon.'

With that, she turned from him and sped away, bounding down the hillside with a swiftness so great the enchanted forest had swallowed her before the boy could blink an eye. As his reluctant footsteps followed the slowly descending sheep, he rubbed his eyes with the backs of his hands like a small boy fighting tears. In his head, as from a great distance, he heard her magical voice again remind him of the rising moon. He smiled suddenly and leapt high in the air before speeding after the distant homeward-wending flock.

IV

Calamity in the Castle –
the Curse Takes its Toll

Igorin's day of ultimate bliss was, of course, the lovers' well-guarded secret. Lost in the hills and shrouded by a magic web, they had been invisible to all. However, the results were felt in other quarters, and felt in the most terrible and disastrous ways.

On Midsummer Eve, all the country yeomanry was gathered in ordered ranks before the Dark King's castle. Barons and nobles of the outlying districts were arrayed on the verges of the huge greensward with their retainers, men-at-arms, provisioners, horses, cattle, equipment, tents and pavilions, all ready to do their annual week's training and exercises in the king's service. It was also the official time for bringing forth the tithes owed to the crown.

The usually peaceful greensward was now become a parade ground festooned with banners, pennants and flags of all descriptions and the clamour and noise of carpenters' hammers and axes smote the still hot air as tents and pavilions were hastily erected. The yeomanry sweated profusely under the noonday sun in their closely drawn ranks. The nobles, on heavily laden horses, nearly melted in the baking ovens of their armour.

A loud blast of trumpets stilled the clamour and the drawbridge was lowered, clanking and rattling the huge chains as it creaked ponderously over the deep moat. A second blast sounded and the royal guards came thundering over the bridge, led by the king's commander, Baron Rodney de Minge. They quickly formed ranks on the far side of the bridge as a guard of honour for the king.

After a short, hushed silence, King Barlocks emerged from the castle, resplendent in coal-black armour, his head covered by a matching helm sprouting black plumes of such length they curled luxuriantly over the flanks of the matchless white steed. As he reached the middle of the drawbridge, just below the royal gallery, a tremendous roar of water was heard, sounding as thunderous as an avalanche or a great waterfall.

Water came spewing ferociously from every chink in the king's armour. The pressure was so great it seemed a geyser had been loosed inside somewhere. Suddenly his plumed and crested helm rose straight up in the air, rising on a fountain-like jet that reached the very parapets before cascading down into the moat. As the first stream of airborne liquid hit the still water, great clouds of steam rose from it and soon the men on the parade ground could not see the royal personage. In no time at all, the entire castle was lost to view, enveloped in a billowing cloud of white vapour.

Gonzola hesitated for only a second, his great surprise quickly changing to a knowing urgency. He thrust through the throng of lords and ladies on the gallery and hastened down the stairs, muttering an incantation to himself. In the centre of his forehead, just above his eyes, a small beam of light appeared, shining with the intensity of a miniature searchlight. A knowing observer, had there been one about, would have guessed that the magician had attained a level of Knowledge bordering on true Elvan Power.

While all about him were flailing and flapping helplessly in the gathering billows of steam, the magician quickly located the king who was trying to quell his panicking horse and undo the straps of his armour at the same time.

Unceremoniously, Gonzola touched the king's armour with a small ivory wand he kept concealed in a secret pocket of the great black cloak he wore winter and summer. The armour shattered in a thousand pieces and the king came tumbling down from his horse. He would have fallen flat on his back had Gonzola not caught him up under the arms.

The king was blinded by the steam like all the others, but the magician saw clearly the huge rent in the king's black velvet hose. The finely embroidered doublet was nearly split in two. From the front of the king's body was suspended a great black penis as thick as a fire hose, spewing steamy liquid in every direction. As the magician watched, the stream quietly petered out and the formidable and unspeakable python-like affair began to shrivel. Hastily, Gonzola reached out with both hands and heaved the terrible thing up over the king's right shoulder, around the back of his neck, allowing the copious balance to dangle down over the left shoulder.

'Make haste, sire, we haven't a moment to lose,' barked the magician, dragging the lurching, weakened king after him. As they stumbled up the stairs, the fog began to dissipate and shadowy figures could be seen running blindly, bumping into one another and bowling each other over. Gonzola dodged this way and that and soon had the king safely locked inside his private chamber.

By the time he had the exhausted king stretched out on his vast bed, the fire hose python protruding from the king's body had shrivelled into many tiny puckers. With a gurgle and a loud pop, there was nothing left but the infantile blob of flesh which usually adorned Barlocks's crotch. Wisps of dissolving steam blew in and out the open window, wafted on a light capricious breeze. From below, they could hear the shouts and lamentations of the confused hosts.

'What happened?' sobbed the king. 'And what is that terrible stench?'

Actually, the royal chamber did smell as though a thousand rotten eggs had been smashed in it. Gonzola fastidiously wrinkled his nose. Until that moment, he had been too preoccupied to notice the awful odour.

'I am afraid, my liege,' the magician rumbled deep in his chest, 'this unbearable aroma is an aftermath of your recent astounding performance.'

Barlocks sat up and groaned. 'Will you stop your infernal riddles and tell me what happened?' He coughed a few times before releasing a tremendous sneeze. 'Sun preserve us and shine benignly upon us,' wheezed the monarch, 'I nearly drowned inside that dratted armour. And now I am coming down with an accursed cold. Was any man so afflicted!' He turned his head to stare at the magician whose form was shimmering in the evaporating vapours. 'Speaking of armour,' he growled, 'what the drat happened to it?'

'Which riddle do you wish solved first, my lord?' asked Gonzola with a certain amount of patient irony. 'As to the armour, it yielded to forces too great to withstand. 'Tis a pity, I know how highly you prized it.'

'Prized it?' wailed the king. 'That armour cost at least five years' worth of your princely wages. Now, will you tell me what happened out there?'

'I can tell you little as yet,' the magician mumbled,

pacing slowly across the floor, his bushy white brows knitted together in concentration. 'Even a magician must think at times. But I warrant you, it is but a new twist to the same old curse. An outraged Elvan King is not easily appeased.'

As he paced, an insistent voice inside the old wizard's head kept repeating: 'It must be that boy, he is come of age. And someone has got to him, yes indeed. Who could that "someone" be?' His mind raced round all the possibilities he could think of. Bumbree? That lascivious old witch would love to get her hands on him, but she was just a low-level black sorceress, no Elvan Lore there. And this whole thing smacked of . . . yes! The Elvan King's household. Where else would the knowledge lie? He thought about the Elvan King, the king's wife, his sister who was the boy's mother. None of them fitted. Why should they wish to awaken the boy's secret powers?

Gonzola scratched deeply inside his beard and began mumbling under his breath. 'Somebody . . . somebody I don't know about. Now, now, let's not become scattered where logic will do the trick.' As he concentrated still harder, the answer began to dawn. 'Someone . . . someone young, someone who would be bound in soul and blood to the seemingly innocent shepherd. And that could be only one, one only in all of Time. What a fool I've been! How could I have been so blind?' He scratched more furiously. 'Had I foreseen that, what a perilous journey it would have meant with that boy. Yes, to somewhere even Glortan fears to tread. Or Glortan's . . . yes, by my beard . . . or Glortan's daughter!'

'What are you muttering about now?' demanded Barlocks.

Alarmed, the magician's head came up sharply. The king was on his feet, rumaging through a gigantic chest in search of new raiment. An assortment of hose and doublets flew over his shoulder, aimed in the general direction of the bed.

'Where are you going?' asked the wizard.

'Where am I going, you old fool?' roared the king, running to the window and pointing down. 'Where do you think I'm going? Do you want them to start grumbling? If I don't appear soon, they'll likely as not break camp and go home. With all the tax money. Now, you go down there and entertain them till I'm ready. And you'd better have a very good story to cover that — that embarrassing incident. One chuckle from the ranks and you will pay dearly, O learned wizard.'

'If you leave this room before the sun sets, your royal highness, you will learn meanings for — uh — "embarrassing incident" you never dreamt existed,' Gonzola intoned in his deepest spellbinding voice.

The magician was not absolutely certain, but his logical mind declared that the first display was only the beginning. He also knew that the mystical Midsummer Eve would start at sundown. The fair hand guiding the young shepherd would be off for the Sacred Glade before the setting of the sun.

The king's bravado collapsed as he sat disconsolately to pull on fresh hose. 'What did you mean by that, good Gonzola?' he asked, his face haunted.

The magician closed his eyes and threw his head back. He tried to picture the exact event which had caused the torrential fire hose evacuation of a short while ago. His mind calculated quickly how long it would take for something new to happen.

'Sire, if I do not miss my magic, by the time you are fully dressed, the next horrendous Elvish prank will descend upon us. And so it will go, in fits and starts, like the waxing and waning of young passions, until the — uh — day is spent.'

The king rose from the chair pulling up his hose. No sooner was everything in place than a loud ripping noise echoed through the chamber and the fresh hose split asunder. A huge sheath bolted out of the king's abdomen so suddenly that it bowled Barlocks backward on to his bed. As he fell, the gargantuan sheath flew up from the floor and extended itself until it pierced the canopy over the bed and came to a quivering halt against one of the overhead rafters, pinning the king firmly to the mattress.

'Help!' shrieked the king. 'Gonzola, do something. Quick, man, it's killing me. The pain is excruciating.' At these words, the magician ran across the room and took a huge broadsword from the wall.

'No, no, not that!' yelped the monarch. 'Get some of the scullery maids. But blindfold them first. Get some ladders too. They must climb up there and do something to relieve it. It burns me fiercely, it will burst if it is not relieved.'

Barlocks's groans followed the old wizard as he slipped out the door and carefully locked it. In no time at all he had a team of stout, buxom scullery maids marshalled together, all wearing blindfolds and carrying ladders. Gonzola threw open the door and the girls rushed in, bumping into one another, the ladders becoming entangled and they all started shrieking at once. Gonzola ran first to one, then to another, trying desperately to sort out the hysterical mêlée.

With great gasping and panting, the ladders were finally set against the overhead beam and the girls started scrambling up, goaded on by the magician's bellowed directions. Five girls in all, they began panicking with the sense of height, one after the other trying to back down. Gonzola flew about, pinching bottoms viciously, whacking and thumping to drive them back up again. One girl, in her terror, toppled backwards

65

and landed on the wizard's head, bowling him over and smothering him in layers of petticoats and soggy under-garments. Obviously, from the smell that burned his nostrils, the girl's panic was so great she had been unable to contain herself. None the less, she became quite excited in her new predicament and began wriggling her hips and moaning, attempting to catch the old man's head between her wet, exposed thighs. He sank two of his good teeth into the ripe flesh and she screamed, rolling off him as if scalded by boiling oil.

'Rub! Rub as hard as you can,' gasped the old man, urging on the four girls who had reached the tops of the ladders. Eight hands flew up and down the enor-mous pole, yanking the sheath back by degrees until an ugly black wart-covered head and part of the slimy, oozing shaft were exposed.

A great scream from the prostrate king heralded a rumbling like an underground torrent. The poor girls held on to the thrashing shaft for dear life as it jumped and jerked wildly. A splintering crash tore through the chamber as the overhead beam parted. Cascades of an evil-smelling black fluid poured out of the ceiling and inundated the girls until they looked as if they were covered with black mayonnaise. Great puddles of it ran off the bed and wobbled jelly-like across the stone floor. Anguished cries and blubbering wheezes filled the room as one by one the half-drowned and smothered girls toppled backwards from their perches.

Fortunately, none was hurt seriously, a bruise here and there being the worst they had suffered. With all haste, Gonzola hustled them out of the room and sent them blindly down the stairs with their ladders. Next, he collected a group of chambermaids with mops and pails and bade them wait outside the king's chamber until he had had a chance to survey the damage.

The king's proportions had returned to 'normal' and he was huddled on his haunches as far back against the headboard as he could go. The room looked as though it had been savaged by muddy water buffaloes.

Gently Gonzola led the ashen king into the royal toilet and brought him some towels and a change of clothing. When that door was securely closed, he turned the chambermaids loose on the room. By the time the king was ready to return, the room was spotless and the maids, with their pails full of muck, had departed. Gonzola and Barlocks stood in the centre of the chamber with awe-struck faces, staring at the shattered beam overhead and the shreds of the torn canopy hanging down over the bed.

'Is it over yet?' whispered the king, trembling.

'I am afraid not, my lord,' Gonzola admitted sadly. 'We forget what it is like to be young, to be at the very peak of youthful exuberance.'

'What did you say?' Barlocks queried with quizzical brows.

''Tis nothing, your majesty, just that I feel it is still but the beginning. The sun is a long way to setting.'

'Oh no. No, no, no,' moaned the king, sitting weakly on the freshly made bed.

'My lord, I suggest I use this time to inform the throng outside, for the interlude may be briefer than we know. Shall I not tell them you have graciously declared a holiday feast due to the extreme heat? That they shall all be dismissed until the morrow when the exercises shall be reconvened at an early hour? Give your word quickly, your highness, for I wish to be back at your side before the next onslaught begins.'

The king whimpered and nodded a meek assent before sinking down to stare wide-eyed at the ceiling overhead.

Before the sun finally sank that day, the exhausted

Barlocks was gasping like a man on death's doorstep. The ceiling and roof overhead had been smashed completely and those parts of the floor not covered with broken stones and rubble were piled high with small mountains of what appeared, to the best of Gonzola's knowledge, to be reeking hillocks of goat dung.

The rising moon shone down through the gaping roof, silhouetting the great tower against the sky. All was silent and the king cowered in a small bed in one of the lesser guest rooms.

Eagles in the Moonlight

❀❀❀❀❀❀❀❀

Igorin perched himself gingerly on the very edge of the chimney top and crossed his legs. He hugged himself with his bare arms and a shiver of delicious anticipation ran from his toes to the hair on his head, tightening his skin like a charge of electrical fire. He was facing the exact centre of the enchanted forest and his eyes, half-closed, peered straight ahead. He listened to the faint woodland sounds attuning themselves to the utter stillness of the night. At last, a pale silvery light crept along the roof-top and rose up the boy's back, bathing him bit by bit in a shimmering glow. With the rising of the moon, he looked like a pale bronze statue covered in a thin patina of silver. Soaring free of the low hills, the moon filled the horizon behind him like an enormous opal; the moon was to be much closer in those days.

The boy felt the currents rising in his spine and centering as he directed them. The picture of a huge eagle filled the space right behind and between his eyes. Slowly his arms extended out from his body and when they were fully stretched an aura of blue flame, tinged with orange, obscured his form. A small puff of smoke, as would be made by the last ember bursting in the fireplace below, wafted skyward and with it a splendid

69

eagle who deftly caught the light breeze from the forest and soared with it, hardly moving its wings at all. As the trees fell away below, a dark shadow appeared directly over him, a few scant inches away.

'Well done, my brother,' a harsh voice like the cry of an eagle sounded in Igorin's mind. He opened his mouth in alarm to speak.

'No need for that,' the rasping voice spoke silently inside him. 'We do not need speech, you and I. For I am in a way, you. I am your expanded self. I am inside you and yet outside too, moving like your shadow. I am the eyes of your past and of your future, the light on your path. I am your teacher and your protector.'

'Why have — why have I never — met you before,' the strange words formed in the depths of Igorin's mind. The words came slowly for this was a language he did not know. Yet he seemed to know it, he could understand it clearly, but the words took time in forming.

'Until today,' the separate thoughts flowed down through his mind, 'you have lived exclusively in the world of men. Today you reached the highest Elvan attainment and all that is Elvish is yours. You already understand the language because it has always been there. Deep inside you, as is all our history and ancient knowledge.'

'But I cannot seem to think of it,' Igorin's thoughts protested. 'You say I am of the Elvan People, and so does Astra. But I don't seem to know about it.'

'If you think about it you will know,' the other thought-voice told him. 'Do you see that brilliant star over the White Mountains? It is called Topar, the home star of the Ancient Ones. Gaze steadily upon it as you fly and see what it tells you.' The shadow above wavered slightly. 'And you must stop thinking of yourself as Igorin. From this moment hence, you must think of yourself as Flondrix.'

Flondrix thought the name over to himself a few times and then gazed at the bright distant star. It changed colour as he looked, the hues brightening until it became pure silver.

He saw the Ancient Ones travelling through space on the awesome force named Ra-Chand, visiting many worlds and bringing wondrous Knowledge with them. Somehow, he knew one of these worlds was called Elvanhome. Something ached inside of him as the word formed. Then he understood that the Ra-Chand of the Ancient Ones was the greatest of all Cosmic Forces, truly beautiful when treated with love, yet potentially the most destructive power when used improperly.

He felt that the great energy in his spine, the one which had brought him so many wonders and joys during the day, was connected to the great Ra-Chand. The word Io-Chand formed in his mind. All Elves had it and could invoke it at will. Men once had it too, but they so abused it and turned it to such destructive purposes the Ancient Ones had sent them forgetfulness lest they upset the whole Cosmos. It would remain dormant in the race of men until they could be trusted. This was why the Ancient Ones had returned to their favourite children in Elvanhome and imposed a great burden on them. They were to send a colony to the world of men to watch over them as the Ancient Ones had watched over Elvanhome during the long evolution of the Elves. In gratitude, the Elves were granted great power and the ways of travel known as the Other Paths. And in the full blooming of the Elvan Io-Chand in perfect harmony with the master Cosmic Force, Ra-Chand, were the very seeds of Elvan immortality.

Many pictures flashed through his mind as the

powerful wings beat the night air. Unerringly, he veered slightly to the south to correct his course, making a perfect line for the Sacred Glade.

'Well done again, my brother,' the hoarse voice said in his mind. 'You fly well and you are remembering the history inside yourself.'

'Yes, but I don't understand everything. How does it all work?' the worried boy inside the eagle asked.

'Rise up until you and I are one,' came the answer. Flondrix made a slight adjustment in his tail and pinion feathers and he merged with the shadow. Suddenly he understood many things about matter, energy and illusion. And how at one and the same time he must be the doer and the observer. What any other eyes might have missed as an indistinct patch below, signalled to his mind that he had reached the Sacred Glade. He started the long glide down, knowing exactly which tree and which branch of that tree to alight upon.

VI

A Taste for Mischief
in the
Enchanted Forest

۞۞۞۞۞۞۞

Flondrix clambered down through the branches of the tall tree, his sharp little faun hooves landing accurately on each succeeding bough until he stood upright on the ground below, in the middle of a path near the Sacred Glade. He looked up once to the top of the tree wistfully, sorry for leaving the majestic guise of the eagle; it had been wonderful skimming along high in the air under the brilliant moon.

A soft muzzle rubbed along his curly goat flanks and gentle teeth nipped his short tail.

'You're here at last,' whispered a familiar voice. 'How glad I am to see you.'

The faun whirled about and embraced the lovely doe's neck. In the dark, he saw that her eyes were no longer violet, but her own true flashing emerald, sparkling even in darkness like icy flames. He felt a strange sensation going through his mind and then extending itself, coursing through his entire body. It was as though their very wills had blended and he existed as much inside her person as she existed inside his. Confirming this revelation, the dark green fire leaped in her eyes as she nodded her head with satisfaction.

'We are now as one,' she confided. 'You will know I am here and I will know you are close to me, but to all others we will seem as one, in my person.'

'That sounds very nice,' he said beginning to sidle around her.

'Behave yourself for a moment,' she ordered. 'Don't you make light of this, my dear, for it would be disastrous to have you discovered here, to have anyone question your presence at our most sacred rites and celebrations. True, you have that right by birth, but the time is not yet come to announce your true identity. Stay close to me and all will be well.'

'What about your father?' he asked, her words having sent a small chill through him.

'We will arrive at a time when he is too occupied to concern himself,' she assured him. She went on to explain that there were but three with the power to detect him: her father, her mother and her aunt. The two women would be busy helping her father and later, when the feasting and revelry got under way after the more solemn rites, they would retire and not return until just before dawn. By that time he would be winging home again as the great eagle.

Without another word, she led him along a path which circled the Sacred Glade. Trotting along, his nostrils were suddenly filled with a splendid fragrance, a scent something like the one he had smelled before in the hills near home. He tried to identify it and reached out to hold the doe's ear.

'Did you drop your water on the path?' he asked innocently.

Her deep musical laugh answered him. 'Lovely Flondrix, you were so excited you did not even notice.

How well you act out your role of woodland faun! That was *you*, my dear. As we were standing and chatting, you deposited a goodly quantity of your golden liquid on the ground . . . and quite a number of droppings too.' She turned her head and licked the end of his long, firm priapus. 'Without even thinking, it seems, you have made perfumes of everything, just as I told you to.'

Tantalized by the soft touch of her tongue, he was about to run behind and mount her, but she admonished him to wait. There was something important they had to do first. Whimpering like a disappointed child, he trotted along after her when she broke playfully away from his grasp.

As they disappeared among the trees, a large shadow began to materialize over the spot where the faun had dropped from the tree. The shadow loomed larger and its ominous shape filled the path, the shambling movements disclosing what seemed, at first vague sight, to be a great hulking bear attempting to sneak close to the tree on tiptoe, silently, surreptitiously, like a thief in the night.

As the beast came into full view in the etiolated light of the moon, some of the features appeared less bear-like. The low hindquarters, covered in shaggy grey hair, were those of a bear, but the forelegs were too long and dangling, ending in huge hands with long thumbs. The ears were halfway between a bear's and an ape's, but the muzzle was very blunt and wide with slobbering great lips which pulled back to reveal ugly yellow fangs. Three great paps hung down from the apparition's chest and patches of hair were missing there, disclosing the doughy, wrinkled skin of an old woman. As the beast turned to sniff the air in all directions, it could be seen that similar patches of furry hair were missing over the broad hindquarters, exposing roughened, pimpled buttocks of an unmistakably human cast.

Satisfied that no one was about, the disgusting beast shuffled behind a tree and reappeared almost immediately with a large kerchief, the four corners of which were tied up to form a lumpy bundle. She squatted in the middle of the path and untied the kerchief with deft movements of the hands which belied their clumsy look. Taking a small iron pot and a wooden ladle from the bundle, she quickly scooped up all the droppings left by the faun and dropped them in the pot. Drawing the ladle over the ground, she caught up as much of his liquids as she could, emptying them into the pot too. A hoarse murmur of delight broke from her throat and the ugly, irregular yellow fangs glistened wetly in the moonlight. Behind the still clinging aroma of perfumed gardens, her keen nose could detect the pungent seminal fluids which pour so freely from excited, priapic fauns.

Hastily, the grotesque creature gathered up the corners of the kerchief in one hand and took the pot and ladle in the other. She lumbered off into the thicker part of the enchanted forest; when she was sure she was well out of sight of the Sacred Glade, she dug a hole in the ground with a trowel from the kerchief. With a few mumbled words and some powder she scattered in the hole, she soon had an eerie fire going, a fire that gave off an intense heat and yet the light from it was so pale it could not be seen from five feet away. Over this, she placed the iron pot and, with the kerchief spread out on the ground, began grinding odd herbs, powders and foul substances in a small mortar. When this mixture was ready, she poured it into the pot and stirred vigorously. Soon the pot simmered and bubbled and she lifted it up. Immediately, the fire went out. Placing the pot on the ground near the kerchief, she continued to stir the mixture, blowing frequently at the unsavoury contents.

When the brew had cooled sufficiently, she delicately dipped the ladle in and sampled the stuff. She licked her lips appreciatively and tried another taste. Hideous, reddened eyes rolled ecstatically in the gloom. As the right hand with the ladle reached out for the third time, the left hand shot forth and grabbed the right wrist. Noiselessly, the two hands struggled for supremacy. Inside the now febrile brain, a furious dialogue was taking place.

'Leave off, blast you, leave off — it is mine!' 'It is *ours*, you miserable dung-eater, you will spoil everything.' 'No, I won't, I want just one more delicious taste.' 'I know you, you greedy scavenger, you'll lick the pot clean. Bind him! Bind him! If there is anything left over, you may have it.'

Slowly, slowly the left hand drew the right hand back. Weakened, the right hand let the ladle fall to the ground. For a moment it seemed the huge beast went into a trance, the red eyes glazing over. Abruptly, the head snapped up and the two hands busied themselves as though there had never been a struggle at all.

Back on the path, the hideous thing dropped on all fours and dipped a small brush made of twigs in and out of the pot as she painted an invisible circle over the earth and around the spot where she had originally gathered the droppings and wettings. Completing that, she took the metal trowel again and held it tightly until it began to glow a deep red colour; quickly she began to dig the earth out of the area inside the circle. In no time at all, she was so deep in the ground she could hardly be seen. Yet the earth she threw up scattered soundlessly in the undergrowth and seemed to disturb nothing. That job finished, she put the trowel back in the kerchief and squatted, admiring her handiwork.

The seemingly inexhaustible kerchief now produced two strange small black boxes which she placed on either side of the path, close to the edges of the circle Next, she extracted a heavy chain made of linked plaques of metal, a metal of incredible imperviousness. She placed the chain in a semi-circle along one portion of the edge of the hole, imbedding it in the soft earth so that the plaques stood upright. Gathering up a handful of powder from the kerchief, she sprinkled it carefully on the ground, linking each black box to the chain itself.

When the beast had stored all the implements and paraphernalia on the open kerchief, she shuffled to the edge of the hole opposite the chain and placed one hindpaw on either side of the path. A great gush of liquid started to pour from a gaping orifice between the hind legs and straight down into the hole. On and on it poured like a torrent. And as it poured, each of the black boxes began to glow, a faint, eerie humming noise surrounding them. Higher and higher they hummed, the glow going from deep red to orange and finally to a stark white. As the last drop fell from her body, the powder on the ground flashed blue, shooting from both boxes to the ends of the chain and then everything was extinguished. Only the strange metal of the chain glowed softly for a few minutes more.

Calmly, the terrible beast took the black boxes and stored them away in the copious kerchief. Then she bent over and brushed dirt from the path over the liquid-filled hole. Somehow, it did not sink and she smoothed it and smoothed it until the path appeared as if it had never been touched. All one could detect was a perfectly normal path and perhaps, if one looked very closely, a chain lying there.

Satisfied at last with her handiwork, she tied up the ends of the kerchief and picked up the pot and ladle, shuffling rapidly into the underbrush to her hiding place under a large tree. Seating herself comfortably, she settled down with her hind legs spread and her head nestling into an accommodating depression in the bole of the tree; there could be heard a long sigh of contentment.

Idly, the right hand reached out for the ladle and began scraping the bottom of the pot. In leisurely fashion, the ladle came up and the lolling tongue thrust itself out to lick it. Back went the slow, deliberate hand and once more the ladle returned from the pot. Just then, the left hand snaked out and slid the ladle from the other fingers. A soft grunt of surprise escaped from the disappointed mouth; the eyes watched fascinated as the left hand moved the ladle down, aimed it carefully and plunged it into the orifice between the hind legs as far as it would go. The beast began trembling as the left hand plunged the ladle in and out, faster and faster.

Bumbree, the disgusting witch of the enchanted forest! In the guise of a bear that had slipped halfway towards being an ape, the whole image was a bit patchy because of her inveterate carelessness. It was difficult to tell which aspect of her was the most horrid. As she licked her lips and manipulated the ladle, her slitted eyes did not stray from the circle on the path, nor was her mind fixed on anything but her expected prey.

Midsummer Rites
in the
Sacred Glade

◉◉◉◉◉◉◉◉

The doe halted without warning as she approached a small clearing. The faun, running behind her, stopped short and came to rest at her flank. Staring ahead, he noticed a splendid silver table on which was mounted a large golden urn, ringed about with small golden goblets. Fascinated, he watched a shimmering giraffe glide slowly to the table and raise a forefoot to fill a goblet from the urn. She lifted the goblet and drained off the potion; he blinked and when he looked again, the giraffe was gone.

Unhurriedly, the doe led him to the table and bade him fill two goblets for them. The delicate glowing nectar caught at his nostrils and he thought his head would float away. She whispered to him that he must drink very slowly since this was his first taste of their magical nectar. Unlike the ales and wines of men, it did not intoxicate the senses, but so expanded the vision and awareness that one could be stunned by the beauty and intensity of everything.

He looked down into the iridescent fluid and felt drawn to it by a power stronger than his own will.

Impulsively, he raised the fragile goblet and let the liquid trickle down his throat. A riot of sensations started immediately, a cool, white fire suffusing his body from head to foot. When he put the goblet down, he turned to the doe.

The body of the doe was but the vaguest, shadowy outline. Standing inside the faint animal-shaped aura stood Astra in all her true, radiant beauty, the matchless Elvan Princess. She smiled at him with unconcealed delight.

'You now have true Elvan sight,' she whispered, 'the true sight that is withheld from all others. Should an intruder happen upon the Glade, he would see naught but countless beasts cavorting and mating and he would be so stunned his senses would desert him and he would flee in terror. Come, my love.'

Gently she took his hand and led him along the rest of the path until the trees thinned and the spaces between widened. Soon they entered the mystical place, The Sacred Glade, at the very heart of the enchanted forest.

His eyes illuminating his face like small moons, the boy's head made a slow, hesitating sweep of the vast Glade. Hand in hand, breathtaking forms moved in stately cadence, stopping to touch and caress one another lovingly. Groups flowed together and broke apart only to reform again, the shining males and females touching, fondling and kissing one another. Astra squeezed his hand and before he knew what happened, two radiant girls swept them up and he was being kissed and touched and just as suddenly, the girls drifted off, leaving him with the feeling he had never seen two such loving smiles.

As the girls moved away and Astra drew him further into the Glade, he became aware all at once of the haunting music which filled the forest clearing; at first he thought it to be music, but the more he listened, the more it seemed to be the sounds of the stars coursing regally through the skies.

'There is my father,' he heard Astra's voice whisper, but the whisper was inside his mind. It was like listening to the other eagle, his other self on the long flight to Astra's side.

'Where?' he thought back to her.

'Up there. Do you not see the high dais with the four large thrones?'

He looked and was so astounded he stopped dead in his tracks. Had it not been for Astra's urging, he would have stayed conspicuously rooted to the ground.

Majestic beyond men's dreams sat Glortan on the second throne from the left. His body was surrounded by millions of tiny pinpoints of light which whirled so rapidly that at moments they seemed to be standing still. A small crown of golden leaves was twisted about his brow and it coruscated in the sparkling moonlight. In the throne to his left was Aureen, his wife and Astra's mother. Like her husband, she was totally wrapped in star fire and her beauty made a sigh catch in Flondrix's throat. There was an empty throne to Glortan's right, and in the one next to it sat . . . the boy looked at the glorious woman around whose splendid body the first minute starry pinpoints were beginning to ignite.

Beyond this woman's beauty, beyond the splendour of the sight before him, something about her moved him so deeply his neck began stretching as his hesitant footsteps moved on. It almost seemed his body was moving but his head remained behind. An ache greater than any he had ever known went through him, shaking him to the foundations of his being. As he stared, the woman's body on the throne began to tremble and quiver. She seemed to be struggling to pull herself out of a trance. At the same moment, Glortan's body began to shake and there was an ominous rumbling note in the music of the stars.

Quickly, Astra whirled him about and pulled him along, plunging him into the thick of the Elvan revellers, dancing in rhythmic slow motion around them. In a few moments she had spirited him to the far side of the Glade. He caught up both her hands and pulled her to him.

'Who was that?' his fervent, silent thought demanded.

'The one next to my father?' she answered innocently. 'That was my mother, of course. She is Aureen. Queen Aureen.'

'No, no, the other . . . that — that lady sitting off by herself,' the frantic thought flew back to her.

'Oh. That was my Aunt Glortina, my father's sister. Why do you ask?'

'I — I don't know,' his mind answered. 'Something so very strange happened when I looked at her. It was as though I had known her — I don't know — in some other time and place. But I know that isn't right,' he broke off, completely confused.

'I am beginning to see the light,' she chided prissily. 'Ah, well, that's how it goes. A young man vows his love for a young maid, then he goes chasing after some older woman he finds more attractive.'

He opened his mouth to protest, forgetting he didn't need speech, but before a word was uttered, she had climbed into his arms and covered his mouth with her own. She kissed him so fervently that others came close to them and stroked them, warmed by the depth of their love.

At least that is how it seemed to Flondrix. What the others did see was Astra alone, standing on the tips of her toes and then rising a few inches above the grass, shimmering in a moment of ecstasy. The Elves stroked her with love and Flondrix felt the strokes, but they did not feel him. He tingled wildly, caught up in the full sharing of her joy.

Suddenly a great chord of music sounded from above and a hush fell over the Sacred Glade. All the glowing Elves turned as one and faced the dais of the Elvan Thrones. As they turned, their true forms vanished; a horde of jungle and woodland beasts in great profusion stretched out on the grass and fixed their eyes upon the dais. The lights surrounding the thrones intensified blindingly.

Before his eyes, Flondrix saw Glortan's beautiful image change. From that slender, majestic form grew the body of a giant, rippling with the muscles of Hercules. The lights around his head glowed and then dimmed. When they brightened again, in the place of Glortan's head was the head of a mighty bull. The lights radiating about the thrones continued to intensify and it was then Flondrix noticed the women's bodies changing too. Gone was the wraith-like and ethereal slenderness that is Elvan and in its place the bodies assumed the bold and awesome fullness of mythical goddesses, lush and inviting in hips and breasts, the flesh glowing like fire opals and ivory blending together. Their true heads grew pale and were replaced by the heads of two great eagles. The three Royal Elves, so fearsomely and excitingly arrayed, grew and grew to at least four times their previous size, the thrones and dais growing with them until the over-whelming spectacle towered over the Glade.

As the full path of the moon moved across the dais and began mounting up the base of the empty throne, a great sigh rose from all the beasts. No other sound was heard, but the excitement contained in that sigh was enough to send the blood pounding through

Flondrix's temples. Pressing closer to Astra's doe, he wanted to ask what was happening. Her mind answered his unspoken thought: 'Watch!'

When the moon's path reached the seat of the empty throne, a hushed gasp rose from the assembled host and lights greater than any seen before began to expand in the enormous moonbeam. Something which seemed to consist of nothing but the ghostly and majestic light filled the chair and overflowed it until it touched and irradiated every part of the Sacred Glade.

As the gasp still trembled in the air, the faun heard a thought from the doe that seemed to echo throughout the Glade. 'He is here! He is here!'

'Who is here?' Flondrix demanded inside his head.

'Elvanlord is here!' she beamed back. 'Elvanlord, the Patriarch, the eldest of all the Elves. He is come from Elvanhome, over the Far Paths, to be with us tonight. Usually, he has only time to send his greetings and blessings across the trackless heavens. But he is here now. He truly loves his long-lost children.'

She tore her eyes away from the dais for the beat of a butterfly's wings and looked at her beloved faun. 'No more messages now, not until the ceremony is over. Just watch, I will explain it all later.'

By now the whirling, glowing and fiery moonbeam filling the empty throne had condensed until a vague and venerable figure materialized in the seat. But the outline in dancing lights was so pale it was more like an illusion, a prank of the very lights themselves. Again a hush fell as Glortan's great hand raised itself skyward. As at a signal, the eagle-headed, voluptuous body of Aureen rose regally and moved towards him. When she stood before his throne, two golden phalli shot up from the base of his torso and rose quivering in the night until they stood six feet up from his huge body. Aureen faced the awful presences and wafted up from the dais until her feet were placed on each arm of the throne. There she stood, her arms raised high above her head, the fingers arched and tapering, pointing to the Sacred Star, Topar. Flames of blue and green leaped up from her fingertips.

Glortan placed his huge hands under her buttocks and lifted her higher still; there she was suspended, her knees flexed and thighs raised. When Aureen's feet were firmly planted on Glortan's shoulders, Glortina rose, as Aureen had done, and walked with stately undulations until she faced the throne filled with mystical light. There, she performed the same rite, rising up until she too was suspended high in the air, held by hands which were all but invisible.

A great and glorious chord rang through the Sacred Glade, to be echoed by all the shadowy creatures simultaneously. This in turn was drowned by a new and urgent chord with the force and volume of one thousand organs. As the new chord sounded, every male in the Glade covered a female. Before he realized it was happening, without even knowing how or why, Flondrix had leaped upon the doe's back, his quivering priapus sheathed in her honeyed, flooding orifice. He wanted to move, but he was held there, transfixing her and transfixed himself. As he reached the very limit of her envelopment, the two great pairs of hands above the dais, the visible and the ethereal, released the two pairs of luscious and star-glowing buttocks at the same instant. Slowly the buttocks lowered, until each Elvan Princess was impaled so deeply there seemed only one body in each seat.

The heavenly music soared, the multitude of Elvan voices joining in a chant that began with the word: 'Chandrala!' and was followed by the whole lovely paean to the beauty of Four as Two as One, the ultimate bliss.

86

Up from the dais rose ring upon ring of iridescent vapour that curled and coruscated, filled with the myriad pinpoints of mystical light. The dais was obscured as was the heaven above, the glow of the vapours becoming more and more intense until they were nearly opaque. The moon appeared as a faint disc and all the stars were snuffed out save Topar, which glowed more brightly silver than ever. From the centre of this vast cloud, a voice in the sky reverberated. As Flondrix turned his eyes towards the cloud, he noted that all other heads were likewise lifted. In the centre of the cloud a picture began forming. The picture was still vague and shadowy when a very thin thought reached Flondrix.

'Keep pressed closely. It is all our earnest joinings together which creates the vast force needed to connect us to Elvanhome.'

As he pressed himself deeply inside her, he saw a picture form of a land almost beyond imagining. Great silver-hued trees rose to the sky and gentle meadows dotted the landscape. Nestling upon treetops wherever the trees grew densely, clouds of different colours supported cities whose buildings were made of some marvellous material that glowed like pearls in the pure purplish blue of the heavens. When the picture enlarged itself as one city, Elves could be seen moving about their various tasks. They walked along paths no wider than silver threads lacing in and out between the magnificent buildings.

A few Elves dropped off the edge of one building and floated down to the supporting cloud where they bounced slightly and continued their airy descent to the ground below. There, many were tending fields and gardens while others were busy piping water from the many sparkling streams and rivers to the fields.

A large bee circled the city and Flondrix saw that

there were three Elves sitting astride the bee's back, guiding him. Slowly the bee settled on the rim of a large vat and emptied the great quantity of nectar he had been carrying in his body. When the vat was full, the three Elves dismounted and stroked the bee's huge head and antennae. Quivering with pleasure, the bee spread its wings and darted off into the far fields where the wildflowers grew.

Individual faces and groups appeared, sending thought messages of encouragement to their long-exiled cousins. They were filled with praise for the selfless task Glortan's people had accepted in watching over the world of men.

The picture changed and a sad note sounded in the voice above. On Midsummer Eve, the voice said, it was important that the exiled children of Elvanhome remembered how important their task was and what a great service they were performing for the Ancient Ones.

He watched awestruck the splendour of the Ancient Ones as, like shining giants, fair and calm and all-wise, they first left their great vehicles and stepped out on the earth of man. He watched as they tamed the bestial savages and took them to great laboratories on their sky ships. They worked miracles on man's shape and looks, expanding his brain across aeons of time as they exposed and inured him to the great Cosmic force, Ra-Chand.

The picture faded and was replaced by a view of a very ancient city. Men moved among the elegant white buildings, themselves wearing long white robes which touched the ground. Flondrix was appalled to see how pernicious the race of man had become, the faces he watched passing seemed filled with callous cruelty. In a room near the outskirts of the city, a few men moved between ovens and furnaces, stirring things that steamed in large crucibles. An old and learned wizard consulted ancient manuscripts and gave directions to his workers. Soon they left the building and mounted camels, riding off into the desert. When evening fell and the column of camels was many miles' march away, a terrible explosion ripped the city to shreds and an enormous billowing cloud rose over the charred remains.

With his heart in his mouth, the boy watched city after modern city of man be destroyed until there seemed nothing left alive on the ravaged face of the earth. But some men did survive, though very few in numbers, to rebuild simple civilizations patterned on the ones which had existed in earlier times. Gone were the great industries, the rockets which flew man to distant planets, and in their place the farms, the horses and weapons of antiquity.

The voice in the cloud told them that man had lost his history when he had reached the brink of destroying his world. But once before, as they had seen in the first age of man, their wizards had been able to break down the structures of matter and energy. There was no guarantee this would not be attempted again.

The cloud began to lighten as the voice told them how much the universe was in their debt. All of Elvanhome honoured their unselfish devotion in the far off world of men. Soon Glortan and Aureen would be returning to Elvanhome, their reign in the Sacred Glade over at last. There would be further news of this later in the summer.

With a crash of cymbals, the heavenly music ended and the clouds dispersed. The moon shone brightly and the stars twinkled down on Glortan, Aureen and Glortina, standing hand in hand smiling out at the Elvan host, in their normal guises.

'As you can well imagine,' the melodious voice of Glortan sounded over the Glade, 'we are deeply fatigued by our efforts and so profoundly moved by the visit of our Elvanlord, that we needs must rest. Please enjoy the feasts and revels and we will rejoin you just before dawn. We bid you good night for now, dear children.'

As the three beautiful figures disappeared from the dais, Flondrix noticed for the first time that he was no longer on top of the doe. He was sitting next to her in the grass and his faun's bladder seemed about to burst.

'I have to make my wettings again,' he murmured. 'Where shall I go?'

She silently warned to him to think instead of speak. Her unspoken instructions reminded him of the path they had used from the tree where he had landed. He was to return there and make his sweet liquids so that he could bring them back a goblet of nectar on his return. One would suffice for both of them. He must hurry, however, since his presence might be detected accidentally.

The Dwarfs
Make an Unpleasant Discovery

() () () () () () () ()

'You're thumping it!'

'Am not!' came the gruff answer. Under the heavy black mantle a scuffle broke out.

'Stop it, you two. Nobody's thumping it while I'm in charge,' another voice admonished. Two muffled slaps were followed by whimpers.

The thick black mantle was draped over the branch of a tree very close to the one where Flondrix had landed earlier. Thousands of small linked chains, part lead and part Antertium 99, had been forged into a covering so dense and impervious as to give virtual invisibility. The strange fusion of the two metals was also capable of screening out the most violent heat and radiation known. The secret of how to blend and work the materials in such fine forms was one well-guarded by the dwarfs.

The mantle hung from the upper branch to a lower one, and under it sat four small dwarfs. They had been peering intently through the minute spaces between the links, watching whatever they could see of the Elvan Rites of Midsummer. Their names were Dimbek, Hogbek, Dogbek and Rimbek. About three feet tall, they had long arms, rather spindly legs and pot bellies. Their beards were very black and curly and their bodies sprouted odd tufts of wiry hair the same jet colour; it even sprang profusely from between their naked toes and, strangest of all, the palms of their hands were covered in short, stiff hair.

The four dwarfs wore nothing but brief, sleeveless jackets, more like waistcoats without buttons, which were rounded and tapered at the bottoms. These unusual garments were made of goatskin, the furry sides worn next to their swarthy, yet slightly sallow bodies. The outer surfaces of the jackets were covered with exquisite needlework in pure gold. The elaborate and painstaking designs contained practically every mystical symbol and character known.

Dimbek, the eldest of the four brothers and their leader, sat closest to the trunk of the tree, his long toes clutching the small twigs which grew from the branch. Like the others, his pointed bottom squatted on the wood between his heels and his arms dangled below the bough itself. Rimbek, the youngest, was seated furthest from Dimbek, at the outside of the group, since he had been appointed their lookout. They felt secure with their precious mantle, knowing that no Elvan eyes might penetrate it, but dwarfish custom dictated that guards, sentries and lookouts should be on duty at all times. No doubt, this was a gnome-like quality born of count-less ages in charge of great stores of gold and precious gems.

In the centre of the group, huddled together, were the twins, Hogbek and Dogbek. It was Hogbek who had accused Dogbek of thumping it when the scuffle broke out. Naturally, as their leader, Dimbek had been forced to slap each of them in the interests of discipline and the maintenance of strict silence. Privately, he had enjoyed the disciplinary measures immensely and the hairy palm of his hand still tingled with pleasure. Once or twice after that, he had cast his beady black eyes in the direction of young Rimbek, hoping to catch him out in some infraction while the good sensation still glowed in his hand. Rimbek watched the path diligently, but he also inched a bit further out on the limb, just beyond Dimbek's reach.

Young Rimbek *did* sneak glances towards the Sacred Glade when he felt sure Dimbek's attention was riveted there. They saw nothing but what the Elves wanted them to see, of course. Scores upon scores of misty beasts mounting each other and thrusting furiously, pairs and groups rolling on the ground in ecstasy, twisting their bodies into wild contortions to perform all sorts of abominations on each other with tongues and tails and horns and trunks. The very ground beneath the beasts seemed to flow and quiver, inundation after inundation of a thick, milky fluid splashing up over their legs and flanks.

The righteous dwarfs were properly disgusted with the sights unfolding before them, still they reckoned there was more going on here than met the eye. Each year, for as long as anyone could remember, King Schtoonk had sent a party of his wiliest scouts on the dangerous mission. And each Midsummer, the dwarfs had spied carefully, hoping that something would be revealed about the real magic behind the obnoxious scenes. This was the first such mission for the four brothers and their briefing had taken nearly six months.

It must be admitted, however, that all was not righteous indignation on the part of the four brothers. Their ears could be cut off and their tongues torn out, but they would never admit to the secret lust and yearning the sights they witnessed could provoke. Such baseness was not tolerated among the dwarf people and it was unthinkable that such a horrifying scene could stir anything but disgust. Just the same, despite all the veiled warnings during their training, things stirred and stirred lasciviously.

It was actually true that a few minutes earlier Dogbek had started to thump it secretly. It was not so much that Hogbek, his twin, had detected this, but since the same idea was pounding in his own head, and since he was worried about being caught out, he had accused Dogbek out of hand, hoping to distract attention. It so happened that he had been right.

When the dwarfs had alighted on the branch, they had coiled their long somewhat sticky penes the correct twenty times about their torsos and placed the sharp barbed steely tips in contact with the golden screws in their navels; there they were held firmly by magnetism. These long penes were extremely elastic, somewhat like the webbing strands spun by spiders. On arrival at the base of the tree, all they had had to do was to uncoil them from about their waists and throw them over the branch above where the barbed point held fast. By turning the little golden screw a fraction to the right the dwarfs sprang straight up, pulled aloft by the corkscrew action of the penes, or 'schlongs', as the dwarfs referred to them. When they landed on the limb above, they released the screw slightly to the left and the 'schlongs' fell slackly to the ground, from whence they were deftly coiled about their torsos again.

Quite frequently, while performing some amazing feats of agility like this, a dwarf would underestimate the strain and stress that would occur; the penis would snap off, invariably at the base. However, since a full half turn of the golden screw to the left and two or three days' quiet meditation were all it required to grow a new one, this did not pose too awkward a problem. None the less, thumping with the schlong in a coiled condition can be dangerous.

The two most popular ways of thumping it are either by heel or through lower grade vibrational energy impulses. In the heel method, the sharp hard tip is released instantaneously from the magnetic grip of the navel screw by a sharp sucking in of the sphinctral muscles. Of its own accord, the end of the schlong slides down imperceptibly and slithers under the selected heel, which in turn begins to thump. This is usually such a gentle, supersonic thumping that even the most sensitive of dwarfs find it almost impossible to detect. The other method uses the magnetism in the golden screw to set up an internal thumping.

To start this vibration, a small amount of wind is drawn up through the rectum and forced under great pressure directly behind the golden screw. By far the most secretive method, particularly in crowded rooms since the tip has not changed location and seems at normal rest, it does have one drawback. If the secretly thumping dwarf is asked a question, the answer usually has a breathless, wheezy sound. At this point, most dwarfs flush terribly and complain of acute indigestion, running off in great haste to search for a glass of fruit salts.

The danger in attempting a thump with a fully coiled schlong is due to the peculiar erectile action, which is expressed best by comparing it to a corkscrew or a tightly coiled spring. If the schlong is coiled about the waist when this occurs, and the 'happy-happy', or 'zunk-zunk' as it is known in the older dwarf tongue, does not occur, the python-like constriction can be most uncomfortable indeed. Of course, the dwarf can always release the magnetism, but then the schlong, in its maddened condition, coils itself like a tight spring in front of his body. He then becomes fair prey to any marriageable dwarf lady who might pass by. That is, if her internal threads match his. Since there is no way of knowing until birth which way a dwarf or lady dwarf may be threaded, this can lead at times to confusion. It is by no means the male dwarf's preferred solution.

Dimbek was staring straight ahead, wondering what the large cloud hovering over the Sacred Glade signified. It made any further view of the proceedings impossible. Suddenly, he saw it lift as if it had been pulled up on strings, and the shadowy activity of the disgusting beasts started once more. Dimbek gnashed his teeth silently and wished his three stupid brothers had stayed home in the White Mountains. He needed a thump very badly. Dogbek watched his twin, Hogbek, out of the corner of his eye. He sensed the twin was watching him every time he looked ahead. Thump-madness made their temples feel tight and hot like abused anvils.

Unaware of all the torture assailing his elder brothers, young Rimbek diligently scanned the paths and grounds below him, hoping for something to report. He wanted everyone to pat him and stroke him, saying: 'Good old Rimbek, you are the hero of the day!' Just then, he detected something moving far down the path. His ears picked up the faint sound of small hooves; first they went a few steps this way and stopped, paused a moment and backtracked, hesitating again.

'Something with hooves that stands up on its hind legs is trotting back and forth down there,' hissed Rimbek. 'It may be lost,' he added.

Dimbek turned his head and snarled for silence. 'You know very well our mighty king has his heart set on capturing one of them. We can't ever do that in their Sacred blasted enchanted Glade, but this may be our chance. Be prepared, everyone. If we succeed, King Schtoonk will reward us richly.'

'Why does he want one of those silly animals?' asked the twins in unison.

'You stupid ninnies,' growled Dimbek, 'there is an Elf inside each and every one of those animals. All we have to do is skin it. Then we will learn the great secrets. That's what the wizard Sordo says, and the king listens well to him. Sordo says the only way we can capture one and bind it is to wrap it in our magic mantle. That's how we have to get it back to King Schtoonk's Schtronghold. Let's hurry before it runs away.'

The twins started to argue once again, their heads still hammering with thoughts of thumping. Dimbek slapped them both furiously and all argument ceased. He snapped his fingers in command and all four dwarfs uncoiled and sprang lightly to the ground. In the blink of an eye, they were recoiled and slipping through the undergrowth, the heavy mantle left folded on poor Rimbek's shoulders. At the edge of the path, they heard the hoofbeats sounding more clearly and they sank down behind the screening bush, each holding a corner of the mantle, ready to spring out and net the quarry.

They saw the young faun round the last bend in the path and halt. Then he sprang forward as though recognizing something. The shocked eyes of the dwarfs doubled in size as they saw the very ground open to receive him. He sunk down until his chin was level with the earth of the path. All they could see now was a young faun's head, the eyes glazing over. Then there was an ominous Snap! A chain had leaped clear of the ground and fastened itself securely about his neck.

The dwarfs were too stunned by what they had witnessed to move or make a sound. They felt rooted to the spot and a good thing, as they discovered immediately, when the large bulk of shaggy horror loomed up on the opposite side of the path. It took Dimbek only a second to identify the terrible witch, Bumbree.

The four dwarfs stealthily drew the mantle over their heads.

With unhurried motions, the frightful creature put a large kerchief down on the path and extracted a trowel. She described a circle on the ground with the trowel, moving it around the faun's head. First the trowel glowed dully, then the ground itself. There was a bitter smell in the air as the beast stored the implement and a few other things in the kerchief before knotting the four corners together.

The brothers watched her place one hindpaw on either side of the faun's head and reach down to grab his horns and ears. She tugged and tugged so mightily, it seemed that the long, pointed ears must surely rip loose. With one last great heave, the faun was abruptly freed and came sliding up from the ground, completely encased in a cylinder of thick yellow ice. With a grunt of approval, the witch heaved the ice-encased faun over her shoulder and stooped to pick up the large kerchief. With another grunt and a snort, she went lumbering off down the path, away from the Sacred Glade.

When they could hear her no longer, the dwarfs pulled back the magic mantle and stepped out on to the path. Dimbek scratched his head and beard, looking first up and down the path, then at the round hole in the ground before him.

'What do you make of all that, big brother?' asked young Rimbek.

'Yes,' echoed the twins, 'what happened?'

'What happened, indeed,' retorted Dimbek. 'What do you think happened? That beastly Bumbree had a trap set — a trap to capture *our* Elf before we could get our hands on him. I'd just like to get my hands on her,' he growled, pounding his fist into the palm of his other hand.

The other three started asking questions until he had

to administer judicious slaps to right and to left. The questions stopped with a few scattered whimpers.

'Now, listen to me, you silly fools,' Dimbek ordered. 'This is serious, very serious. When the king finds out about this, we are going to be in a great deal of trouble. The king will say we had our chance and failed. Only twice before were our people ever able to catch an Elf. And we didn't hold on to those for very long either. This was the chance of the century. And we missed it, do you understand? We have to get that animal back. We must make a plan, so start thinking.'

The twins began crying and Rimbek sat disconsolately at the side of the path and buried his head in his hands.

'Does that mean,' Rimbek asked at last, 'that we have to go to Bumbree's Creepy Cottage and – and face *her*? She will destroy us. She *hates* dwarfs, everyone knows that. What could we do against her magic?'

'That's why we have to make a plan,' stormed Dimbek. 'Don't make me repeat that again. Start thinking!'

Astra Faces
the Wrath of Glortan

❀❀❀❀❀❀❀

Stretched out on the soft, milk-white grass dotted with purple clover that grew only in the Sacred Glade (the very grass which had seemed to the base minds of the dwarfs a sea of creamy fluid), Astra tapped her tiny tapered toes nervously and impatiently. Wettings and droppings, yes, but this was ridiculous.

The annoyance she felt was short-lived. Being in the early throes of first love, Astra was feeling and very nearly exhibiting some definitely non-Elvan reactions. Jealousy, suspicion and possessiveness are virtually unknown among Elves. The slight signs of petulance gave way almost immediately to premonitions of evil done and terrors yet to unfold. Slipping away from the undulating crowds of radiant figures, she worked her way unnoticed to the edge of the Glade. Something in the air warned her and she avoided the normal path, seeking a more circuitous route through the thicker trees. She paused in the dense undergrowth, a few feet from the last bend Flondrix had manoeuvred before his fateful plunge into Bumbree's diabolical trap.

She flattened herself against a broad tree and concentrated her magical forces, sending them whirling up her spine to gather themselves between and just behind her eyes. In less than three seconds, nothing more was to be seen of her. Astra was no longer there. Invisible, she sped out from the thick cover and virtually flew over the ground until she was standing, undetectably, a few feet away from the vicious deceitful hole in the path. She drew her breath in as she caught sight of the four unlikely looking dwarfs. Under normal circumstances, she would have enveloped them in a coma-producing vapour and sent for the guards. As it was, she was too distraught to think about that; besides, she had concentrated the greater part of her forces on the tasks of invisibility and divination. As she pondered her next move, the three dwarfs sitting on the ground moaned and the one pacing back and forth stopped long enough to slap them, evoking a moan from each.

'Are you thinking? About what? Your next meal, I warrant. Well, there will be no more meals until one of you comes up with a plan.' With that, he turned on his heel, clasped his hands behind his back and continued pacing up and down the path in great agitation, missing the rim of the gaping hole by mere fractions each time he turned.

'Careful,' piped up Rimbek, 'for if you fall in there, *you* may be frozen in a cylinder of ice and Bumbree will come back for you. Then there would be but three of us to free you and that – uh – funny creature with the hooves and horns who runs around on his hind legs.'

'Yes,' chimed in Hogbek and Dogbek, 'then we would have to make a plan without a leader. We'd *never* be able to do that.' On this dire note, the soft wailing started once more and Dimbek was forced to administer slaps to left and right.

'Shut up, you fools,' he commanded. 'The Elves have ears everywhere. What if they should hear you?

Then they'd know what happened and off they would be, straight to Bumbree's Creepy Cottage. We'd never be able to think up a plan in time.'

Her spirit feeling as though it had splintered into a thousand fragments, her mind whirling with confusion, the unseen Astra melted through the trees and sped across the Sacred Glade. As she began racing up the vine ladders to her father's great tree house, her form began materializing. But so great was her sense of horror and the keen identification she felt with Flondrix and the terrible fate that had overtaken him, she did not realize she was moving rapidly up the vine paths on a doe's hind legs. From the hips up she was Astra, from the hips down . . . a doe.

It was not until she had run through the lower levels and began mounting the forbidden ladders to the royal sanctus sanctorum that she became aware of her ridiculous image. The tremendous surges of power in that mystical room overwhelmed her and, for the moment, she was powerless to exert any counter-forces to correct her own image. She sank to her haunches, somewhat uncomfortably, and gazed at the awesome scene before her.

The top room of the house was built as a round observatory with a sliding dome of ebony. The dome's opening was controlled in such a clever fashion that an aperture of any required size could be selected, widened or narrowed at will, and set to follow the course of the moon or any star. When Astra entered the room, the path of the moon was crossing the path of the star known to the Elves as Topar, as it did but once a year on Midsummer's Eve.

Glortan was stretched out on a golden couch covered in purple velvet. Coverlets of velvet hid all of him save a narrow circlet on his brow, just above the bridge of his nose. The combined beams of the moon and Topar were focused on that spot. Round the darkened chamber, the hollow noise of the winds of space set up a frightening drone as the concentrated forces of the great Ra-Chand poured into the Elvan King. This rite was the annual renewal of Elvan Wisdom and eternal life he would share with his people. It came from afar, from the Stars Beyond the Stars, via Topar and Elvan-home. To disrupt this sacred rite was the worst offence any Elf could commit.

Trembling with panic and terror for her loved one, yet overcome with awe at the miraculous rite she was witnessing, Astra waited silently, counting her breaths with intense anxiety. Suddenly, a melodious bell tinkled and the dome opened wide, admitting the light of the moon-laden sky which poured into every corner of the darkened chamber. Aureen and Glortina, who had been standing clasped in each others arms over a low brazier of green fire, glided to the golden couch and took the coverings from Glortan's body. He was white as marble and in the profoundest of trances. The two women crossed the room and raised the trembling girl, embracing her with love.

Her mother looked deeply into the girl's eyes. 'What is it, my precious child?' she asked. 'You took a great risk in coming here now, as you well know. It must be very important.' Aureen and Glortina stroked and kissed Astra, their faces smiling. But behind Glortina's smile there was a faint premonition of something unpleasant. Something not right in the vibrations which stirred in the chamber.

'How — how soon will father return to us?' the girl asked breathlessly. 'One — one of our people is missing. He — he has been spirited away.'

Her mother began chiding her softly, laughingly reminding her of the stories of her childhood. Yes, on two occasions the foolish dwarfs had found an Elf

asleep and thrown their silly metal mantle over him . . .
At this point, Glortina interrupted, saying something
was definitely wrong and they would have to awaken
Glortan. Hand in hand, they moved to Glortan's side
and began rubbing his body with sweet-smelling salves
that made his skin glow radiantly. His body seemed to
rise up from the couch with no physical effort and he
stood before the three women.

He held up his hand for silence and closed his
eyes. A minute later he opened them and shook his
head.

'My child, your thoughts came to me, saying one of
our people has been captured,' he said softly. 'I have
just counted our people and none is missing.'

'Oh, yes, father —' But as Astra's voice faltered,
Glortina's body twisted until she was facing towards the
path where Flondrix had disappeared. Her eyes turned
back deeply in her head and she watched a phantom
vision, a shaggy beast with a heavy burden arriving at
Bumbree's Creepy Cottage far off in the enchanted
forest.

'The child speaks the truth,' Glortina intoned from
deep inside her body. 'An Elf has been captured and is
now the unconscious prisoner of Bumbree, the horrid
servant of Daemon-Baalim, he who is the enemy of the
Ancient Ones.'

'Preposterous,' thundered Glortan. 'He is chained
and bound in the world beneath. As for Bumbree, no
one of our true people could be put under a spell with
that twaddle she calls magic.'

Coming back to them from the depths inside herself,
Glortina faced her brother. 'This one who has been
captured is one of ours, this I know. Yet, in a way, he
is not. I do not know how to explain it. But there is one
fibre here in my Io-Chand which aches mightily because
of it, as with a great sorrow. This one is ours, yet we

104

know him not.' Glortina turned and looked fully at Astra. So did her mother and father.

'He is one of us,' Astra admitted tremulously. 'He is — he is Flondrix, the mortally conceived child of Glortina. The one who is meant to be mine, the one whose name is written for me in the stars.'

A devastating silence struck the three who stared incredulously at the stricken child. The pained hush stretched on and on until the room quivered palpably with foreboding. Finally Glortan spoke.

'How came he here?' he whispered.

'At my bidding,' Astra sobbed, casting her eyes down. At the words, Glortina's eyes clouded over and she would have collapsed had not Aureen caught her about the waist and held her close to her own body for support.

'If an Elf dies accidentally, under the rules of Elvanhome, an Elvan woman is selected to conceive his replacement; his life force returns to Elvanhome until his new form is born. No Elvan woman can conceive until the permission is given and she attunes her essential life force to it. You know this, Astra, and I believe you know the one exception . . .' The King paused there and looked to his sister. She nodded her assent.

'. . . If she could become contaminated with the dangerous, fiery spirits consumed by men — and this can be done only through the most cunning subterfuge — then her life force is disturbed. Only with a disturbed Io-Chand can the seed of man come to us. This child Flondrix is dear to us for the sake of his mother and all she suffered at the deceitful hands of the Dark King of men. You know, my child, his Elvanhood was withheld. Only Elvanlord and I could change that. How came he here?'

With much stammering and confusion, her cheeks burning brightly, Astra told them the whole story, begging for their love and understanding. When she finished, Glortan was astounded.

'You performed the great rites of initiation with this boy? You conferred full Elvanhood upon him? How? How did you come by such tremendous stores of power? This is the highest Elvan attainment, a degree of attainment still ages away from one so young.' Had he not loved his daughter above all things, the king's voice would have been shaking with fury.

Aureen took his hand and begged him not to be so harsh. Had he not always prided himself in her great learning, had he not always said she was a brilliant student? How he had boasted when she spent all her waking hours poring over the ancient tomes and practising with endless hours of meditation. How often he had said there was none to touch Astra, the most precious of them all. Would he now chastise her for learning so well?

'The purpose to which she put her great learning has defied not only her father, but Elvanlord himself. You know the penalty. I cannot stay that, not even for my own beloved daughter,' the king reminded his wife.

'My lord,' she reminded him in turn, taking his hand between her own, 'well you know that one circumstance must always be considered in the fair administration of our justice. That circumstance is love. This is no ordinary deceit. Astra has not indulged a mere fancy. Perhaps beyond our knowledge, even beyond that of Elvanlord himself, there is an ordained purpose in all of this. Astra would not love so deeply for no reason at all. Remember, soon we will be leaving, soon our stewardship here for Elvanlord will be ended. It was not said who would replace us. Think upon it, my dear lord. In exacting the letter of the archaic Elvan Laws, we may be thwarting the Ancient Ones we so love.'

In great agitation, Astra looked from one to the other as they talked on. In her mind, horrible pictures formed, pictures of unspeakable tortures Flondrix might be suffering at the hands of the terrible witch. Finally, Glortan turned to her.

Ordinarily, she would be banished, sent into the world of men with no memory and deprived of all Elvan powers, there to wander to the end of her mortal days, the king told her. But his judgement had to be tempered with mercy for her great love and the higher designs that might exist. Thus she was to go forth to find Flondrix and free him, never to return until the task was completed. And she might well perish in the attempt. In no way could she call upon her family for help, no matter how much their hearts might be aching to send that help speedily to her. She would have to rely on her wits and devotion to see her through. All magic was to be denied her, save in the form she took.

The king paused and looked down at the doe legs of his daughter. He concentrated deeply and the doe legs disappeared. Astra stood there as her beautiful self, but missing that special sparkle of silver and gold in her hair. The hair on her head and on her body was a lovely, deeper burnished gold. She also had acquired all the usual physical characteristics of a human female.

'You will go forth as a mortal woman,' the king explained, 'albeit, the most beautiful of all. You may change your form to escape great danger, but think well on it. Each time, the power will be diminished. By three or the most four changes, this power may dissipate entirely.'

As the saddened Astra began to turn away, her aunt's hand held her shoulder, drawing her close again.

'One more thing you bring with you, sweet niece,' Glortina smiled. 'The ache in my heart for the son I've never known. And the hope that, through your devotion, I shall see him here. All the strength of this bond, all the encouragement I can send you throughout your perilous journey, this I shall do. That, even my beloved brother cannot deny you.'

Father, mother and aunt enfolded Astra lovingly in their arms and kissed her fondly before they stood aside to let her race towards her destiny. Long after she had gone, they were still standing there, each trying to comfort the other.

A Sly and Unlikely Bargain

☉☉☉☉☉☉☉

Astra stopped in her own room long enough to take a gossamer golden dress and a petite pair of golden slippers of the type Elvan ladies wear when they leave their own part of the forest. As she was about to rush out of the door, she remembered two things she had made when she was still a small girl, two trinkets which had remained untouched in a little coffer on the table. One was a pendant made of a large pearl caught in the silver claws of a lion and attached to a fine silver chain. The other was a bracelet of ivory with a small oval of mother of pearl imbedded in it. She slipped these two cherished items of childhood on, hoping desperately they might still retain their magical powers. Her father just might have overlooked such childish trinkets on purpose. Surely, he wanted her to succeed.

When she arrived at the spot on the path where Flondrix had disappeared, she slowed down to compose herself before rounding the bend. She could hear the dwarfs whispering among themselves a little further on. Astra tried to straighten the dress and smooth it into place. She could not yet get used to the rather voluptuous breasts that jiggled when she ran or walked rapidly. She was also uncomfortably aware of the fuller growth of maidenhair and the pouting cleft hidden beneath it. That and the tiny hole just behind it made her nervous and fidgety as she moved. The new fullness of her hips, plus the swelling of her breasts, made it difficult to keep the dress neatly and clingingly in place. Although she had seldom worn such dresses, she now felt she needed something more; she tried to remember the stories she had been told about the women of men and the strange things they wore under their clothes.

Putting aside the concerns with her own new-found discomforts, Astra moved slowly and noiselessly along the path, rounding the bend to see one of the dwarfs still pacing back and forth, the other three seated much as before. They all looked miserable.

She stood very quietly, watching them and trying to be as inconspicuous as possible. While she could not quite make herself invisible in the usual way without using up the scant amount of magical power left to her by her father, she felt she had to test the pearl pendant immediately. If it did not work, this was the time to find out. She reached down cautiously, raised it and popped it into her mouth. She turned her profile towards the dwarfs and moved quite close to them.

The dwarfs did not turn around. The pendant had retained its power! She was now, to all appearances, like a thin shadow, no thicker than a delicate leaf. In the early years of her childhood experiments, that was as far as she had been able to go. Suddenly, the pacing dwarf stopped in front of the other three; she listened carefully as he addressed them, regretting that she did not understand their speech as instantaneously as she had earlier when she had her full powers. Still, because of her long training, she could master a concentration of mental forces that in itself was incredible.

After a few minutes of listening to the words flowing back and forth among them, she felt quite at home with their language. The last few sentences were perfectly clear. Dimbek was speaking.

'All right, then,' he concluded a long harangue, 'I will give you just five more minutes to think up a plan. If you are under the impression that I've been a tough captain up to now, you wait and see what happens at the end of five minutes . . . if you numbskulls still have thought of nothing.'

With that he turned back on to the path to take up his restless pacing once more. Within her own mind, Astra practised the vocal intonations of the other three. When she felt she had their individual pecularities of speech perfectly duplicated, she watched Dimbek approach the hole in the path and turn around to march in the opposite direction. She sidled up to the hole and dropped down. From there she projected a perfect imitation of Hogbek's voice, but she beamed it so cleverly that only Dimbek could hear it. He, of course, thought it was one of the twins speaking.

'What we need is someone to help us. Someone who is as different from us as day is from night. We need a lovely young virgin from the land of mortal men.'

'What for?' muttered Dimbek without breaking his pace.

The other three brothers' heads came up and they looked at Dimbek quizzically. But he passed them by without so much as a glance. They scratched their beards and shrugged their shoulders. When Dimbek turned and was heading back up the path again, he heard 'Hogbek's voice' following him.

'As a decoy, you big ninny! What would Bumbree do with the likes of us if we came near her Creepy Cottage? She would smell us a long way off and she would snare us and throw us into those awful pots of hers. We would never be seen or heard from again. She would turn us into strange beasts and make us do terrible things to her with our . . . you know. But if we had a decoy, a beautiful innocent young decoy, Bumbree would drool and quiver all over. She would be so intent on capturing the decoy, she would never notice us. Then, when all was clear, we could pop that funny animal into our magic mantle and cart him off as fast as we could.'

Dimbek rumbled threateningly as he pounded back down the path. 'By the gleaming gold of our fore-fathers, where do you think we are going to find a "beautiful virgin decoy", whatever that is,' he squeaked, mocking Hogbek's high, nasal voice.

Hogbek, Dogbek and Rimbek looked up stunned as he passed. They all said: 'Huh?'

Dimbek ignored them, pulling roughly at his own beard. As he turned, the 'voice' reached him again.

'Well, smart brother, where did the funny animal hide? Down in that hole, correct? Does not the great King Schtoonk say: "Wherever you find a problem, look close by, for there resides the solution too?"'

'Are you serious?' demanded Dimbek, stopping sharply in front of Hogbek.

'Am I serious?' repeated Hogbek in astounded, uncomprehending surprise.

Dimbek grabbed him by his beard and yanked him to his feet. 'If you are so smart, you look down there and see what you can find. Go ahead!'

'Look down whaaa . . .' Hogbek's voice rose to a quavering yelp as the strong hand holding his beard lifted him clear of the ground.

'Look down that hole and find us our lovely "inno-cent virgin decoy",' commanded Dimbek furiously. With that, he twisted poor Hogbek's arm and sent him sprawling across the ground. The surprised twin emitted one more piteous yelp as he skidded up to the edge of the hole. He released a terrified scream when he came eye to eye with Astra.

'Who are you?' he managed to squeak.

'I am — Barletta,' she answered, feigning great terror. 'I am the Dark King's daughter and I am in terrible distress. Please help me out of here.'

'How did you get down there?' Rimbek asked foolishly, his vocal cords constricting he was so entranced with the beauty of her face.

'Oh, please help me, whoever you are. You shall be richly rewarded by my father, the king. I will tell you what happened as soon as I am safely out of this dreaded place.'

Before Dimbek could mull this over and arrive at a decision, Rimbek reached down and put his hands under her delicately fragrant underarms. As he lifted, he saw Dogbek and Hogbek reach out and place their hands over her swelling bosom and delightful hips as she emerged with a struggle from the narrow hole. When they placed her on the ground, Rimbek kicked at both the twins' ankles in a fit of jealousy, but they didn't seem to notice. The lovely young girl stood at the rim of the hole and, with gentle firmness, removed the no longer needed hands from her body. She demurely brushed her dress and arranged it in a more orderly fashion. The four dwarfs craned their necks to look up at her.

'Ahem . . .' Rimbek began, but his thoughts and voice were still too muddled to create a whole sentence.

'Oh, please let me tell you what happened,' she begged, 'and maybe then your hearts will be moved to help me. I need all the help and every friend I can get. You do want to be my friends, don't you?' she pleaded. The dwarfs began nodding uncertainly. Her beautiful green eyes grew large and limpid in the pale light of the setting moon. 'Please,' she added plaintively, 'you will help me, won't you?'

The dwarfs' heads went up and down and then from side to side in utter confusion. Finally they seemed to be describing eccentric circles in the air. They simply didn't know what to say.

She told them she had been on a picnic with her friends and had strayed from them when they started picking wildflowers. The next thing she knew, she was deep in the enchanted forest and quite lost. Then she heard a beautiful haunting melody in the distance and decided to follow it. Deeper and deeper into the forest she had strayed when at last, at some distance away, she had seen a woodland faun playing a reed flute. He beckoned to her and she followed until she was exhausted, begging him all the time to stop and lead her from the forest. But he kept dancing on ahead of her, playing his bewitching music.

She must have fallen asleep then, for the next thing she remembered she was in a large clearing, surrounded by the strangest collection of wild beasts she had ever seen. Of course, the young faun was among them, seemingly very pleased with himself. Suddenly, one of the biggest of all the beasts had touched her with a magic wand and she had turned into a doe. It was then she realized she had been brought to an enchanted place and a spell had been cast on her. Again, she remembered nothing until she awoke all alone in the clearing. Everyone was gone, even the faun. It was only then she discovered that her magic necklace was gone. It was the very one the court magician had made for her to keep her young innocence from all harm. Frightened, she had run from the clearing in search of the wicked faun. A few moments later, she had stumbled and fallen into a hole in the ground. She had found herself in a maze of tunnels and had wandered aimlessly until she had eventually seen a small ray of light in the distance. This she followed until the moment she had poked her head above ground and seen the four of them.

'So you see,' she concluded, 'I must throw myself on your mercy, since you are the only friends I have here. I must find that wicked faun and retrieve my precious necklace. I was too silly to remember when all this started that if I had only touched the magic necklace and wished with all my might to be home in my father's castle, the magic would have taken me there. I don't know how it works,' she said, pausing and lowering her head, 'but I know it will not fail me if I can but find it.'

The four dwarfs looked at one another searchingly, then down at the ground. A cunning smile played briefly over Dimbek's mouth, but none could discern that beneath his full beard. Rimbek could not tear his eyes away from the lovely girl. They were filled with longing and adoration.

As he looked, he felt the strong magnetic currents in his navel's golden screw begin to weaken, as though they would shatter at any moment. For one fleeting moment, his mind's eye saw him sitting there with the whole schlong uncoiled and lashing about until it stood stiffly in front of him like an enormous corkscrew. He knew he needed a thumping very badly, he knew it was dangerous beyond measure to keep watching the lovely princess, but he could not tear his eyes away from her. 'Why?' he wondered, thinking about how many times he had run away from dwarf ladies who had been eyeing his coiled up schlong. He shuddered ... just as Dimbek's hairy hand landed on his cheek ... Thwack!

'Are you listening to me?' the big brother shouted in his ear. The magnetism in the golden screw shot up to top level.

'Please help me to find him,' the golden-haired girl was saying. 'I know my father will reward you handsomely. He would pay my weight in gold just to have me back home now.'

Dimbek smiled and bowed. Then he beckoned to the others and they walked a short distance down the path where they began whispering among themselves. They did not notice Astra – or Barletta, as she had told them her name was – lift her wrist and place the mother of pearl disc near her ear. Every word came through to her as though they were shouting.

'You were right, Hogbek, absolutely right,' exclaimed Dimbek.

'I was?' answered Hogbek in great surprise.

'Yes,' Dimbek assured him, 'and the king will be told how clever you are. Everything fits together, don't you see? The Elves enchanted the girl, they must have known the power of the necklace. And that – that faun, as she calls him, must have dropped it when he fell in Bumbree's hole. The magic must have made it snap closed around his neck. King Schtoonk will reward us beyond our wildest dreams if we capture the – the faun *and* the magic necklace. Now here is what we must do . . .'

In a few minutes, they returned to the lovely princess who was leaning against a tree with her eyes closed.

'Ahem –' Dimbek made himself sound as dignified as he could. 'We, my brothers and I, are deeply moved by the story of your great distress, fair princess. Although we do not trust men as a rule, since men are for ever seeking to discover our hidden Schtronghold and rob our precious treasures, we are willing to make an exception in your case and come to your rescue. We will help you recover your necklace. You are now officially a dwarf-friend, and as such . . .'

'Oh, how wonderful,' Astra gasped, but before she

could say another word, Dimbek held up his hand with great authority.

'Enough time for thanks when we succeed,' he told her sternly. 'Right now, we must make all the haste we can. Undoubtedly, Bumbree wants that necklace too. Why else would she make off with that — that faun all packed in ice? We have no time to waste. Can you run like the wind, Princess Barletta?'

'I'll try,' she said gamely, stepping to the middle of the path. She was laughing to herself, knowing she could still muster the leaping swiftness of a doe, even though she could not waste the power to change her form. That is, if these new swelling discomforts of her human body did not get in her way. But how would the dwarfs follow on their bandy little legs?

At a signal from Dimbek, the dwarfs rolled up the magic mantle and quickly strapped it to young Rimbek's back. At another signal, they all made a funny motion with their buttocks and she noticed the great coils around their middles as they unfurled and coiled up on the ground. With a shock, she realized the sharp, pointed tip of Rimbek's was slithering towards her and twitching suggestively. She heard the loud slap of Dimbek's hand against the young dwarf's cheek and a twinge of pity for the poor little dwarf touched her generous heart.

Fascinated, she watched each of them extract two pieces of wood from pockets inside their odd jackets. The wooden pieces were wide at the centres with holes drilled through them, the wood tapering to each side to form tiny platforms. With deft movements, they inserted the barbed tips of their penes through the holes in the wood and drew one up high on the shaft, the other to a point about two feet below the upper-most. Then they began tightening something on each side of the holes in the wood.

'We're off!' commanded Dimbek. The four brothers leaped into the air, their feet landing precisely on the tapering ends of the lower pieces of wood, their hands firmly grasping the upper ones. The penes corkscrewed instantly on the ground, then uncoiled like huge springs. Away they flew down the path, bounding like giant hares, covering twenty and more feet in each rapid bound.

Startled, Astra took off like a deer herself, her legs moving so fast that the dress seemed like a golden blur. And as fast as she ran, she could just about keep the dwarfs in sight.

XI

Early Morn
at the
Creepy Cottage

With the dwarfs well hidden near her in the thick underbrush, Astra stood behind the last tree at the edge of the clearing before Bumbree's Creepy Cottage. And creepy it was, a disgusting yellowish brown; it reeked with unhealthy emanations in the first brightening streaks of dawn. The dwarfs explained that for countless years the birds of the forest had bombarded the sunken, sprawling house until none of the original wattle and daub could be seen. Nor the thatching, for that matter. Mounds upon mounds of bird droppings had covered every inch, thickening with time.

Unconcerned, Bumbree merely sprayed the entire cottage at regular intervals with a special solution she concocted from her own wettings and a mixture of magical powders. Tons of droppings had been smoothed and hardened until the cottage, on close inspection, had the adamantine look of tempered steel. No weapon could penetrate the walls, no fire could mar it or burn it down. Still, from a few yards away, it looked a hapless and aged heap which might collapse at any moment. Very few Elves and certainly no dwarfs ever wanted to inspect the place that closely.

The dwarfs had believed Astra's story and they did not guess the truth concerning the necklace chain fixed tightly about Flondrix's throat. Astra knew it blocked his Elvan powers so completely he was hardly aware of his own identity. A tear rolled down her cheek as she wondered if he would be able to recognize her. Even at the height of her powers, she would not easily overcome that accursed chain.

Grimly, she bit her lip. The first thing was to get him out of there. The dwarfs' plan would work, she was sure. She could draw Bumbree out of the cottage and lead her on a wild goose chase. The dwarfs could then wrap the faun in their magic mantle and cart him off. The problem was to give them enough time to escape Bumbree, but not enough time to reach that Schtronghold, as they called it, in the White Mountains. With her own limited powers, she must rescue Flondrix from them before they reached there . . . and before Bumbree caught up with any of them. How? How to pin her down here longenough? If the dwarfs did get him inside their mountains, would they really try to skin him?

Astra shuddered, then admonished herself sternly. 'Get first things done first,' she scolded. 'What would your father think of you, dithering about like this?'

Softly, so the dwarfs might not observe, she slid her hand up along the bole of the tree until her wrist was level with her eyes. Casually, she leant forward slightly and placed her left eye over the mother of pearl insert on the ivory bracelet. Her other eye focused on the open upper half of Bumbree's door, two hundred yards across the clearing. In the single beat of a heart, she saw the interior as closely as if she had been leaning through the doorway.

She gasped involuntarily and her shoulders shook; quickly, she got herself under control lest the dwarfs wonder at her shock.

Stretched out on a great hollow log raised on stout pegs was the long yellow cylinder of ice. The top of the cylinder faced the door and Astra saw the faun's tousled head, black curly locks wildly dishevelled and the long, pointed ears twitching uncomfortably. The head jerked back abruptly and Astra could see the harsh metal digging into the throat — that infernal necklace! She noticed too that the lovely eyes were closed. What mercy that he still sleeps, she thought.

A cloud of smoke billowed across the room, blotting out the view and another burst from the chimney above, belching its ugly blackness at the morning sky. As the smoke cleared in the room, she saw a darkened hulk loom up from the background. Thick shoulders, muscled and sooty like a blacksmith's. Heavy arms sprouting hair which ran up and over the shoulders, then down between the three huge dugs which dangled to the waist, swaying from side to side with every lurching step. Hips of great circumference leaked down into swollen, knotty thighs, thick with purple veins, wrinkling and buckling, looking ready to burst at each movement. More hair started growing profusely somewhere between knees and crotch; it thickened and twirled like writhing snakes, sweeping up over the multi-potted abdomen and spreading out from the protruding navel until, more like fur and porcupine quills, it reached beyond the hips on either side, curling like an ornate pair of moustachios.

The girl's horrified attention was torn from the grotesque body to the gigantic right hand rising up over the tube of ice. In it was a huge double-edged battleaxe glowing white hot and showering sparks all about the room.

121

Astra's eyelids slammed together as the mighty axe came down. She heard hisses of steam as the clanging blows struck again and again. The horror of her imagination could be worse than what was actually happening, she realized, forcing her eyes open again.

Bumbree had hacked into the ice with the cunning of a smith, fashioning an intricate pattern of precise cuts. From the faun's neck to his groin, she had made a clean incision down the centre of the ice. Two more longitudinal ones had been made on either side of the central one. She made three more cuts across the ice, one at his groin, one just below the navel and the last over his collarbone.

The witch leaned the blackened, smoking axe against the wall and hunkered down to survey her work, one eye closed, the other squinting. Satisfied, she stood up, wiped her hands together and lumbered to the head of the wooden trough. Facing the door, she froze suddenly and went into a crouch, her narrowed eyes sweeping the clearing from one side to the other. Her head rose slightly and she sniffed the air, twitching her nose from side to side like a dog searching out a scent.

Astra quickly moved her head back and the cottage receded to its full two hundred yard distance. She waited a few moments, not daring to breathe, before she eased her head forward and brought the mother of pearl disc back to her eye. Bumbree's powers are nothing to sneeze at, she thought, if she can detect my scrutiny from here.

The appalled girl strangled a cry at the sight that met her telescoping vision. Bumbree had backed up to the wooden trough and her legs were spread around the faun's head, the great mass of matted hair between them draped over poor Flondrix's face. A gaping ditch opened and clutched at the beloved face. Bumbree stood there with her ham fists on her hips and wriggled

122

provocatively. In another moment, an enormous clitoris, longer than a finger and every bit as supple, came snaking out of the cavern and wrapped itself around one of the faun's delicate horns. The little head began lurching erratically as it was pulled higher and higher, the face clutched by the maw itself.

There was a tremendous cracking sound, like hundreds of glass goblets being smashed all at once. Bumbree laughed maniacally and smacked her hips with her fists. Evil joy puckered the folds of fat surrounding her piggish eyes and drops of yellow sweat stood out on the low, pimpled brow. The thick rubbery lips drew back, slobbering, and the long yellow canine teeth slithered over the lower lip.

Retracting her clitoris and sliding forward over the faun's wretched head, the witch turned round to admire her handiwork. On the floor lay four perfect quarter sections of thick ice, hard as steel and not one corner had been chipped. And standing proudly, like the mast on a ship, the faun's great priapus shuddered and jerked spasmodically in the air. Still laughing gleefully, she picked up the longer two sections which had encased the faun's chest and had kept his priapus imprisoned. These she rubbed gingerly in her gaping maw, back and forth, until the edges were well saturated with the copious drippings. She clapped them over the faun's chest and stuck five fingers of one hand into the trench and rubbed the fingers back and forth over the seams in the ice. They disappeared in no time. The ice was as solid as it had been before cracking. Only the small square, from below his navel to his groin, was exposed.

The happy beast picked up the two shorter pieces of ice and ran from the room. Loud squealing and scraping sounds rocked the cottage for a few minutes and then Bumbree returned. Each piece of ice had a perfect, matching semi-circle cut in it. Once more the edges of ice were rubbed vigorously in her saturated trench and then slapped into place over the faun. Up through the hole in the ice stuck his glorious priapus.

If such a lumbering creature could be said to skip about with joy, this she did now. As she flew about the room, she caught up a length of heavy rope coiled in many loops from a peg on the wall. Bending over the ice tube, she fashioned an intricate harness with the rope and found a pair of iron stirrups to attach to the rope ends. With a shriek of joy, she put a foot in each stirrup and heaved her great bulk high in the air. The wooden trough groaned as the knots tightened round it. Bumbree raised herself high over the priapus and dropped crashingly, impaling herself on the full length.

Astra turned her head, hot tears of shame and betrayal streaming down her cheeks. She was about to run away when a thunderous noise came from the Creepy Cottage. As she looked quickly into the disc on her bracelet, she saw Bumbree slide off her perch and collapse, cowering on the floor.

Bumbree was crouching in fear . . . but of what? Something rumbled dreadfully in the fireplace, but only the edge of that was visible from where Astra stood. The sight that tore her heart with grief was the faun's lovely priapus completely covered in a thick green fluid which rolled down its length slowly like malevolent honey. Large drops of it fell on the ice casing and caused it to sizzle. The fluid actually burned into the ice, melting it. Before she could think more about that another horrendous noise sounded across the clearing.

With a deafening crash, the whole hearthstone raised itself, scattering fire all over the earthen floor. The heavy stone was pierced by two huge black horns and sat squarely on a flat, black head. Astra could barely make out the most horrifying profile she had ever seen. One blood-red eye gleamed so brightly Bumbree turned a crimson colour in its reflection. The mouth opened to speak and enormous ruby tusks flashed and glistened, dripping a black saliva.

The girl yanked the disc away from her eye and placed it over her ear.

'What about my sacrificial chickens, you bloated stinking fat swine?' a terrifying guttural voice croaked. 'Fetch them, before I make you even more ugly than you are . . . before I rip out your clitoris and strangle you with it, you snivelling, stinking excuse for a witch!'

'Oh, Daemon-Baalim, darling,' cooed Bumbree, trying to sound humble and seductive at the same time, 'please forgive my careless, thoughtless negligence. I never dreamed you would be here so early. I do know how you like to sleep late in the morning. I'll go out right now and get the chickens for you.'

'You were "doing it" again, were you not?' the voice shouted accusingly from beneath the hearthstone. 'Every time you are supposed to be preparing my great feasts and rites, you impale yourself on some poor helpless beast instead.'

'Oh, no, Dreaded Prince,' she whined, 'I got this one for you. He's *perfect* for the chicken ritual. I went through so much trouble to capture him for you. I was just keeping it warm and firm for the sacrificial rites, it was no pleasure to me, I promise . . .'

'Shut your lying mouth, you foul beast-defiler,' the terrible voice thundered menacingly. 'Fetch me my chickens! Now!'

Bumbree jumped to her feet obediently and ran out of the door, disappearing behind the cottage. She returned almost immediately with two large chickens in her hands, one snowy white, the other coal black.

She charged through the door in such panic that she left the lower half of it swinging open.

The Creepy Cottage was silent, so Astra brought the magic disc back on a level with her eye. Horrified, she saw Bumbree standing on top of the column of ice which rocked under her great weight. She had the black chicken pinned securely under her left arm and the white fowl grasped firmly by the neck in her right hand. She inched the fingers of her left hand under the white one's belly and started tickling it vigorously.

Eventually, the fluttering chicken strained and an egg popped out in the witch's hand. Quick as lightning, Bumbree broke it over the tip of the faun's priapus and jammed the still dilated chicken down over it. As the fowl squawked piteously, the grinning witch rammed its head and neck into her waiting cleft and strangled it, twisting the head off as she did.

The chicken's death spasm had a startling effect on all the participants. Bumbree groaned and ground the chicken's head inside her maw. The unspeakable head beneath the hearthstone filled the room with deafening, maddened laughter. Poor Flondrix lost control of his best intentions, sending a gigantic inundation of pearly fluid up into the chicken, bloating it to more than double its previous size. Bumbree tore the chicken loose and pitched it with deadly accuracy at the face in the fireplace. The huge black jaws swung open, revealing the rows of terrifying ruby teeth, and snapped closed with a tremendous clang. One gulp and the chicken was gone. With a delirious smile, Bumbree took the black chicken from under her arm and started stroking its belly.

Astra twisted her head violently, choking on a loathing so great it sickened her heart. As she turned, her ear brushed the mother of pearl disc and she heard the dreadful guttural voice again.

'No matter where you go or what you do today, be here at the stroke of midnight for our most sacred and solemn celebrations. Remember, this is the night we bury Midsummer. And keep that iced beast in good condition, it will be perfect for the feasting later.' There was a clatter as the hearthstone fell into place. Not another sound smote the air.

Astra knew the fateful moment had come. She stepped out from behind the tree and signalled a warning to the dwarfs. Smoothing her dress, she took a few hesitant steps, then broke into a skipping run, her legs flying with utter abandon and her arms merrily flailing the air. As she skipped across the clearing, she did not hear the hearthstone grate once more or the dreaded voice hiss at Bumbree.

'. . . And don't you dare forget our human sacrifice. This year I don't want some dirty old man, I want a lovely young virgin, do you hear? Get one, if you know what is good for you!' Clang! went the stone again.

'Tra-la-la, pretty birdy in the tree, don't fly away, come back to me. When you sing, I am as happy as can be. When you fly away, how sad, O woe is me.' Astra stopped singing and shielded her eyes, peering around the clearing as if in search of a bird.

Bumbree loped to the door and stared out, amazed to hear such a clear, high voice singing so sweetly. She couldn't believe her eyes as the lovely girl started skipping nearer and nearer the Creepy Cottage. Twittering inside herself nervously, the old witch pulled a wrinkled Mother Hubbard outfit off a peg behind the door and wrapped it around her grotesque body. She pulled the lower half of the door close to her hip so the young thing would not be able to see the ice-encased faun lying in the trough.

'Good morning,' Astra called sweetly. 'Pray tell, have you seen a small bird flying about? He was such a beautiful bird, all covered in golden feathers that sparkled in the sun. I've been chasing after him until I shall surely drop with fatigue.'

'Now, now, my child,' Bumbree cooed, trying to sound like a sweet old nanny, 'you must bide a while and let me bring you a refreshing bowl of milk.' The witch picked up a jug from the small table near the door and held it up invitingly, all the while sending a strong beam of mesmerizing vibrations towards the girl. Astra's head dropped, but surreptitiously, she caught at the pendant hanging about her neck and held it a few inches in front of her. The vibrations were neatly cloven a few feet in front of her and passed harmlessly to either side.

With downcast head, Astra felt the large, swaying body moving closer and closer. Just as Bumbree dropped the empty jug and threw out her ham-like hands to capture the girl, Astra sped like a deer to the far side of the clearing. Caught off balance, Bumbree dropped to all fours and growled horribly. When she looked up, she saw the young girl stretched out on the ground near the trees, holding her ankle and rubbing it piteously.

With an animal roar, Bumbree sprang forward and closed the distance between them with amazing speed. When she got there the girl was gone.

Many hours later, and many, many miles from the cottage, Astra leaned against a tree, enjoying one of the few respites she'd had all day . . . and in truth for most of the night, for it was rapidly approaching midnight. During the past few hours, Bumbree had assumed the guise of a great forest wolf and the speed she could attain was exhausting Astra. Still, she had to hold out until midnight.

Bumbree had to be at the cottage at midnight. The voice had commanded it and the witch obviously lived in fear and dread of Daemon-Baalim, also known as the

Beast Beneath. How long would she stay there when they discovered the faun was gone? And would the faun be gone? What if the dwarfs had failed? Only if she had her true Elvan powers could she know the answer from such a distance. There was no other way; she must get back to the cottage before Bumbree to make sure Flondrix had been successfully removed by the dwarfs. Then she had to catch them before they reached their Schtronghold. And how soon would Bumbree be finished with her horrid rites and celebrations? Would she then be off in hot pursuit again?

Before Astra could ponder any more, she heard the sound of the hot wind building up near by. She pressed herself as far into the contours of the tree as she could and popped her pendant in her mouth. Then she placed the mother of pearl disc in the centre of her forehead, between and just above her eyes. She knew this would block any emanations the witch might detect. A few moments later and the wind howled as the great furry beast sped by like a comet. When the sounds had diminished in the distance, Astra reversed the wrist and aimed the disc outward from her brow, forming a diadrom she hoped would confuse Bumbree when she turned and backtracked.

Astra looked up at the moon as it sailed out from behind a large white cloud; then she turned her gaze towards Topar. She wished with all her might that she had bought herself enough time to pass the cottage and be off before Bumbree returned.

*

The dwarfs had waited until the sounds of the chase had faded in the distance. For good measure, they waited another five minutes, straining their ears to make sure no returning sounds could be heard. Satisfied at last, they crept out of the heavy undergrowth,

Dimbek in the lead, the twins right behind and little Rimbek bringing up the rear, the heavy magic mantle over his shoulders.

They tiptoed into the Creepy Cottage, every hair on their heads, beards, bodies and palms standing on end. But there was nothing to terrify them. Then Rimbek stepped on something and when he lifted his foot, he saw the severed, mashed head of a white chicken. The plaintive scream was hardly out of his mouth when Dimbek's hand found its unwary mark.

'Hsst!' Dimbek snarled, 'bring that mantle over here and help us.'

When they approached Flondrix with the mantle, they realized that something had changed drastically. Ruefully, they stared at the towering priapus, then down at the neat hole in the ice and scratched their beards. No matter how they tried to arrange the mantle, it simply would not cover everything. When Hogbek suggested they try to cut the huge mast off, Flondrix emitted a plaintive scream. The dwarfs jumped and Dogbek was told by Dimbek to hold his hand over the faun's mouth. Flondrix, who hardly knew his own identity let alone his whereabouts, began to struggle as the stiff hairs on the dwarf's hand tickled his sensitive nostrils.

Finally, three of them cut loose Bumbree's complicated harness and managed to tie the large mast down with the pieces of rope until it was parallel to the ice cylinder.

'All right, everybody, let's hoist him up now,' ordered Dimbek.

With copious heaves and grunts, the strange procession moved through the Creepy Cottage door; as they walked out into the sunlight, labouring mightily under their burden, they resembled nothing quite so much as four small pallbearers struggling under a large, black-draped coffin. Groaning and grumbling, they worked their way back to the edge of the clearing and a few yards into the deep forest cover.

'In the name of good King Schtoonk and all his ancestors,' sobbed Rimbek, 'it will take us for ever and a day to get back to the White Mountains like this.'

Dimbek called a halt and ordered them to lower the cylinder gently to the ground.

'We shall certainly not travel home like this,' Dimbek intoned, imitating his little brother's woe-begone tone. 'We shall all uncoil now and do the corkscrew spring-leap all the way home. Understand?'

'What?' shouted the twins with one voice. 'Uncoil and try to do the corkscrew spring-leap with this heavy burden on our shoulders? Springing with one hand? You must be mad!'

Dimbek walked calmly over to the twins. Twice his hand moved like lightning. The twins yelped.

'Orders are orders! Who is in command here?' he demanded. The twins pointed to him. 'That is correct. Now, no more insubordination. You uncoil, you mount the wooden platforms and prepare to spring-leap. Left side: Hogbek front, Dogbek rear. Right side: I will take the front, Rimbek the rear. You must all start on the word, Go! Hold on to the captive for dear life and keep the rhythm ... do you understand that? Keep the rhythm.'

Rimbek looked behind him towards the clearing. 'I feel guilty about leaving that lovely young girl at the mercy of ...'

'Will you take your place!' roared Dimbek, his knowing palm finding its mark.

After four false starts, each one sending the ice-encased body of the unfortunate faun crashing to the ground, they prepared grimly for the fifth attempt.

'It would be a lot easier,' Rimbek suggested

humbly, 'if we could untie him and get him to spring-leap a little. It is certainly not for lack of . . .'

'Silence!' shouted Dimbek. They hoisted the burden to their shoulders once more. 'Besides,' grumbled the leader, 'he is not a dwarf, he is an Elf. Whatever made you think a mere Elf . . . oh, never mind. Ready? Go!'

The movements were finally coordinated without further mishap. It was slower going than the journey from the Sacred Glade, the leaps covering no more than ten feet, but it was immeasurably swifter than the snail's pace they had made up to then.

XII

When all Seems Lost
New Friends are Found

When Astra slipped swiftly across the clearing, she knew from the moon and stars above that it was almost midnight. Her sensitive ears also told her that Bumbree, still in the guise of a great grey wolf, was not far behind. One look inside the Creepy Cottage door made her heart soar. The trough was empty! She didn't pause an instant longer than it took to ascertain this; running behind the cottage, she stood for a moment fully exposed at the opposite side of the clearing from the direction she reckoned the dwarfs had sped towards the White Mountains. Concentrating as hard as she could, she emitted vibrations she knew would attract the bloodthirsty witch. Then she popped her magic pendant in her mouth and screened herself with the bracelet as she circled around the clearing. In only moments she was pursuing the dwarfs as fast as her legs could go.

The great wolf hurtled out of the forest and stopped dead in its tracks, the long foaming snout pointing immediately to the trees behind the cottage. With a howl, she started racing towards the trees. When she was abreast of the cottage, a frightful crash echoed through the clearing. The hearthstone sounded as if it

133

had been smashed to smithereens. A blood-curdling howl tore the night air.

'Where are you, you filthy slut? Where is my beautiful ceremony? My human sacrifice, my great feasting and rejoicing?'

The wolf form disappeared and a terrified Bumbree stumbled to the door, dragging her Mother Hubbard outfit along the ground behind her.

'Here I am, dearest,' she panted, plunging through the door. 'He's gone!' she screamed so loudly the grass outside paled. 'He's gone, he's gone! That horrible little girl has stolen him!'

'What in the name of thunder are you talking about?' roared the voice from under the fireplace.

'The faun,' she sobbed, 'the pretty faun with the great — I mean the one encased in ice, the one I brought for your lovely ceremony, the one I captured just for you last night.'

'What?' The very house shook and the chimney threatened to collapse. 'I told you to take good care of that, you filthy, bumbling animal-doer. Who took it?'

'It must have been that little girl . . . the virgin you wanted,' Bumbree sniffed through her tears. 'I've been chasing her all day and all night. She came to the door just after you left this morning, just after you told me . . .'

'A little girl?' the terrible voice croaked. 'You could not catch a little girl? You filthy, clumsy idiot, how could . . . wait!'

The hearthstone rattled and an incredible snuffling began somewhere beneath the fireplace. It was so strong that odds and ends on the earthen floor were sucked under the hearth by the vacuum.

'Aha! You fool. You blind, stupid fool. A little girl, eh? A faun, eh? You blundering great idiot excuse for a witch! They were Elves, you scum-ridden slob! Do you hear me? Wait . . . Hah! Not only Elves, but ones precious to my hated immortal enemy, Glortan.'

'Oh, beloved, how was I to know . . .' Bumbree began sobbing.

'Shut up, you miserable fat filthy swine. This chicken head . . . hmmm.' The voice stopped and a crunching noise filled the room. 'Yaaah! Just as I thought. There have been dwarfs here too. *They* stole your faun. You have been duped. You are the most worthless witch in my entire collection.'

'Please, darling,' Bumbree begged. 'I'll leave now, I'll catch them. I promise.'

'Before the solemn rites?' the horrendous voice howled. 'You have bungled every other part of the ceremony, you shall not spoil the solemn rites. Prepare yourself!'

Wailing and sobbing, howling and pleading, Bumbree threw her great bulk over the empty trough. Hissing eerily, a huge serpent emerged from beneath the fireplace and slithered across the floor. The head reared up and one ugly, crusted eye gleamed dully from the centre of it. It struck the huge, gaping trench that sagged between the witch's thighs and buried itself there. Horrifying garbled noises came from Bumbree as the python-like thing pushed and rammed, squirming higher and higher. Abruptly, the sounds tearing from her throat were muffled.

The ugly snake head burst from her mouth and swayed, its one eye glaring about the room. More of the snake emerged and began coiling itself around the thick wrinkled neck, stretching it until Bumbree's face turned purple and the eyes started from her head. When the last coil was tightly wound and the full length of the snake's body was extended taut upon the earthen floor, the head turned to face the witch's popping eyes.

135

'When this is over,' hissed the snake, 'you will be gone with all haste. You are not to return until you have captured those two, do you understand? Bring them here to me. If you don't, you will be subjected to the Ultimate Horror. I do not have to tell you what *that* is, do I?'

Impossible as it may seem, at these dreaded words Bumbree's popping eyes widened to twice their already dilated size.

'Yes?' hissed the snake. 'Are you ready?' Without waiting for an answer, the vicious serpent struck, burying its head in her right nostril. It forced, pushed and squirmed until the nostril appeared ready to burst in twenty places, but it held. When the snake's head was deep inside her own, the hideous pumping began. Before it was over, the inundations had expanded Bumbree's head to the size of a grotesque pumpkin and it glowed a fiery red.

'What do you say now?' the voice rumbled from beneath the fireplace; the same words were hissed inside the great, inflamed ball of her head.

'Oh, darling,' she gurgled indistinctly, 'I love, I love you.'

*

Flying over the ground swifter than the swiftest hind, Astra saw the blurring trees thinning as she approached the great White Mountains. Placing her mother of pearl disc before her eye, she could clearly see the four dwarfs nearing the base of the mountains. They were still spring-leaping in unison, but they were obviously so tired they could not go much further without another break in the long, wearisome journey. Calling on her last ounces of strength, she sprang forward.

Bursting through the last of the trees at the base of the mountains, she was just in time to see the great stone portals clang shut. When she reached the spot, tripping and panting, Astra saw that there was no way ordinary eyes could tell where the doors were. The surface of the mountain base was one expanse of smooth, unseamed stone.

The poor girl collapsed on the ground and wept with all the bitterness and frustration in her heart. She railed at herself for being too slow . . . if she only had not gone back to the Creepy Cottage to make sure the dwarfs had succeeded . . . if she had loved her dear Flondrix as much as her father had told her she must . . . she stopped there, knowing that thoughts of defeat would solve nothing.

She closed her eyes and before she was able to reopen them, she fell asleep. She was aware of nothing until a sharp, insistent pain in her little finger woke her. When her eyes popped open, she was amazed to see a small grey and brown mouse sitting on her leg, nibbling excitedly at her finger.

With a gasp, she pulled her hand back, expecting to see the mouse jump off her leg and run away. Instead, he continued to sit there chattering in a squeaky voice, shaking a forepaw at her. She blinked her eyes when a half dozen more mice came running up to sit on the grass next to her, all chattering at once. They were terribly upset and trying desperately to tell her something. They were all pointing towards the forest.

Astra stood up and stared ahead, her eyes moving across the vast forest. At the edge of her thoughts, she knew this situation was not accidental. As a mortal, the mice should shun her . . . yet? 'Why am I dithering so?' she asked herself. Lifting her wrist, she placed the disc over her eye.

She saw a terrible shape moving with blinding speed towards the White Mountains. Outwardly, it appeared to be a gigantic bear with certain gorilla-like aspects.

But there was no mistaking the wicked eyes or the three great dugs that hung loosely from the matted chest, swaying wildly as the hulking beast slipped past the trees. Bumbree! Bumbree was after her ... and Flondrix.

'Oh, by Topar's sacred Midsummer light,' she whispered to herself, 'what shall I do now?' Bumbree would be there in a matter of minutes. As her anxiety increased, the girl felt a griping cramp in her lower abdomen, then a hot flush that burned its way down through the unfamiliar tubes in her lower body.

'Excuse me,' she said to the mice, and retreated behind a near-by boulder in confusion. She remembered at the last moment to hitch up her lovely golden dress when she squatted. Tears of mortification welled up as she felt so many strange things pouring out of her body at once. Oh, those poor humans, she thought to herself as she gathered up as many thick ferns as she could. Her face turned crimson when she realized the last of the ferns was stained red.

Astra stood up quickly, hoping against hope that she would not stain her lovely dress. What, she wondered, do mortal women do when this strange phenomenon occurs?

She heard the approaching rumble of the bear and saw the mice gathered about a tiny hole near the base of the invisible portals. She had not noticed the hole earlier because a small, inconspicuous stone had been placed before it. The mice were chattering with great anxiety and the one who had awakened her ran over and tugged at her slipper, pointing first to the hole in the ground, then towards the noise building up in the forest. Next, he pointed at Astra, making gestures with his forepaws that indicated she should become smaller and smaller. Once again he pointed to the hole and squeaked as loudly as he could.

The message was perfectly clear. She would have to use up some of her frighteningly small reserves of personal magic. She shrugged, and seconds later she was standing on delicate paws near the hole, a beautiful golden mouse.

'Chalk for cheese, I thought you would never get the message!' boomed a loud voice in her ear. She turned and saw the mouse who had been beckoning her. He stood taller than the others and glowered at her with small black eyes, tinged with red.

Her new companion sniffed the air and the hair round his neck bristled like a mane. 'Bacon rinds and bitter nuts, you are on heat!' he exclaimed. 'What marvellous timing, my dear.'

Thunderstruck, she saw the other mice circling about, trying to get behind her. A scuffle broke out and the big mouse cuffed two or three of the smaller ones, sending them sprawling.

'In there, all of you,' he ordered. 'We have enough trouble as it is. Hurry! The witch will be here any moment.'

Mice flew past her and the next thing she knew, she was being pushed roughly through the hole and down a tunnel. Light disappeared as two of the mice, under their leader's direction, jammed the stone securely in place, blocking the hole. Astra's small eyes grew accustomed to the darkness rapidly, but not before two noses began investigating the delightfully aromatic spot under her tail. During the next brief scuffle, she was nearly bowled over as the two bold mice were sent barrelling down the tunnel.

'Stay next to me,' the large mouse ordered, 'for these young fools cannot be trusted for a moment. But I certainly wish you had not chosen this dreadful day to play the irresistible lady.'

'I did not choose it,' Astra protested hotly. 'I – I

have no idea how it works. Something happened just before I changed into a mouse.'

'No use complaining,' the big mouse admitted gruffly, 'we'll just have to put up with it for the next few days.'

'The next few days,' she echoed dismally, 'I can't wait that long. I have to find the dwarfs' Schtronghold. My—my—someone is there I must save. He is a captive of the dwarfs.'

'Yes, yes, I know,' the big mouse answered absently. Just then, a rumble and a crash reverberated through the tunnel, nearly deafening them. 'Your friend Bumbree has arrived. Let's move along . . . quickly!'

They scurried down the passage and did not halt until they were deep, deep down inside the mountain, screened from the witch's penetrating senses by thousands of tons of solid rock.

When they arrived at a broad antechamber of some sort, Astra noticed that none of the other mice was around. The big mouse sniffed the air cautiously and then nodded his head towards an entrance in the rock facing.

'What's in there?' Astra asked.

'My lair,' he replied. 'Now, before you get upset, I'm taking you in there to my wife, Binny. Can you understand it isn't safe for you, wandering about like that? Why, every bachelor in the kingdom would be climbing all over you. To say nothing of the married ones who lose all scruples when they get away from their lairs.'

'Please don't misunderstand—I'm so grateful,' Astra assured him, 'but tell me the truth, who sent you to my rescue? It was no accident.'

'Nobody sends me,' the big mouse declared. 'My name is Boff and I'm pretty much king round here. But it is true, someone loves you very much.'

'Glortan, my father . . . no, it was Aunt Glortina . . . please tell me,' she begged.

'I have nothing further to say on the subject,' Boff told her firmly. 'Now inside you go. Hurry it on.'

The lair was rather sumptuous, with wall hangings and floor coverings of rich design, deftly made up of scraps stolen from the dwarfs, no doubt. In a back corner, a rather portly lady mouse was stretched out on a soft bed made of woolly fluff, covered with a gold brocade spread. Gathered up under her, making a terrible racket of suckles and squeaks, were five healthy, glossy-coated youngsters.

'You stay here until I get back, girlie,' Boff ordered. 'This is my wife, Binny. She'll take good care of you.'

'Where are you going now, darling?' Binny called from the far end of the lair.

'I want to check on our reconnaissance crews, Binny. Our guest here in the somewhat "indelicate condition" is concerned about someone the dwarfs have captured.' Boff turned to Astra. 'What is it they call him? A foon?'

'A faun,' Astra corrected him demurely, casting her eyes down.

'A faun?' sniffed Boff. 'Well, one thing's certain, he's really — uh — constructed in a fascinating fashion. According to the boys, he had to be tied down . . .'

'Boff! Don't you dare talk like that in front of our guest,' Binny warned. 'Her faun is her business. If I hear any more rowdy talk from you, I'll cuff your ears smartly.' Biddy called out to Astra, 'Come over here and rest awhile, my dear. I'll tend to your problem as soon as the children are fed. What an unfortunate time to have this happen to you . . . dear, dear.'

With a huff and a couple of snorts, Boff scampered through the entrance of the lair and disappeared.

XIII

King Barlocks
Plays an Uncertain Trump

✦✦✦✦✦✦✦

'Drat it all, Gonzola, *do
something!*' the Dark King's voice shuddered through
the bed chamber, the sentence chopped into little
pieces by the chattering of his teeth.

The bed was piled high with the sheepskin and bearskin robes and three enormous charcoal braziers blazed
near the quaking king. The magician circled the bed,
heaping fresh charcoal on the fires, his nightshirt
sticking to his skin, his face sweating profusely. A pig
would roast easily in the room, he felt, but the king
was shivering and whining about freezing to death.
What could be happening to Flondrix? At the very
least, he must be encased in ice, the wizard thought.

'For nearly two days,' the king complained, 'I have
been sealed in this blizzard none but I can detect. All
your fiery ointments have had no success. Can't you
do something?'

'My liege,' Gonzola answered with infinite patience,
'it is the Elvan curse again. And there is no cure save
Glortan's forgiveness.'

'Well, get it then!' Barlocks screamed, his extreme
discomfort putting him beyond rational thinking.

'Yesterday morning that dratted thing was slamming into the ceiling again . . . and cackling! Eggs broken all over the floor. Headless chickens running about spraying blood all over the chamber. Now the dratted thing is slammed against my chest as though it were bound with chains. No man can endure it, I tell you.'

'I weep, my lord, I weep for your plight. But what can I tell the Elvan King that will move him? If you command, I must go. But empty-handed, I face his further wrath. I put my aged head in a noose and may never return. What can I tell him?' the wizard asked reasonably, heaping a last shovelful of charcoal on one of the fires.

'When you have finished that, come over to the bed and lean that hoary old head close to me. I think I know what you can tell that blasted Elvan egomaniac . . . yes, something that may knock a bit of the pompous starch out of him.'

Fifteen minutes later, Gonzola rode across the moat on a gigantic black horse, a steed that seemed charged with a strange and mysterious essence. Steam blew thickly from the animal's large nostrils and the guards standing to attention almost expected to see flames leap from the beast's nose. Huddled inside his sweeping black cloak, the ancient travelling hat jammed down on his head, the magician shivered almost as violently as the king. Fear and loathing filled his eyes, and it was not fear of the enchanted forest or its denizens. The weight on his heart was profound, his ears still ringing with the dreadful words Barlocks had uttered.

Early the next morning, horse and rider halted near Bumbree's Creepy Cottage. Gonzola reached inside his cloak and pressed a small button on the back of a thick iron star suspended from a heavy iron chain around his neck. He closed his eyes for five minutes and focused all his attention on the base of his spine. When he opened his eyes, a faint, eerie glow surrounded the man and the animal.

Dismounting in front of the door, the wizard paused and sniffed the air before entering the cottage. Inside, he moved across the floor carefully, noting the feathers, bits of egg-shell, the ashes scattered about. He bent low over the fireplace and extracted the small ivory wand he kept secreted inside his cloak; when he touched it to the hearthstone lightly, an ugly gash of lightning flashed from it, slamming into the side of the chimney and breaking loose a bit of stone. He sniffed at the strong sulphur smell and nodded grimly.

Straightening up and stretching, he walked to the trough, covering each inch of it with his uncanny eyes. He noted every chafe of rope, every footprint and analysed the dampnesses and traces of fluids. When he stepped out into the still pale morning sunlight, he saw the pallid outline of the White Mountains in the distance, something he had never confided to the treasure-hungry Barlocks. His eyes blazed as they remained fixed on one point where the mountains rose above the trees. Eventually, he shook his head sadly and remounted the huge horse.

The horse's long, untiring strides headed unerringly for the Sacred Glade. At one point, a branch which hung low over the path touched the glowing aura over the magician's head and hat. The bough splintered and fell behind the horse in a shower of burning chips. Soon after, Gonzola was bent low over the horse's mane, sound asleep.

*

The magician's eyes opened and he gazed round Glortan's large observatory. If he was surprised, nothing showed on his face. His hand slipped idly under his cloak, but the chain and star were gone. He was seated in a beautifully carved chair covered with a gossamer material that radiated warmth and eased the aches and travel weariness he felt. Three empty thrones stood on a dais in the centre of the circular room. Without even testing the chair, he knew he was held fast. In the dim light, he sat back and waited. Soon, pale lights with no visible sources began playing along the walls, changing colours through range after range of rainbows, becoming brighter with each second.

Although he could detect no apparent door, his eyes shot up to see three radiant figures stride into the room: Glortan, his wife Aureen, and his sister Glortina. The old wizard bowed deeply, indicating his profound respect.

'Greetings to our worthy and unexpected guest,' Glortan's thrilling voice filled the room. The three sat down and the dome slid back to bathe them in shimmering moonlight. 'We will return your clever iron toy when you leave our domain, Gonzola,' the Elvan King added. 'But we do find it strange that you should arrive here surrounded by a force such as that.'

'I am truly sorry, your majesty, it was an oversight. I stopped at Bumbree's Creepy Cottage — well, you know her. I fell asleep and forgot to turn it off.'

'Bumbree's cottage?' Glortina asked, her mischievous laugh tinkling like little silver bells. 'Was that not a bit out of your way?'

The magician spread his hands and nodded, smiling ruefully. He looked at the three regal Elves and knew the question was serious. They were not playing games with him.

He ticked the points off on his fingers. Daemon-Baalim had been to the cottage. They had obviously celebrated the hideous rites of burying Midsummer. There had also been four dwarfs there with an anti-radiation mantle. Something half man, half beast had been abducted in a cylinder of ice by the dwarfs. Obviously, it was an Elf, and a very important one at that. There was also the clear impression of another Elf, a female one in human form. There were many indications that these two Elves were in mortal peril and the girl was trying to rescue the boy.

A long silence followed during which the Elvan King stared deeply into the magician's unwavering eyes.

'I credited you with much, worthy Gonzola,' Glortan said at last, 'but you have now surpassed even my expectations. Rare indeed the mortal who can penetrate so deeply the Elvan Domain of Knowledge. Speak and fear not, Elvanfriend, what are your precise conclusions?'

'Briefly,' sighed Gonzola, not feeling the least bit safe, 'I believe your sister's son has come of age and has been given full Elvanhood of a high order. How this happened was not easy to discover. But I also believe the gracious Queen Aureen produced a daughter at the exact moment the boy was born.' He paused and looked up through the dome, regarding the stars. 'Something in this has ordained each for the other, a Cosmic plan which has yet to unfold. Shall I go on?'

'By all means,' the Elvan King spoke softly, but his eyes had assumed a very serious look.

'This young maiden is now banished according to Elvan Law,' Gonzola continued, 'for in the guise of something like a faun, she brought him to the Mid-summer Eve Rites without your knowledge. Bumbree captured him, and it became known that your daughter had given him full Elvan Knowledge. It would seem that she lured Bumbree off while the dwarfs spirited away the hapless one. She is now in the White Mountains trying to rescue him. I have scried his name to be Flondrix. I do not know hers.'

146

'Her name is Astra,' Aureen said, averting her head for fear of exposing her emotion.

'Gonzola, you display great powers of divination. Among others. I trust you will never misuse them,' Glortan spoke sternly. 'Now tell us what brings you here.'

'I have come to plead for the remission of the curse on King Barlocks.' As Gonzola spoke, he felt the tension mount in the room.

'You are no fool, yet you come on a fool's errand,' Glortina said, her tone brittle.

Glortan held up his hand. 'Gently, dear sister, for our friend is deeply disturbed; this is no prank, the chamber fills with foreboding.' He gazed up through the dome, his wondrous Elvan eyes roving from star to star. 'Look! Watch how they dim and waver. The very Cosmos senses fell news. What is it, Gonzola?'

'It is news of Kranz, noble king. The dread magician to the Under People. And of Daemon-Baalim, the Beast Beneath.'

'Daemon-Baalim is no longer free to roam the world of men, Gonzola. You know that. He must find mediums, like that wretched Bumbree. This has been so since the end of the first age of man. Kranz was sealed in the time trap of the Under People, with your help. Elvanlord and the Ancient Ones stopped their time on the final day of destruction. The Now of the Under People is eternal and repeats eternally. Kranz cannot escape. Daemon-Baalim was bound Beneath for all time.' The Elvan King stood up and glared at the magician. 'Do not provoke me, Gonzola.'

'Sire, hear me, please,' Gonzola requested politely. 'There is a key. A key which can unlock both doors. A dreaded one, and you know its name.'

Glortan sat down slowly and took a deep breath. He watched the magician for a full minute without speaking. Aureen and Glortina sat in their thrones like statues.

'If you know its name, speak, magician,' the king commanded.

'Tritertium 333. Kranz knew that the sciences of the first age had worked out the theoretical bases up to 332. Kranz has produced Tritertium 332. Now he knows that the ultimate stage is possible and he plans to make it a reality.'

'Gonzola, Tritertium 333 will be the most devastating force in the Cosmos. If unleashed, it could destroy the Cosmos as we know it. Do you realize what you have said?' Glortan sat back in his throne and fire fairly danced in his eyes.

'Only too well, your majesty. Kranz will know how to upset the balance of everything. Our universe will be gone and Kranz, on the other side of Time, will be supreme. Time is pressing, sire.'

'How did it happen?' Aureen whispered.

'Kranz has worked tirelessly through these ages. A scrap of information here, another there. Strange things exist even in the ancient tomes of the dwarfs but they value little that is theoretical. Bit by bit, he has gathered it together,' Gonzola sighed.

'All of it?' demanded Glortan.

'All but the last little fragment. For some strange reason I cannot fathom, that fragment is locked deep inside the race memory of ... King Barlocks.' The magician looked down as he announced this. 'Kranz knows this and now Barlocks has become – well, aware.'

The Elvan King closed his eyes and pondered deeply. To succeed totally, Kranz would have to break the bonds which held him imprisoned in the time trap, in the Eternal Now of a previous age. He would have to be able to manifest himself fully in the here and now of the Sacred Glade. Daemon-Baalim would be his willing helper in a bid for his own freedom, but Kranz would still need the aid of two willing mortal accomplices in this age. One of those accomplices must be of very high attainment — like Gonzola or Sordo. The other . . . Barlocks? Yes, if he could not be dissuaded. What if Kranz could obtain an Elvan medium? Glortan shuddered. Through all of time, the advent of the Fallen One had haunted the Elves. One throwback in the service of evil. Until the Fallen One finally appeared among them and was vanquished, the Elvan evolution would not be complete.

Glortan opened his eyes and looked deeply into Gonzola's. He knew immediately that much of the same thought stream had been passing through the magician's mind. Perhaps even the last part.

'Sordo?' asked the Elvan King.

'He has been called a fool,' mused the magician, 'but fool he is not. Kranz knows his weakness, knows that he can be swayed. In the Order Most High, it has always been thought that Sordo might one day exhibit a slight shade of grey.' Gonzola coughed self-consciously. 'Yes, he could be the weak link.'

A long low breath was heard to leave each Elvan body. The room remained absolutely still for many minutes on end. Gonzola watched Glortan's face lifted towards the stars and he knew the Elvan King was in communion somewhere beyond most mortal ken. In the silence, the old sage's attention focused on Sordo, the magician to the dwarfs. Had he passed information to Kranz already? How far had Kranz wormed his way into Sordo's vulnerable mind? Through his long imprisonment, Kranz had trained his mind to travel anywhere though his body was trapped . . . but was it still trapped? Gonzola wondered.

Glortan looked down again, his troubled eyes once more fixed on the venerable magician. 'So,' he said sadly, 'Barlocks will hold us to ransom. Does he realize what Kranz is up to?'

'I have told him nothing, great king,' Gonzola answered, 'nor could I detect anything more than the elementary cunning that sensed how something in this new, vague awareness of his would affect us as nothing else might.'

'I know how Kranz can communicate with Daemon-Baalim or Sordo . . . or you, for that matter, good magician,' Glortan added significantly, 'but how did he reach this unenlightened king? He is no adept, steeped in the knowledge of sages and sorcerers.'

'Sire,' sighed the weary magician, 'I am afraid it all goes back to the curse you afflicted him with. Over these recent days, the torture he has endured must have unhinged his mind in some way. The fragment of information buried deep in his race memory came to the surface. It was like a beacon to Kranz, for his limitless scanning power is phenomenal. Now, Kranz is locked into King Barlocks's mind, probing like a ferret for the last key to Tritertium 333.'

'Gonzola, please wait upon us a brief while, there is something we must discuss privately.' The Elvan King bowed graciously and a moment later, the three thrones were empty.

When Glortan returned, his sudden appearance made the phantom lights in the chamber crackle with an enormous charge of energy. Gonzola felt the currents running through his body with such intensity he nearly lost consciousness. When his eyes cleared, he knew he contained forces and powers greater than he had ever known before. It was then he noticed that the two other thrones were empty.

'My wife and sister asked me to apologize on their behalf,' Glortan announced softly. 'You will understand your news has created great turmoil here' The magician nodded as the king spoke. 'Oh, you will be pleased to know that the curse has been removed, I'm sure.'

'Your majesty, you must divine that the Dark King will be sending me back here shortly . . .'

'Yes, good magician,' the Elvan King interrupted, 'he will demand that my sister return to him. It was predictable. She is already on her way to him, but this time she goes as a mortal woman.'

'Your majesty!' the old sage gasped, rising from his seat. 'Is — is this wise? I ask most humbly . . .'

'Sit down, Gonzola.' Glortan looked briefly at the stars overhead and the magician was sure he detected tears in the awesome eyes. 'You are concerned with an ancient Elvan legend, are you not? You wonder if it is wise to send Glortina in mortal guise to a king who has already been touched by Kranz. We send our sister to persuade your king not to be a fool. We send her in mortal guise as she would be too aloof in her Elvan form, too aloof to reach the king's innermost being and make his love for her stronger than any blandishment Kranz could offer. And you wonder, do you not? What if Glortina should be the Fallen One who is predicted to come among us?'

'Oh, your majesty.' Gonzola dropped his head in his hands, the king's words biting deeply into his heart. 'But in telling me my thoughts, you tell me yours too, great king.'

'Just so,' Glortan shot back. 'And we must cleanse this foul thought from our minds. There is no Fallen One until the Fallen One is among us. Glortina is now making the greatest sacrifice she can in our behalf. To believe otherwise is to betray her.'

'I accept the mighty king's decision,' the magician agreed. He cleared his throat and looked at Glortan searchingly. 'Glortan the Great has filled me with

151

immense powers. In my very bones I feel he is about to ask of me all that borders on the impossible.'

The Elvan King smiled bleakly. Great as it was, Elvan power had its limits where Kranz and the Under People were concerned. In the battle of human wills, a mortal medium would be required, but a medium of such dauntless strength and power, of such unflinching integrity, that he would walk into the very maw of the Beast Beneath, as Gonzola had done once long ago. He would have to be able to pit himself against Kranz, in will and resources, and win. On the shoulders of such a mortal would rest the fate of the whole Cosmos. As would the fate of Flondrix and Astra, now languishing in the mountain halls of the dwarfs. Such a magician would also have to dominate the mind and will of Sordo.

'I see,' Gonzola breathed after a long and contemplative silence. 'I presume I must start shortly for King Schtoonk's Schtronghold. Freeing your daughter and nephew may prove sticky indeed. Can I effect that and still bargain successfully with Sordo?'

'By the time you arrive,' Glortan informed him, 'they will be gone. Your arrival, on that score at least, will be above suspicion.'

'Shall I watch for Flondrix and Astra along the way and send them back to you with all haste?' Gonzola asked hopefully.

'Unfortunately,' sighed Glortan, 'I fear they will become involved in the great struggle ahead. By the time you leave here, they may well be heading in the opposite direction. They may be going . . . where you will be going . . . when you leave Sordo.'

'Oh, no . . .' Gonzola rose and took one step towards the dais in protest. Glortan held up his hand in a sad salutation, then lowered it to hold the magician's in his own strong grasp.

'Time has already started spinning its enigma, Elvan-friend,' Glortan intoned. 'You are filled with vast Elvan power as you know. But on your wit and resources alone will depend the result. Rest you well here for the night. You will leave at dawn's first light. Go well, Gonzola.'

As the king released his hand, the magician called out to the fading Elvan figure.

'Sire, how will my absence be explained to the Dark King?'

Glortan's voice had a distant quality by the time he answered. 'Glortina will tell him that you are my hostage in safe keeping till I am certain that all goes well with her.'

Gonzola sank down in the large chair and pulled his cloak more closely about him. He could hear those last words repeating endlessly through the dark chamber. Over and over in his mind the words formed — what if . . .? He tried to blot the vision of Glortina from his mind, to obey the Elvan King's request that he ponder no more on the legend of the Fallen One. Awake and asleep, as the night galloped across the sky, neither legend nor vision would desert him. Before he put the dreadful thoughts to rest, the first pale hint of dawn found him.

As he busied himself preparing for his departure, Gonzola's mind raced ahead to the days which would unfold. Though Kranz was imprisoned in a time trap many lost centuries back in man's history, the era itself was one of man's highest peaks of technological development. Total atomic destruction had only been averted by the Ancient Ones when those last twenty-four hours were sealed off in a simulated eternity. Each day that world was atomically pulverized and reconstituted, only to begin the cycle anew. Now, Kranz was on the verge of creating Tritertium 333, the final deadly element. If he could do that, he could develop a vehicle to send it in, a vehicle which would be impervious to the cycle of the time trap. The vehicle would be aimed at Topar, the sacred star of the Elves, of that there was no doubt. With Topar and Elvanhome destroyed, Elvan power would vanish from the Cosmos. Glortan's hosts would be vulnerable.

The old sage stood tall and strong beside his horse, making the last adjustments on cinch and stirrups. Elvanlord could stop such a vehicle in mid-flight, long before it reached Topar, he told himself. He could stop it and destroy it with its own deadly power. With Tritertium 332, yes. With Tritertium 333? What could possibly stay Elvanlord's hand?

As the mighty steed thundered towards the White Mountains, the question asked itself over and over. Only one answer came back: Astra and Flondrix, hostages on that vehicle of Kranz's. Finally Gonzola knew the awful immensity of Glortan's premonition and the mission ahead. Elvan power flowing through his body communicated itself to the horse; the great beast neighed furiously into the wind and fairly left the ground.

XIV

Pandemonium
in the
Halls of the Dwarf King

Astra moved slowly and carefully along the very narrow, high ledge of rock which followed the walls of the great central cavern. Moving in single file, before her were the large hindquarters of Boff, and behind her she could hear the quiet breathing of Tup, one of Boff's most trusted captains. Under the circumstances, she was happy indeed for the neat and fastidious cloth pad extending down from the base of her tail to cover her swollen orifice. Binny had secured the pad deftly with strands of thread knotted tightly over her back and under her belly. Whatever the pungent herbs Binny had packed inside the pad, Tup moved behind her in utter unconcern. Even Boff, who had a keen nose for such things, had had to compliment his wife for her thoroughness.

As a dozen loud cymbals crashed below, Astra scrabbled to retain her footing on the narrow ledge. All three mice sank down on their bellies and peered into the great vaulted hall below.

A large portal had been thrown open at the far end of the hall, and hordes of dwarfs came dancing in, following the cymbals, drums, flutes and horns which were sending a tremendous din echoing through the cavernous feasting hall. Masses of dwarfs cavorted, leaping over chairs and benches, forming dance circles and whirling about wildly to the raucous, insistent thunder of the musicians.

Dancers were followed by dozens upon dozens more, holding long festive boards high over their heads to place them end to end around the hall. Then chairs began to appear, sliding crazily over the smoothly polished stone floor. They were sent skittering from one dwarf to the next, passing in the fashion of a bucket brigade, until all the tables were ringed with chairs. Another clamour broke out as, splendidly dressed and sparkingly armed, the royal guards entered, pushing the royal thrones before them. Soon, they had the two large and two small thrones placed properly at the very top table, just below where the mice were squatting. No other chairs were placed near the thrones, but on the opposite side of the royal table a numbers of chairs, much grander than all the rest, were placed by the guards. From that point, the tables ran back the length of the hall, one line of each at right angles to the royal table. The far end, near the portals, was open so that people could pass freely up and down between the rows.

Another crashing and blasting from the musicians, and through the portals passed four large carts drawn by teams of matched, pure white donkeys. A retinue of dwarfs in white aprons and coats followed the carts and, as they passed up and down outside the rows of tables, great steaming tureens, bowls of meat and all sorts of gastronomic delights were piled on every available inch of the tables' surfaces by the cooks. When they had departed with their donkeys and carts, the musicians created their most resounding fanfare and all the revellers stopped dancing and cavorting and stood in even lines expectantly, their heads bowed respectfully.

The royal guards entered for a second time, pushing the expectant rows of dwarfs back to clear a path. Then King Schtoonk and Queen Schtenkah entered the hall, followed by their son and daughter, Prince Schtark and Princess Schrink. In stately procession, the king turning his head to left and right to nod and greet his subjects, the royal entourage forged ahead until they arrived at the head table and took their places on the thrones. At a signal from the king, all the other diners quickly scuttled to their appointed places and sat down with much laughing and joking, backslapping and raising of full goblets of wine to drink the king's health, and a health to the rest of the royal family.

When all the diners were finally seated and the noise had subsided somewhat, the king raised his hand once more and the royal guards trotted back out through the portals, to reappear a few moments later pushing a long and imposing wagon made of gold, solid gold, even including the wheels themselves. An awed hush fell over the room as the wagon was moved to a spot near the centre of the great hall, about fifteen feet away from the tables. A buzz started in the festive hall, running like fire from one end of a row of tables to the other, then back up the opposite row. It hushed itself again as the king signalled. The musicians blared forth and through the portal, dressed in splendid waistcoats and capes, came strolling four dwarfs. Astra gasped from her perch as they approached the golden wagon. She recognized the four brothers, Dogbek and Hogbek, with Dimbek in the lead and little Rimbek following up in the rear. When the four brothers reached the wagon, they each took a grip on what seemed to Astra, from that height, a tissue of cloth that covered the interior of the wagon. In fact, it was the magic mantle. With a great heave, they pulled it loose.

A roar went up from the crowd and they all stood up, then climbed on their chairs to get a better look. From that distance, none of the dwarfs could hear Astra's cry. In fact, it was really a small squeak and Tup nipped her tail to warn her to be quiet. She was in tears and didn't even notice, so sad was she to gaze down and see, far below, looking terribly tiny, the beloved form of her Flondrix, still encased in ice and still with the dreaded necklace caught tightly and cruelly around his throat.

'Come on,' whispered Boff, 'we've seen enough. We have a big job of work to do.'

'Oh no,' pleaded Astra, 'we can't desert him now.'

'You want to free him, don't you?' demanded Boff. 'Follow me!'

A few seconds later they entered a very tiny hole in the solid stone and were tunnelling up and up over the dome of the hall until they squeezed into a low vault that had been carefully cleared. Hundreds of mice were hurrying back and forth, carrying as much rubble as they could in little baskets suspended from their sharp teeth. All around the edge of the vault, spaced at intervals of about twelve inches, were small holes that had been drilled with clever precision. As Astra watched fascinated, she could see piles of dust and rubble forming at the rims of each hole. Mice with empty baskets came running back to fill them at the holes, then went off again carting the full baskets. The vault was so low in places she had to flatten herself on her belly.

'What are they doing?' she asked Tup; Boff was nowhere to be seen, having slithered off to supervise another group. Tup led her with difficulty to the rim of one of the small holes. She looked down and saw the tail of a silver-coloured insect just below her eyes. The tail was vibrating at fantastic speed.

'Those are rock-driller termites,' Tup explained. 'Their proboscises are as hard as the finest diamonds. And they vibrate at a tremendous rate. As you can see, there is little room in here, so we have to keep cleaning out the rubble or we wouldn't be able to move at all.'

'But why are they doing it?' she asked.

'They've always worked for us. We feed them and take care of them. For as long as mice can remember, they've been drilling through the mountain. We probably have a better tunnel system now than the dwarfs. And the very best of the emeralds and rubies and diamonds the dwarfs dig out of the mountain just disappear.' Tup laughed happily as he told her this. 'You should see our hoard! The dwarfs fight among themselves all the time about how many of their precious gems disappear. But they'll never be able to find them.'

'Oh,' exclaimed Astra, 'that *is* interesting. But what I meant is, why are the termites making these holes now?'

'For Boff and a special trained squad to put the black powder in,' he answered, wondering why she asked such silly questions.

'Black powder? I still don't understand,' she pleaded.

'I keep forgetting,' he apologized, 'you're not a real mouse. The dwarfs have a black powder they use to blast loose sections of their mines below. When we first came across it, some of the boys tried eating it. Made 'em pretty sick. But worse, when a lady came on heat, there was nothing they could do about it. Not for a few days, anyway.'

'Are you going to blast this place loose?' she asked, her eyes widening. She turned her head to seek the way out.

'Yes,' he replied, 'but not just yet, don't worry.

Boff's a born engineer. He figures out every detail. This piece of stone we're standing on is just about the size of the space between the rows of tables in the festive hall. Well, a little bit smaller. And this spot we're standing in is precisely over the area between the tables. When the blast goes off, Boff figures that this one big block of stone will come crashing down. We hope none of the dwarfs will be hurt, although they've killed a lot of us.'

'What will happen then?' Astra was concerned, in fact terrified, that if the calculations were off, the great block might come crashing down on her beloved Flondrix.

'Knowing the dwarfs, they'll be out of that hall so fast the stone floor will give off sparks. And they'll lock and seal off the portals for fear of more structural weaknesses. Then they'll get to their treasure vaults at the base of the mountain as fast as their bandy legs can carry them. I warrant you, if I know my dwarfs, they won't venture out until morning.'

'But what if it falls in the wrong place?' she gasped.

'Don't be silly,' jeered Tup, 'our Boff is an expert. He'll drop that huge slab right between the tables. Chalk for cheese, he never misses. And when the room down there is cleared and sealed off, we'll get busy freeing your friend. To say nothing of the delicious dinner we expect to get.' As he mentioned the dinner, his small hindquarters began wagging happily. But Astra had no time to ask more questions. Boff came crawling back into the slim vault, followed by a large crew of workers carrying baskets, long coils of some sort of string and an assortment of other things she could not readily identify.

'All right,' called Boff, 'everybody not engaged in the next operations clear out. Rejoin the invasion forces below. Nobody moves out into the festive hall until the sentries give the all clear signal. And nobody eats until the prisoner is free. Is that understood?'

*

Meanwhile, unmindful of the furious preparations going on overhead, the dwarfs had crowded over to the golden wagon to inspect the prize which had been brought back by the four heroic brothers. The king banged loudly on the table with his goblet, commanding order and quiet. The royal guard shoved and pushed and the musicians struck up a deafening blast on their horns and drums. The crowd quieted down as the king stood.

'Now hear me well,' King Schtoonk announced, 'nobody is to go near that wagon or touch anything until Sordo gets here. Your carelessness might cost you your lives. Back to your places everyone.'

Reluctantly, the crowd surged back, eventually finding their places and reseating themselves. Then the four brothers were marched up to stand in front of the king on the opposite side of his table. The king read off a speech proclaiming them as heroes and promising that they should have titles and rewards beyond their wildest dreams. The crowd cheered. Golden necklaces with huge medallions, on which the king's own crest was engraved, were hung about each of the heroes' necks. Amid further cheers and a fanfare of music, they were seated at the royal table among the half dozen nobles and venerables of the kingdom.

While the commotion subsided, a tall smiling figure in a long robe and skullcap walked into the hall. His full white beard came down almost to his waist, covering a good part of the front of his robe. It could still be seen that the robe, made of a pale silvery grey fabric, was encrusted everywhere with magic symbols and characters, rather like the waistcoats of goatskin and embroidery worn by the four brothers. A wide purple belt circled his middle, clasped by a buckle in the design of a serpent's head made of gold and set with large emerald eyes. The snake's fangs were sunk into a huge ruby in the shape of an apple. There were few dwarfs, the king included, who did not fear the mysterious powers locked up in the extraordinary belt that never left the magician, awake or asleep.

Sordo smiled, for this was indeed the magician of the dwarf kingdom, and his pale almost colourless grey eyes twinkled. He strode directly to the golden wagon without greeting anyone and commenced a detailed inspection. Up and down he walked, touching the ice here, leaning over to sniff at something there. When he had circled the wagon completely, he paid the first attention so far to the faun's head sticking out of the ice at the back of the wagon. Flondrix was dimly aware of a new presence standing near him, but identifying it was more effort than he was able to muster; he didn't turn his head or open his eyes.

'Chooch,' muttered the magician, an expression he was forever making absent-mindedly. In fact he frequently seemed to give the impression of a rather addled and dotty old man who forgot from one moment to the next what he was talking about or what was going on around him.

'Chooch,' he said again softly. 'Bet you can hear everything I say.' Sordo scratched his ear for a moment and then snapped his fingers. Two young dwarfs came racing through the portals at his bidding. These were Farful and Fertig, two distant cousins of the king who had pleaded to be apprenticed to Sordo. They never did anything but make messes in his sorcery rooms or burn things accidentally. And Sordo meticulously avoided teaching them anything. Farful was carrying a smallish cauldron which bubbled and sent up clouds of blue smoke. Fertig followed behind with a long staff.

'Put it down,' ordered Sordo. Fertig put the staff on the ground and Farful stood there wide-eyed, holding the cauldron in both hands. It was getting terribly heavy and the blue smoke bothered his eyes.

'Chooch! No, no, you idiots, put the cauldron on the ground and hand *me* the staff. You're hopeless, the pair of you. Now, stand back.'

The two cousins moved back rapidly, standing out of the way. When he thought no one was looking, Farful, the younger of the two, turned towards the royal table and, trying to appear quite casual, began adjusting the coils of his schlong around his waist, setting the barbed tip more carefully in the golden screw in his navel. The gesture was not lost on Princess Schrink. She lifted her head slightly and sniffed with disdain. Fertig kicked Farful in the ankle and hissed to him to pay attention.

Sordo cocked his head first to one side, then to the other. Finally, he dipped the tip of the slender staff into the bubbling cauldron. When he raised the tip, it glowed fearfully, scattering sparks of every hue. Lightly, he touched the tip of the staff to the ropes wrapped around the ice cylinder. A flash of blue flame and the priapic phallus bolted up like a catapult, sending the remnants of the ropes flying across the hall and into the far wall, very close to the royal thrones. And there stood the dreadful mast, straight up and quivering like a dagger in a wooden door.

A gasp went up from the crowd. Dwarf ladies regarded the member with stricken eyes. 'It doesn't corkscrew,' was heard echoing from first one corner, then the other. 'It's absolutely straight,' more voices joined in. 'What possible use is that?' came another, a high-pitched female voice. Sordo smiled and watched the last few quivers peter out.

'You equipped yourself well, didn't you, my good

Elf?' whispered Sordo. 'Not that I blame you. In similar circumstances, I might have been tempted the same way myself. No doubt.'

Sordo dipped the tip of the staff back into the cauldron and waited. As he did, he noticed a slight commotion at the royal table. Princess Schrink was terribly distressed. She was clutching to her flat bosom, Sordo noted with raised eyebrows, the very ropes that had been catapulted across the room. The king was signalling frantically to Sordo. Sordo turned and beckoned the two apprentices.

'Do you think the pair of you can hold this rod, just like this until I get back? You don't move it, you don't walk away, you don't drop it – Chooch?' They both nodded energetically and grabbed the rod. Sordo shook his head and walked in slow, stately strides towards the king.

When he arrived, Sordo saw that the young princess was close to hysterics. She was biting determinedly at the stout cord, gurgling in her throat and rolling her eyes about wildly. Her brother tried to get the strands of rope away from her and she gave him a vicious kick under the table that started him howling. He was still terribly young, as dwarfs go, so nobody paid him much notice.

'Sordo, would you ever do something about this daughter of mine?' screeched the king. Queen Schtenkah was trying to calm him and control her own tears at the same time.

'What seems to be the trouble, your majesty?' inquired the magician.

'It's that – that monster out there. When you cut those ropes, when she saw that – that thing, she said she wanted to marry him immediately. Do something, man, *do something*!'

Sordo laughed long and softly, setting his bottom

down on the corner of the table rather unceremoniously. As he chuckled away, he scratched at his ear.

'Not to fear, majesties, not to fear,' he said at last. 'It would never be possible.'

'I told her that!' barked the king. 'Her mother told her too. She doesn't believe it or she doesn't care. Every other proper dwarf lady in this room is appalled by the sight. It makes no sense to them. I can't understand what's got into the girl — I mean her royal highness,' the king corrected himself.

'Ah well, chooch and all that,' commented the magician, ''tis but a temporary flight of fancy, a mild madness. If it does not pass soon, and with your majesty's permission, we can prove the grim truth to her highness when you announce the marriage ceremony.' He turned at this and winked at the four brothers sitting opposite the king and queen. They blushed and cast their eyes down.

'What do you mean?' asked the king. Sordo didn't answer, but crooked his head slightly. The king rose and stepped down, joining the magician near the golden wagon, out of earshot.

'If his majesty will be patient for a few moments longer, until I have completed a couple of experiments, I will explain all.' The king nodded and put his hands on his hips imperiously.

Sordo stepped over and took the staff from the cousins, Farful and Fertig. The tip of the staff sparkled more brightly now than it had at first. Sordo, with his sharp eyes, found the icy seams that Bumbree had fitted together in the Creepy Cottage. He pressed the point of the staff into one of them and the light at the tip dimmed and dimmed. With a sputter, the staff flew up, nearly tearing itself from his grasp. He pursed his lips and shook his head, plunging the staff back in the cauldron. Out it came a few seconds later, glowing and sparkling brightly again. He carefully moved the tip to a spot between two of the links on the faun's mysterious metal necklace. The collar's links seemed to tighten as the staff came close. Then as the tip of the staff touched the metal, the staff shattered into a thousand pieces with a blinding flash.

Sordo shook his arm up and down, feeling the acute and painful throb moving all the way up to his shoulder. It felt numb and stayed that way for some hours.

'Just as I thought,' he muttered when he stood again at the king's side. 'Bumbree's usually sloppy witch-craft has been fortified by – uh – someone who shall remain nameless. Not so easy, this.'

'What has that got to do with the idiotic notion in my daughter's head?' demanded the king.

'You'll see, you'll see,' the magician assured him. 'Now, even though I am a mortal man, I do know the laws of the dwarfs backwards and forwards. She cannot marry him unless she is capable of completing the ceremony, is this not correct?'

'Yes, of course,' replied the king.

'Chooch!' Sordo smiled and stroked his beard. 'So, when the four brothers complete the ceremony with the brides you've selected, then the young Princess can try her luck with our faun here. I guarantee you, it won't work. Even if she were unthreaded, left or right, it wouldn't work. But it will accomplish something very important. Without it, we will have no advantage from this captured Elf.'

'I simply do not understand,' the king stamped his foot as he spoke. 'Will you kindly stop the riddles and explain yourself?'

'Your majesty, it is quite simple. Because of the nature of the witchcraft, it can withstand mortal magic. Because of that little metal collar around the Elf's neck, his powers are arrested. He cannot free himself, nor can he change his form to escape. The one thing we need to break the ice is the powerful Elvan fluid that will come gushing out of the huge phallus waving about up there. With that, I can conjure up an element that will break the ice and reduce the force intensity in that collar just enough.'

'Just enough for what?' the king demanded.

'Just enough,' Sordo answered, 'to give him back some very important powers, but restricting those powers to *our* control.' Sordo had selected the word 'our' very carefully. The king did not stop to wonder if this control might be limited to Sordo's wisdom only.

'Oh well,' the king answered easily, 'if that's all that's needed, let somebody thump him. That should do the trick . . . it always does.'

'For dwarfs, yes. For Elves, no.' Sordo shook his head for emphasis. 'We would not be able to evoke that, no matter how we tried. He would *resist*.'

'Are you trying to tell me that Princess Schrink is *irresistible*?' the king asked, frowning at Sordo.

'I will not comment on that, for it would be out of order. What I meant is, it requires the efforts of a dwarf lady. Otherwise, it won't work.'

'Well then, let some of the ladies here choose lots,' the king ordered, turning to walk away.

'Wait, your majesty.' Sordo caught at his sleeve. 'There are only two things wrong with your suggestion, if I may be so bold. First, this is no ordinary Elf. He is of the highest royal extraction. Secondly, no matter what other lady tries, though she will fail in dwarfish terms, you will still have your lovesick daughter to contend with.'

'Hmmm,' murmured the king. 'I see your point. Sort of killing two mice with one stone, eh? Well, if that needs be done, we shall have to do it later, in complete privacy, after the ceremonies are over.'

'I'm afraid, sire, that this poses another problem,' whispered Sordo, noticing the number of ears at the tables straining to catch their words.

'Now what?' the king snapped huffily.

'In order to know she has failed, your daughter must see herself to have failed and must be seen to have failed. How else shall we do that save by comparison between the four brothers and their brides and your daughter and the faun? After all, she is a pure girl, she would have no way of knowing, would she?'

'But she won't be so pure afterwards, will she?' countered the king.

'Chooch! Of course she will. Nothing will happen,' the magician assured him, 'nothing at all.' He pointed over his head to the priapus in the air. '*That* can never be a corkscrew. As a half man, half beast, the faun follows the reproductive pattern of mortals and animals. The pattern of the Elves is still a mystery to us, but they are not the ways of the dwarfs. The four brides will do the ceremony in approved fashion. They will inseminate the grooms who will immediately produce a valid egg each. The brides will take them off and nestle them and in due time they will hatch proper dwarfs, correct?'

'Yes, of course,' said the king, 'that is the only right and proper way.'

'Your daughter will get nowhere,' the magician continued, 'no matter how she tries. But, because of her birth and genuine dwarfishness, she will evoke from this faun the opposite reaction. It is the male faun who does the inseminating. And that is the fluid we need. A gallon or so of it will be sufficient.'

'All right, all right,' King Schtoonk conceded, 'I'll make the announcement.'

As the king returned to the throne, the magician sent the two apprentices scuttling out to bring back some

168

fresh cauldrons and other equipment he thought he might need, plus a new staff and some ointment for his numb arm.

With a signal for silence (while the king was speaking), Boff, Tup and three other strong mice moved the large stone that had been fitted carefully over one of their widest tunnel entrances in the solid rock wall of the great hall. The spot was about a foot off the ground and ten mice at a time could jump down. The wall in which they were hiding was the wall on the far side from the tables, just about opposite the golden wagon. When the stone had been shifted back a bit, they could see over the top of it. Boff reached a paw out to pull Astra up. As she looked out, she concentrated deeply on the still faun, sending her thoughts out to him.

The faun's head turned slowly, fraction by fraction, until he faced the wall. Then he opened one eye slightly and peered towards the little creatures. A moment later, a shadow of a smile crossed his lips; carefully, he turned back to his original position. Astra saw that none of the dwarfs had seen him. Luckily, Sordo's back was towards the wagon.

'. . . And so, according to our time-honoured customs,' intoned the king, 'we will reward our heroes mightily. As we have no system of inheritance through the male lines, and as no male can be married until he has proven himself worthy by hard effort, devotion to duty and diligence in everything, marriage to a highly endowed lady is the reward of all rewards. In the case of these four heroic and devoted brothers, their brides will be the wealthiest ladies in the kingdom. Each one of them is in the one hundred ton diamond class, to say nothing of all their other riches.'

The king cleared his throat and adjusted a pair of gold spectacles on his nose, picking up a slip of paper with the other hand. 'Now, we have noted here that the twins, Hogbek and Dogbek, are left-handers. The eldest, Dimbek the leader, has a right-handed thread as has his youngest brother, Rimbek. Will the ladies please stand.' As the crowd cheered, four round, beaming faces rose above the crowd in four different parts of the room.

'There they are, the richest and loveliest in the realm. Knarbo and Kniput, you are the chosen brides of the twins. Kneko, the youngest, will be the bride of Rimbek. And you, Knukah, the richest of all, are for none other than the stalwart Dimbek.'

Pandemonium broke out; members of the families of the brides and the grooms hugged each other and clapped each other on the back, the musicians began a rousing march and the king sent the royal guard off for all the trappings needed for the ceremony. Even the most dedicated trenchermen put down their food and wiped their hands and mouths.

No one heard the heroic brothers speaking among themselves.

'We're going to have to "do it",' moaned little Rimbek.

'Yes,' groaned the twins, putting their arms around each other and apologizing for all the good thumps they had denied themselves and each other.

'Stop it, you fools,' ordered Dimbek, 'do you want the king to think we're ungrateful? Think of the diamonds, the untold mountains of gold. We're going to be rich! Think of that. You'll never have to "do it" again if you're careful.'

'Come on, boys,' the king broke in on them, 'here comes the greatest moment of your lives.'

The brothers looked around and saw that the royal guards had placed four low couches side by side in the centre of the hall, just ahead of the golden wagon. Above the couches, like a stout playground swing, passed a bar of iron with heavy legs on either side anchoring it to the floor. From the overhead bar, four pairs of very strong elastic ropes hung down, each one ending in a thick wooden rung.

The four brothers, looking sheepish, marched over to the couches and stretched out on their backs . . . after they had uncoiled, of course. Then, smiling uncomfortably, they corkscrewed and waited. The royal guards led the ladies, one by one, over to the couches and helped them up into the air, until their thighs were firmly fitted through the wooden rungs. As each one took her place, the elastic ropes gave and they came down, then up, then down, then up until they were settled about an inch over the up-pointed corkscrew schlongs. At a command from the king, one royal guard, behind each lady, firmly grasped her hips. For Hogbek and Dogbek on the centre two couches, the guards began winding the ladies to the right. The other two guards, standing at the foot of Dimbek's and Rimbek's beds respectively, began winding those two ladies to the left. When each had been wound down the ritual twenty-four turns, the guards waited. The king raised his hand, the musicians raised their instruments and the whole audience caught its collective breath.

Down came the king's hand, out roared the music and the guards let go. Slowly at first, then faster and faster, the ladies twisted as the elastic ropes raised them. They flew clear, rose way up and came plummeting down.

And down they spun madly, almost a blur, until the tightening elastic slowed them, arrested them, and began twisting them up and up, spinning faster and faster in the opposite direction. As they cleared the corkscrews the sixth time, their heads clanged on the stout iron bar overhead, which was by now swaying precariously. Down they plunged once more, their spin reversed again by the twisted elastic ropes. The seventh time down, they spun so hard that all four of them locked tight. A moment later, the brothers made mighty heaves upward with their hips, and out of each of their bottoms dropped a large brown egg, about the size of a young watermelon.

A deafening cheer went up from the crowd as the eggs appeared and the royal guards twisted each lady strenuously to free her. Moments later, the exhausted dwarf brothers, shuddering from the frightful experience, were recoiling themselves self-consciously. Each of the brides was surrounded by well-wishing admirers and family, all of them leaning in to get a better view of the lovely eggs being nestled jealously to the bosoms of the blushing brides. The brides were then ushered out of the feasting hall by their families and accompanied to the nesting rooms to sit out their confinements. The four brothers went back to finish their meals, accompanied by proud friends and family, all of them vying to give the boys the most resounding claps on the back.

A sudden hush fell over the crowd as the royal guard moved the overhead contrivance to a position above the golden wagon. Questions, surprised murmurs, groans and whistles filled the room as the guards put blocks of stone under the iron legs to raise the entire apparatus high enough. Then they shifted and jiggled the device until they had one of the central pairs of ropes directly over the monstrous priapic mast.

The king called for silence and made a brief and uncomfortable announcement. Breaths could be heard sharply drawn in all around the large hall. The king raised his hand and reminded them all of the princess's royal prerogative. Her choice must be honoured if she could effect a proper marriage.

This time there was no cheering comment, no fanfare from the musicians. In silence, Princess Schrink walked uncertainly out to the wagon and was respectfully hoisted up by the waiting guards. Soon, she was suspended with her legs through the wooden rungs. Two guards, sitting on the iron crosspiece above, hauled the elastics up and adjusted them. Two others spun and spun the princess until the ropes were tightly coiled. Then they let go.

Down, down she came spinning faster and faster until she hit the top of the dreadful mast. Thunk! A groan broke from the crowd as she fell to one side, nearly crashing into the icy cylinder. Then up she rose, hitting her head against a cushion which one of the guards was considerately holding under the iron crosspiece. Up and down she went bouncing, with no spin at all. Each time she hit the top of the massive member with a crunch and bounced off.

The horror of all this could not be resisted by poor Flondrix. Something about the touch of dwarf flesh seared into the abused priapus until, not out of desire or inflamed passion, but purely in a panic of self-protection, the fluids massed and massed as though to drive off a predatory attacker. Out came the gushing torrent, catching poor Princess Schrink on her way down like an angry rising geyser. It spun her crazily upward with such force that the elastic ropes wrapped around the iron crosspiece twenty or more times, unseating the two helpful guards. As they were dislodged, the cumbersome apparatus slid first off one stone block, then another, and the whole thing teetered and came crashing down, narrowly missing the faun's head.

Pandemonium broke loose again as dwarfs everywhere tried to avoid the gushing fluids. Others tried to extricate the princess and aid the hapless guards, in the end causing more confusion than their help was worth. Sordo alone did not lose his head. He rushed in at the final moment with his two apprentices, each of them with a cauldron, and they went leaping here, there and everywhere, trying to anticipate where the next capricious outpouring would land. Ignoring all the racket and confusion around them, they filled their cauldrons and hurriedly left the room.

As the magician and his helpers made their exit, a whistle was relayed through all the tunnels of the mice until it reached Boff at the main entrance. Quickly he sent the message back and, with his helpers, pulled the stone door back into place. He then noticed Astra leaning against the tunnel wall, crying her eyes out. He sauntered over to her and tried to give her gruff reassurance, warning her to hold her paws over her ears, as it would all be over in the flick of a mouse's tail.

No sooner had he spoken than a deafening roar reverberated round every corner of the great cavern, followed immediately by a mighty crash. Screams and shouts, gnashing of teeth and pitiful wails could be heard even in the tunnel of the mice. Without further hesitation the large stone was shoved aside by Boff and his mates. The clatter of hundreds of feet filled the room and hardly a thing could be seen for all the dust. They heard the queen wailing as the guards, fairly blinded with dust, carried the piteous Princess Schrink from the scene of disaster. They heard the king shouting orders to seal off the room, for there was no knowing how much damage that filthy monster had done to the ceiling with his awful gushings.

*

The mice heard the portals slam shut, the locks being ground into place by big winches. Then all was silence.

Boff sent a sharp whistle over his shoulder and they all leaped down into the debris of the cavernous chamber. In moments, Astra was seated on Flondrix's forehead, rubbing her nose tenderly over his eyelids.

'It is I, it is I, my own true love,' she shouted and he nodded his head, a broad and happy smile filling his face. 'Careful,' she warned him, 'or you'll dump me off. It took me over a minute to climb all the way up.' He stopped moving his head, but the glorious smile remained.

'What do we do next, dearie?' Boff's voice called to her. She looked up and there he was sitting on the ice above, shivering.

'It would take us for ever to get this ice off,' she told him. 'But my beloved Flondrix can do it in the twinkling of an eye, if only we can remove this hateful necklace.'

'How can we do that?' Boff asked, eyeing it suspiciously, sniffing as he did so. 'Seems to me that one touch and it's dead mouse.'

'You are quite right,' she agreed. 'But I think I can withstand its power, at least for long enough, if you can get me ten of your best rock-driller termites. You see, there are ten links between each plate of metal. If they can drill through those while I sit on the dreaded collar and draw off most of its energy, we will surely free him. But they have to work fast. From the time I step on that necklace, I will have five minutes at most. After that, I am bound to disappear and then . . . well, I just don't know.'

'Don't worry,' Boff called over, slipping down the side of the cylinder, 'I'll get you ten champions. They'll have it done in three minutes flat or I'll feed 'em to the bats.'

In no time at all, much to Astra's relief, Boff was back with Tup. Between them they had hauled a long piece of string up to the top of the ice cylinder and, when Boff settled there, Tup slid down the opposite side, taking the end of the string with him. As he slid down, up came a small basket with ten little heads peering over the rim.

Squatting carefully at the edge of the ice, Boff called to Tup to stop where he was. Juggling the string in his paws, Boff settled the basket, which swayed slightly, just an inch over the accursed collar.

'All right, dearie,' he called to her, 'go to it.'

Astra nuzzled the corner of Flondrix's mouth as she passed, warming herself in his smile and wondering if it would prove to be the last time she ever saw that smile . . . or anything else, for that matter. She allowed herself one last look at the mast that, to her small size, seemed to tower in the air like a tree. It was slightly askew and still quite damp. A tear dropped from her eye as she lowered herself down from the faun's chin and stepped out boldly onto the collar.

A humming of energy went through her small body and the room began to grow a bit dim, the feeling of painful stiffness mounting from her tiny claws up through the pads of her paws. Her thinking became a bit muddled too, as she nodded slowly to Boff. She was aware of the basket being lowered and rock-driller termites pouring out. In a flash, each one was working furiously at a link. She saw the sparks fly as the diamond-hard drill points bit into the metal.

Oh, faster, faster, she said to herself, trying to hold her breath and calm her fears. The terrible numbing ache reached her flexed heel joint. What would happen, she wondered, when it arrived at that infinitesimal spot near the base of her spine, when it attacked her weakened Io-Chand? On drilled the termites, sparks flying thicker and faster as they worked. She was vaguely aware of Boff's voice overhead, shouting and cursing, spewing down the vilest threats at the poor little insects. They worked as though their insides would burst right through the thick carapaces, but the goadings poured down on them just the same. Good Boff, good hearted Boff, he is doing it all for me, she thought. In her blurry vision, she could see his head, thrust dangerously far over the edge of the cylinder, and his whiskers were twitching violently as he shouted.

As her head lowered painfully, Astra heard a thousand squeaks sounding out all over the room. Boff stiffened on his perch, every hair on his body standing on end. Scurrying and panic filled the room. She watched Boff turn slowly and look towards the wall where the opening to their large tunnel was. She followed his gaze and, even through the vaporous numbness, a great shaft of terror went through her.

Out of the wall was slithering an enormous snake. Head raised two feet above the smooth stone floor, it was nearly halfway to them and still more and more snake was emerging from the wall. Every mouse in the room cowered, watching that vent in the wall, the only entrance or exit to the feasting hall. And every mouse was holding its breath, wondering when the snake's tail would finally show, wondering where it would attack first and how many of them would be able to make a successful dash to safety. They were paralysed. None save Boff had even begun to wonder how such a snake had got itself into their tunnel system or how it had managed to manoeuvre some of the passages which were so narrow only two mice could walk abreast in them.

The answer dawned on the foggy Astra and the terrified Boff at the same moment: Bumbree! As if she had read their thoughts, the snake's mouth opened wide and the double red tongue flicked out mockingly; the hideous reptile was laughing silently.

Transfixed with fear, all the mice watched the tail flick out of the wall, then flick back in again, moving around inside. When it emerged, it was wrapped around the door stone. In a trice, the tail flicked once more and the stone was wedged into place so firmly that only blasting powder could loosen it. As it struck home, the screeching of mice became deafening. Even the brave Boff stepped back a pace, baring his strong sharp teeth.

Undulating slowly, the snake resumed its unhurried progress across the hall. Soon, Boff and the rest of the mice knew that Bumbree had her attention fixed on one thing only. One small golden mouse standing on the magic collar around the faun's throat. As Boff looked out of the corner of his eye, he saw how pale poor Astra looked. Then he blinked. It was more than paleness, he could see the very faint outline of the faun's chin right through her body.

'I'll feed your rotten body to the bats, you filthy cousin of a snake!' he shouted with all his might. Bumbree stopped and looked at the bold mouse as though seeing him for the first time. She was puzzled. Feed her to the bats? Very funny. And *cousin* to a snake? Her guise was perfect this time . . . she'd had very powerful and talented help from . . . hmm. *That* mouse would be the first to go . . . afterwards.

But the chief of the rock-drillers knew Boff had meant that remark for him; he redoubled his efforts, noiselessly urging his companions on.

Bumbree's head swung back to her prime target and she moved closer to the faun's head. When she was within good striking distance, she drew her body in and coiled it, lifting her head high enough to be some inches above Astra's perch. She gauged the position very carefully because she did not want to touch the collar. Nor did she want Astra to dissolve. She had much better plans for her.

'Well, well,' hissed the snake, 'look who's here. Our pretty little maiden who leads friendly people on wild goose chases, hmm? And what do you think you're doing? Do you think you can draw the power out of that collar? Not in what I suspect is *your* current condition. You'll only destroy yourself like that. What a pity that would be, such a pretty little child. Now, we must teach you a little lesson, mustn't we? And we must get your nice faun out of here too, mustn't we?' Bumbree paused and looked up at the magnificent mast waving above. 'Yes, indeed we must,' she sighed.

As she was talking, Boff looked down behind Astra's sinking hind quarters. First one little head, then another and another. Soon there were nine sticking up. The leader looked down to where the tenth termite was, hesitated a second, then nodded to Boff.

'You filthy excuse for a snake,' shouted Boff, 'you lousy, stinking third rate witch, I'll bet your teeth are false. I dare you try me, I'll bite your rotten nose off.'

The snake's head swung, the jaws opened and, without thinking, hearing only the goading threat, the snake instinct drew her into a strike, but a strike at an angle to Astra. As the head came whizzing towards Boff, he jumped high and shouted:

'Leap, Astra, leap!'

With the last strength in her, she jumped as high as she could, landing on Flondrix's nose. As the snake head streaked by, the collar flew off, scattering the drilled links, all of which flew into the gaping mouth of the snake. The rest of the collar wrapped itself about her neck, just behind the head, and stuck fast there.

The snake, mouth closed and jaws locked, dropped to the floor writhing furiously. Around and around she lashed, slamming into everything in her way, sending mice flying in all directions. And as she whipped about, spinning and rolling, coiling and uncoiling, she began to shrink in size.

A dazzling flash filled the room and, with a mighty

crack, the ice cylinder split into a thousand pieces that ricocheted off walls and rained down from the ceiling. One heartbeat, Flondrix was lying bound in a prison of ice, the next he was on his hooves, one of them dug deeply into the snake's neck, just behind the collar. Glowering down at the lashing serpent, he held Astra aloft in his left hand and reached over to the wagon with his right. He tore loose one of the golden spokes and put one end into the spot on his throat where the collar had been. The other end he forced down on the collar around Bumbree's reptilian neck.

He pressed so hard he gasped for breath and tears welled up in his eyes. Dimly, he saw the golden spoke flash against the collar around the snake's neck as the metals fused. Tighter and tighter the collar became until the snake-eyes popped out ludicrously. When the collar and the portion of neck beneath it were about twice as thick as a pencil, he released the pressure and threw down the golden spoke. Bumbree changed size no more. The body, now only about three feet long, moved listlessly, the head gyrating slowly from side to side. Nor could she open her mouth any wider than necessary for the forked tongue to dart out.

'Now,' Flondrix said at last, 'you can see what it is like to be a prisoner in your own skin, hardly able to move and at the mercy of anything that comes along. A fly will be about the biggest thing you can swallow . . . if you can catch one with that wicked tongue of yours.' As he spoke, the chief rock-driller termite moved across the floor, followed by his team of nine champions. Bumbree's tongue lashed out in fury, full understanding coming over her when she saw them. Two of the little insects were caught up on the end of each tongue tip. Before the forked tongue was halfway to her mouth, she hissed and dropped them, two fiery holes burning her tongue miserably.

Flondrix leaned over quickly and put out his hand on the stone floor. The ten termites climbed on to his palm and he brought them up to his eye level. He then put his other hand side by side with its mate and Astra stepped across to kiss each one on the top of his head. She whispered her sincere thanks and assured them she would be in their debt for ever.

When the little creatures were safely stored in one of Boff's baskets, Flondrix went to the wall where Bumbree had jammed the stone and freed it.

'Darling,' Astra called up to him, 'we should be leaving as soon as possible. We cannot trust that no curious dwarfs will return to inspect the place.'

'How long are you going to stay a mouse?' he asked, smiling down at her.

'Until we are safely on our way,' she answered. 'I fear to try any more changes. I don't know how much power I used up on that collar. I was very nearly gone. In fact, I think I should try to stay like this until we are safely back in our own realm.'

At this, Flondrix felt a scratching on his hoof. He bent down and held out a hand for Boff to climb on.

'Tell me,' Boff asked them both, 'how safe is that snake?'

'Quite safe, I should think,' Astra answered. 'In fact, that should be that for Bumbree, as long as she is kept safely in your mountain. But you must make sure she never gets to the outside world again.'

'Leave that to us,' Boff assured them. 'When we're finished with storing our next year's supply of food, we'll get the boys busy. We'll have her stowed away where nobody will ever find her. Hey, put me down, Flondrix, and get on your way with dearie, there. She'll show you the route.'

As Flondrix bent down to release the mouse, he and Astra thanked him and all his friends profusely. They

181

did not notice the sudden cunning look in Bumbree's eyes, nor the way they swelled still further with a supernatural effort. As Flondrix stood up, he felt his eyes drawn once more to those of the snake. Astra's eyes followed his, drawn by the same strange fascination. As they looked, both felt something eerie, something like a memory fading, and then it stopped as quickly as it started, the snake's head falling to the floor with a dull plop. Bumbree, although no one knew it then, would be a long time recovering. But just in time she had remembered something the two young Elves had overlooked. And she had held on to just enough power to send a wisp of subtle deception into their minds.

Shaking their heads, the mouse and the faun looked at each other curiously.

'Come, beloved,' Astra begged, 'we have no time to lose. Put me in the wall tunnel and then change yourself to a mouse, holding my paw in a firm grip. We must be out of here as quickly as we can. It is a very long run and it will take some time.'

A moment later, Flondrix was crouched in the tunnel entrance with Astra, feeling the strangeness of his new form. They shouted and waved down to their friends below, then turned and scampered up the long winding tunnel. At the next junction, Astra chose the path that led downwards, circling in a long sweep and crossing junction after junction. She never faltered as they raced along, never hesitated a moment in choosing the right turning. She was that sure of herself. Within the hour, while the night was at its blackest, she would lead them out of the hole at the eastern face of the mountain, the very one she had entered with Boff — how long ago? It seemed like weeks and weeks.

Flondrix called to her to halt for a respite.

'What is it, darling?' she asked, standing at a

wide spot in the tunnel where four other branches joined it.

'I'm still not up to full strength,' he admitted. 'My imprisonment took a lot out of me and my bones are still deeply chilled and brittle. Can we rest for a few minutes?'

'Of course, my dear,' she answered, curling up and breathing heavily from her own exertions.

Flondrix squatted and released his wettings, following that with quite a number of small pellets.

'There are many disadvantages to being frozen in a block of ice,' he observed ruefully, looking behind. 'How am I ever to thank you for your loving devotion? How shall I express that fully?' She smiled and shook her head; dear Flondrix, he never tired of asking questions.

'Tell me,' he went on, 'what is that thing wrapped around you, that thing under your tail?'

She told him briefly about her experience outside the mountain while still in the form of a mortal woman, and what had happened when she changed to a mouse. When she finished, Flondrix snuggled close to her and nibbled on the threads until they came loose. Then he grabbed the pad and threads and tossed them across the tunnel.

'What are you up to?' she asked in surprise.

'Well, you don't need that any longer, do you? I'm the only one around, you don't have to protect yourself from me.'

'Flondrix, I don't think that was very wise,' she admonished, feeling terribly anxious about any delay in their escape. But he was already warmly mounted on her, thrusting happily at her wetness. She sighed a delighted sigh, knowing she could never deny her dearly beloved anything.

An hour later, neither of them noticed anything

strange about the protective rock they moved, shifting it bit by bit with all their strength until they could just squeeze through into the night air of the open world. As they replaced the little stone door over the hole, Astra did not question the scene or find anything strange about it. She simply had no knowledge that they were outside the *western* face of the mountain. That last exhausting effort of Bumbree's had jumbled their senses of direction!

'Quickly,' panted Astra, 'change yourself now to the great eagle and let us fly with all haste. I will cling to your neck so that I will not be in the way. And still we will be able to talk as we go. Oh,' she added, 'I will feel so happy to see mother and father, so happy to feel their arms about me again. And Aunt Glortina! I'll never be able to thank her enough.'

The great eagle rose up on the night wind, the minute golden mouse clinging to his neck, and soared straight for the west, in the opposite direction to the Elvan Realm and the Sacred Glade.

*

All the time Flondrix and Astra had been racing through the long tunnels, Bumbree had been watching the busy mice hauling food from the tables to the floor, across the great cavern, to be hoisted up into the tunnel in the wall. Whenever no eyes were upon her, she inched her way further and further from the mice. Eventually, she wormed her way to the base of the thrones. She had no trouble identifying Princess Schrink's, but it took many efforts of her wasted strength to gain the seat. Over and over she fell back to the floor. When she finally succeeded, she coiled up on the seat, making herself look as small as possible.

The moment Astra and Flondrix gained the free air outside the mountain, a strange change came over the mice. Their work became less organized, they squatted frequently or sat up on their haunches to sniff the air. They began eating gluttonously instead of storing the food. Glortina's enchantment had left them and they had become ordinary mice once more. This is what Bumbree had remembered and the Elvan lovers had overlooked.

With the first grinding sound of the portal winches, all the mice squeaked furiously and dashed up the side of the wall and into the tunnel. They did remember to seal the tunnel entrance with the stone, but had only the vaguest memory of Bumbree in their now simpler minds. They had even left two of their hard-working rock-driller termites behind in the excitement. One of them got stepped on rather badly by a dwarf and it took his companion nearly a month to carry him back to the mouse lairs.

*

Thundering through the night, a sudden black cloud passed through Gonzola's mind. He slowed his horse to let him breathe and looked up at the dark sky. Two shadowy horses appeared at his side, mounted by riders who were almost totally invisible in the night, so wraith-like were they.

'Did you feel something?' Gonzola asked over his shoulder.

A voice near him replied: 'It is the children. They are flying to the west.'

'So Glortan foretold,' the magician sighed sadly. He touched his black mount's neck lightly and it dashed on like the wind itself, heading for King Schtoonk's Schtronghold.

And far in the western distances, Flondrix looked down from his eagle height, peering into the black depths below where no moon or stars cast their light

185

through the densely clouded night. He identified the clearing and the great tree house of Glortan. 'Was it?' a question niggled at him. Of course it was, his annoyed response countered. He began the long descent, cutting a wide circle in the intense gloom. As the wind whistled past his head, he heard the joyous chattering of Astra, her little mouse claws clutching tightly at the feathers round his throat.

He spread his wings fully, opening the pinion feathers and shooting his legs down to make a perfect stall landing on the uppermost platform. As soon as his talons touched the wood, a blinding light surrounded them. A complete wall of flame hemmed them in on all four sides, even roofed them over in fire. Just as suddenly, the fire died down to an intense, dull glow that solidified into walls and roof of thick, shining steel.

Standing in front of them, as if appearing from nowhere, was a tall, slender man in black boots, tightly fitting breeches and a matching black tunic that fell to his hips. The tunic was attached to a cowl which edged forward to hide most of his face. They could just make out an aquiline nose, razor sharp at the bridge, and a close-cropped beard that had been shaved back from a mouth now twisted in a sardonic grin. Above the grin, they were aware of penetrating black eyes that seemed to peer straight through them. This awesome appearance was heightened by the golden emblem on the breast of the tunic. A large, fiery sun surrounded a star with eight points. In the centre of the star, a heavy-lidded eye glowed with a fire of its own.

'Well, my dears,' a brittle voice lisped at them dryly, sounding like dessicated acorns falling on a tin roof, 'I see you made your way "home" nicely. Allow me to welcome you, most warmly I'm sure.'

'Who are you?' croaked Flondrix. 'Where are we? What have you done to – to our people?'

'Such precocious questions,' chided the sibilant voice. 'This really is not the time nor the place. No, we have a tiny bit more travelling to do first. This is neither the *time* nor the *place*.'

As he repeated the words 'time' and 'place' with insinuating emphasis, Astra began to tremble so violently she nearly lost her grip on the eagle's feathers. The tall man's hand emerged from one of the copious tunic sleeves and two long, delicate fingers began stroking the eye on the emblem of his tunic. As he did so, the steel room began to sink, slowly at first, then more and more rapidly. In a matter of seconds, they lost all awareness of the blinding speed as they accelerated through what seemed not so much the inside of the world, but more a limitless void. When the room began to turn slowly, there seemed no more orientation of up or down; nothing seemed real any longer.

A sobbing gasp broke from Astra's throat. 'It is the Under People! Oh, by my heavenly star, it is the Under People.'

'Aren't we a clever one,' the mocking voice came back. 'And your host, about whom your rugged young man was inquiring, is none other than Dr Kranz. Or Herr Doktor-Professor Kranz, as he was once known in the dear, bygone days.'

Those were the last words the two young Elves heard as they broke through the barriers of light and time, moving through dimensions beyond either. They were not even aware of changes in themselves or the passage of a new time. It seemed only that the mocking voice spoke and they opened their eyes.

Astra looked out into a bright, disorderly laboratory with windows along one entire wall. Work tables were strewn with books and complex equipment. Some of the books were new, others looked as though they had weathered the dust of many centuries. Through the windows, a great city appeared mistily. It took some moments to realize that the building was so incredibly tall that it towered hundreds of feet up, so high that clouds sailed by below the level of the windows. Similar buildings rose up in the distance, stretching as far as the eye could see.

Flondrix gasped and clutched the door of his steel cage. Astra whirled, finding herself locked in a duplicate cage of heavy mesh, adjacent to Flondrix's prison. He blinked, seeing her restored again to her own form. She turned to him, tears streaming down her lovely face, as he pounded impotently on the unyielding steel.

XV

Gonzola Pays an Unexpected Call to Schtoonk's Schtronghold

◉◉◉◉◉◉◉◉

Gonzola stepped carefully through the debris in the Dwarf King's feasting hall, one ear cocked for the commotion he expected shortly; his two invisible friends and the three horses were outside the eastern portals of the White Mountains and guards were milling about everywhere. The king himself must be there by now, to say nothing of Sordo and the corps of engineers, all of them trying to get those stubborn portals to close. Gonzola smiled, picturing the chaos in his mind. But those portals would not close until his invisible friends wanted them to.

He stopped his humorous musings and chided himself for wasting time. There was much to ascertain before the furious king and his entourage reopened the portals to the feasting hall and attempted to arrest the 'intruder'. It would not take Sordo long to put two and two together.

Over the next two minutes, the magician had pieced together the story of the mice and the rock-driller termites. He had picked up the loose golden spoke on the floor and squeezed it with all his strength. When he saw the colours of the sparks and the bolts of energy it shot forth, he had the whole story of Flondrix's release and the capture of . . . His keen eyes located a large scale stuck to the wall at the entrance to the tunnel of the mice. Another scale caught his eye clinging to the edge of one of the thrones. It was one third the size.

Gonzola lost a whole minute looking at those two scales and then he gasped. Whirling around in front of the throne, he surveyed the whole cavernous chamber once more. Bumbree! In the guise of a huge snake. Then a small snake. She must be ensnared in the foul device that had bound Flondrix. But the sensitive sorcerer could not detect Bumbree's presence in the mountain now. He hesitated only one minute more, then plonked his bottom down most unceremoniously on the seat of Princess Schrink's throne. He closed his eyes and rolled them back until it seemed he was looking at the base of his own spine. Drawing heavily on his own forces, he brought the centre of concentration up to that point between and just behind his eyes which could enlarge itself like a screen. Soon vague shadows were solidifying themselves and distinct forms and colours clarified in his inner vision; through the cloak, the hose and the fine linen underpants, he drew up every remnant of the particles of memory left impressed in the seat cushion.

Dwarfs were milling round the golden vehicle which was now empty. Princess Schrink detached herself from the crowd and sidled over to the table to pick up a piece of bread and jam she had not finished before the ceiling collapsed. Then she saw — on the seat of her cushion — Yes! It must be! It *couldn't* be anything else!

'Yes,' a voice hissed to her, 'I was left behind just for you. My master, the lovely faun, has fallen in love with you, but he had to escape when he could. But to prove his love, he left me behind to comfort you until he returns. He taught me to corkscrew so that I could please you in as many ways as possible.'

'He loves me, he loves me,' the princess laughed softly, stealing a glance over her shoulder to make sure no one was listening. 'What am I to do with you, you lovely thing? I must say, you do look a bit different. You are shorter and thinner—and—oh! Did you always have such pretty eyes?'

'You were so excited you missed many good things,' the hissing voice tantalized her. 'This, for instance.' Out darted the red forked tongue.

'Ooooh!' exclaimed the princess, 'what is *that* for?'

'All in good time, all in good time, my dear,' the voice lisped soothingly. 'Just listen, and listen *very* carefully.'

The snake told the palpitating princess that she must hide the faun's precious jewel and then leave the mountain. She would go for a walk in the woods alone and, when she found a secluded place some distance from the mountain, she must lie down and go to sleep. As soon as he could, the lovely faun would return. When he kissed her she would awake and they would be reunited.

'Do you promise to obey the instructions and tell no one?' the snake asked.

'Oh, yes,' the princess beamed happily, clapping her hands. 'But where am I to hide you?'

'Just lift up your skirt, my dear, and sit down on me v–e–r–y slowly . . .'

The thunderous winches clanged and rattled, the portals grinding as they drew apart. Gonzola sat bolt upright, rubbed his eyes quickly, leaving the throne as if it were on fire. The royal guards came storming in, their swords and lances levelled at the magician. He raised his cape and thirty guards found themselves foolishly looking at their blunted weapons which had charged into the solid stone wall. Gonzola was rushing to the portals, arriving just as the king entered, followed by an outraged Sordo.

'How dare you . . .' the king exploded.

'Where is your daughter? Quick, your majesty, there is no time to lose. She must not leave these halls,' Gonzola interrupted.

At a signal from the king, another platoon of guards surrounded the old magician menacingly.

'Hold his cloak down!' barked Sordo, and a number of the guards bent forward and held on to the great cloak with all their might.

'Your majesty,' Gonzola's voice boomed through the caverns like the tocsin of doom, 'your daughter is in great peril. If you don't act now, you may never see her again. I am deadly serious.'

The Dwarf King hesitated a moment longer, then ordered all but a few of the guards to find the princess immediately.

'Gonzola, you are under arrest!' the small king roared, shaking a furious finger. 'How did you get in here?'

'Through the eastern portals, your majesty,' he answered lightly. 'They were wide open. I looked for the guards, but they were not there. I came in here looking for you and Sordo –' Gonzola paused and smiled disarmingly at Schtoonk's magician – 'my worthy brother in the Order Most High.'

'What did you do to our portals?' Schtoonk demanded. 'They won't close. They are jammed and we cannot budge them.'

Gonzola shrugged his shoulders and shook a puzzled head. 'Sire, on my honour, I did not touch them. But if my colleague can supply me with one or two items from his wondrous laboratories, I believe I can have them working before I leave.'

'There are three horses out there, Gonzola,' Sordo insinuated. 'Where are your companions?'

'Companions? I have much travelling to do, Brother Sordo. It is easier on the horses if I change them frequently.'

'That's funny,' Sordo laughed wryly, 'that horse of yours is known to be a mysterious breed, alone of his ilk. Since when did he tire?'

'May I remind my brother that none of us is getting any younger?' Gonzola smiled back. 'My horse included.'

'Enough of this horse nonsense,' the Dwarf King interrupted, 'I want those portals put back in working order. And I want to know what brings you here uninvited, magician.'

'Your recent guests, your majesty,' Gonzola answered soberly. 'I don't know if they could properly be termed "invited guests" either.'

Gonzola watched the Dwarf King grow pale when he described the faun as a very close relative of the mighty Glortan. All the colour drained from that small face when the king learned that Glortan had a daughter who had risked her life to save the faun. None of this was being taken as a pleasant joke in the Sacred Glade.

'We knew nothing of that,' the little king spluttered. 'Some of our boys got carried away, they'd never seen an animal like that before,' he finished lamely. Before Gonzola could remind him of his usual espionage activities at the Sacred Glade during Midsummer, the king swung back, pointing his finger at the magician.

'And another thing, they *rescued* that animal from Bumbree's evil clutches. Glortan should be thankful. We were going to release him.'

A troop of guards came running through the portals. Their leader saluted the king.

'Your royal highness, Princess Schrink has gone for a walk in the forest. She dismissed her maidens and said she would return later.'

'What?' barked Gonzola. He twirled about so rapidly the guards holding him were spun loose. When he stopped, he stamped his foot. 'Your majesty, by your gracious leave, I would speak a few moments with my colleague, Sordo.'

The shaken king just nodded his head and two of the guards supported him as he walked uncertainly to his throne.

'What do you think you are up to, Gonzola, storming in here and upsetting everyone? What is this nonsense about the princess?'

'Did you examine this room?' Gonzola demanded, a deep scowl on his face. 'Did you not know Bumbree was here?' The colour of Sordo's face became ashen.

'Bumbree?' he whispered.

'Yes, Bumbree. In the guise of a snake. And in that guise, she has left the mountain . . . with the king's daughter. Bumbree is weakened. She now wears that high force collar you must have noted round the faun's neck. You also must have known whose invention it was. And who will be rumbling round "beneath" until his slave is free. Think well on it, Sordo.'

'I don't care for your tone, Gonzola. And since when have you been working for the Elves? Since when did *they* need a magician?' Sordo demanded with false bravado.

'Since you and the Dark King have begun to listen to strange voices, Brother Sordo.' Gonzola reached into an inner pocket of his cloak and withdrew a slip of paper marked with alchemists' ciphers. 'Put together these ingredients. Tell the king that if he will give us a good meal and four to five hours, we will have the entire chamber put to rights. But we must be enclosed here for that time with no disturbance. It would take his engineers weeks to do the job.'

'Where are you going?' Sordo asked shakily, still reeling from the impact of Gonzola's remark about the 'strange voices'.

'To see about my horses. *And* your portals.' Gonzola drew his cloak about him and sauntered from the cavernous chamber.

*

Outside the great stone portals which were still jammed open, Gonzola sniffed the air in every direction. He stood near the great black horse and seemed to be assuring himself that the grass in the vicinity was adequate to keep the three beasts going for a few hours more. To all eyes watching him from the portal, he was a concerned horseman with no thought save for the well-being of his charges. He fussed with bridles and cinches, brushed and patted the animals and talked to them encouragingly . . . or so it seemed. None of the dwarf guards near the portal could see the figure standing by his side, talking to him earnestly. It was one of the outriders of the night before, Yana of Elvanhome.

'There is no question the portal mechanism will now respond to your signals?' Gonzola asked softly.

'None whatsoever,' Yana answered, his voice sounding like the muted strings of a lute. 'Themur and I have it so balanced now, so perfectly attuned, it will open whenever we sound this note.'

The incredible Elf made a sound so high it was clear only to Gonzola and Themur, who was leaning against one of the portals and smiling down at the dwarfs labouring with the mechanism. The hinges sighed when the sound reached them and this infuriated the sweating dwarfs further.

'You will hear the other note when you go back inside and we close the portals. Incidentally, do you see what Themur has in his hand?' Yana asked.

Gonzola narrowed his eyes as Themur opened his hand and held out a tiny sphere of clear amber. To the dwarfs, that was just as invisible as everything else about the tall, slender, magnificently radiant Elf.

'It looks like a small yellow stone from here,' Gonzola answered. 'What is it?'

'As you pass, look inside it. You will see the tiniest snake imaginable,' Yana laughed.

'You – you *caught* her?' Gonzola choked with surprise, for a moment losing his imperturbable manner. 'How – how did you know? How did you find her?'

'I was scanning your meditation earlier,' Yana chuckled, 'and just as you got to the point where the princess received her instructions, out she walked. Poor Themur is unusually sensitive to unpleasant vibrations. His hair nearly stood on end. You would never guess where that evil witch had hidden herself.'

'You stopped scanning too soon, I didn't have to guess,' the magician remarked dryly. 'Is she securely held?' He turned to eye the small amber globe in Themur's hand with concern. 'How did you trap her?'

'Since the portals were already adjusted, we followed the princess closely,' the Elf answered blithely. 'We just watched and waited. Then,' he shuddered, 'out it came. It was not very pleasant. Neither the snake nor the exposed parts of the princess. The snake tried to fight us but Themur got his heel on the collar and pressed until it was no larger than the eye of a small needle. We had some of the wax made by the bees of Elvanhome, an extremely powerful element we can form into an adamantine amber-like substance immediately. There is no stronger prison.'

'Do not, whatever you do, lose that sphere,'

Gonzola's colour paled as he spoke. 'From the vibrations I feel beneath my feet, I deem *someone* is not at all happy.'

'Oh, that one,' laughed Yana. 'Daemon-Baalim has been lashing about under there ever since the princess stepped through the portals. Do not trouble yourself about him.'

'I must return now,' advised the magician, not completely reassured by Yana's confident tone. 'That thick-headed Sordo may take hours and hours to break down. I should be back before the day is out.'

'We will be here,' Yana stated calmly. 'Elvanlord is sorely distressed by the events unfolding here. He does not send messengers and guardians lightly. Where you are, we will be.'

Gonzola nodded and forced an optimistic smile before he walked briskly towards the huge stone portals in the side of the mountain. As he passed Themur, he looked down with a slight shiver of revulsion at the amber ball containing the miniaturized shape of Bumbree's snake. The little eyes glowered at him with so much hate he turned his head, giving Themur a quick wink as he did.

The magician stepped inside the entrance and three guards fell into place beside him.

'What about these blasted portals?' hollered the chief engineer over the heads of his sweating workers.

Gonzola looked up, tilted his head and snapped his fingers. As he did so, Themur made an inaudible sound and the portals came crashing shut.

'They will open and close whenever you want them to,' the magician called back over his shoulder. To himself he said: 'And whenever *we* want them to.'

*

Sordo watched and wondered, following Gonzola's every move. He learned much in those two hours, much that Gonzola regretted imparting, but he knew he had to gain Sordo's respect and confidence. Reluctantly, he opened the doors of Great Knowledge a crack, not knowing if he would win Sordo over. At the end of those first two hours, the sharpest eye could never have detected what a catastrophe had struck the vast chamber the previous night.

'You are truly a great wizard,' Sordo beamed with genuine admiration and awe. 'I knew that Elvan attainments could control such forces, but I am amazed that a practitioner in our Order Most High could do this. Is there perhaps something Elvish in our worthy brother?'

'There is nothing I have done here today you could not now do, is there?' Gonzola answered, deflecting the last innuendo. 'Come, Sordo, we have earned our meal and a few cups of cheering wine. Let us refresh ourselves now.'

The hours slipped by with the swiftness of minutes, Gonzola bent over the corner of the table, impressing his presence into Sordo's fibres forcibly, his voice vibrating, his eyes flashing with irresistible power. He reminded Sordo that Daemon-Baalim was a phantasmagoria, an evil power in thrall who needed mortal mediums to further his aims and eventually free him. Kranz was one, and Kranz was trying to reach others. The Dark King, for one. Kranz believed he could make the unreal time of the Under People real time by destroying everything else. Oh, he would promise a golden age of immortality to those who harkened to his call and helped him. By destroying the source of Elvan power in the Cosmos, the hosts of Glortan would become enfeebled, an easy prey for the armies of Schtoonk and Barlocks. Kranz's helpers would know power and riches beyond their wildest dreams. It was all a false and treacherous vision. Kranz would destroy the Cosmos as they knew it (if he was allowed to) and nothing would remain but a dark void, an abyss of horror extending to eternity. Only a greedy, misled fool would believe in Kranz's dreadful scheme.

'Sordo, Kranz must be contained in the time trap of the Under People for all eternity,' Gonzola thundered, 'and the Beast must be chained Beneath for ever.'

'But Kranz can come back here,' Sordo argued, 'he discovered the way a long time ago. And the Beast's chains are weakening.'

'Physically, Kranz cannot leave the ethereal vehicle he comes in. Not without the trapped and bent wills of mortals to help him. The Beast Beneath owes most of his new powers to Kranz's malignant will, but make no mistake – Kranz will use Daemon-Baalim, he will not be used by him. Of the two, Kranz is far more dangerous,' Gonzola assured him.

'What would you have me do?' Sordo asked vaguely, his face momentarily vacant, as though he were listening to distant voices.

'So!' roared Gonzola, crashing his fist down thunderously on the table. 'Kranz knows someone is reaching your mind, doesn't he? He is trying to bend your will against me.' Sordo nodded, his lips compressed and his colour draining. 'Then tear your will loose and listen only to me!' Gonzola commanded. Sordo's eyes cleared and he looked alert again, though terribly shaken by the ordeal.

'Sordo, you must seem to do Kranz's bidding, otherwise the assault on your mind would be unbearable. Soon, Barlocks will be sending messages to Schtoonk. An alliance will be formed. All must seem to be falling helplessly into Kranz's trap. I alone will

199

be the renegade, the dissenter. Kranz would not believe otherwise of me. When dwarfs and men march against Glortan, Kranz will promise that his cataclysmic device will destroy only the Elves of this universe. *You* know better now, but give no indication of this to Kranz. Now, fix all this in your mind and listen to no other voice but mine.'

Gonzola reached out as he spoke and closed his hand over the serpent's head and the ruby apple on the buckle of Sordo's belt. An eerie blue fire glowed through the back of the mighty wizard's hand.

'You will be twisted and bent, Sordo,' his voice rang out hypnotically, 'and you will seem my mortal enemy. But when the final moment comes, this memory will come flooding back to you. You will withdraw your will from Kranz and that will strike the first blow at his new power. My strategies and the great powers of Elvanhome must do the rest.'

Gonzola stood up and watched the dazed Sordo shake his head.

'What did you just say?' Sordo asked meekly, wagging his head from side to side as though he had fallen asleep unintentionally. Gonzola smiled.

'I said I must be on my way now. But I need a good dwarf, a very reliable dwarf to go with me. We must find such a one and you have to convince King Schtoonk to let him go with me.'

Before Sordo could protest, Gonzola strode boldly to the portals of the festive hall and touched them with the ivory wand he whipped out from under his cloak. The winding winches started spinning madly and the portals creaked open. Before they had moved very far, little Rimbek stepped through and looked up at Gonzola. The dwarf had the magic mantle folded neatly and balanced on his shoulders. In one hand he carried a heavy sack.

'Are you Gonzola, the magician?' Rimbek asked, casting his eyes about the hall in astonishment. 'Well, you are a mighty magician, that much is certain,' he added in an awed voice.

Gonzola reached down silently and took the dwarf's free hand, leading him over to the chair in which the stunned Sordo still sat.

Sordo looked at Rimbek, at the metallic mantle and the sack in his hand. 'Where are you off to?' he asked.

'With him,' replied the dwarf, inclining his head towards Gonzola. Sordo looked at his colleague and Gonzola shrugged, as if to say he had no notion of what it was all about.

'Why do you want to go with him?' Sordo asked. 'Furthermore, where do you think he is going?'

'I don't know where he is going,' Rimbek admitted, 'but I want to go with him. I feel upset about the faun because I helped to capture him. My new bride is in the nesting rooms day and night and she hardly talks to me. My brothers are so busy gloating over their new fortunes they have no time for me either. Besides, I like adventures and I just want to go with Gonzola.'

The two magicians looked at each other and burst out laughing.

'Won't your new bride miss you?' Gonzola asked.

'She may miss me, but I won't miss her . . . not for some time. My schlong hurts.'

Gonzola knitted his brows and looked questioningly at Sordo.

'Chooch, you know,' Sordo explained rather fastidiously. He pointed to the coils round the dwarf's middle.

'Aha!' Gonzola mused, nodding his head approvingly. 'What are you carrying in the sack? Oh, I don't even know your name.'

'I'm Rimbek,' the dwarf told him, 'and I have my

best mining tools in here. Never can tell where you may strike something valuable.'

'That's true, that's very true,' Gonzola agreed. Mining tools were exactly what he had intended asking a dwarf to bring along.

'Well, come on then, Rimbek. We're off.'

XVI

A Plunge into the Dreadful
Maw of Time

◉◉◉◉◉◉◉◉

Gonzola drew in his great black steed at the rim of the high ridge and looked out over the valley below. The moon was just reaching the tops of the hills in the distance and would soon be sinking behind them. But the stars were bright and clear in the crisp, dry night, sending their sparkling light down to give form to the shapes being slowly deserted by the moon.

The magician's attention was focused on a spot halfway across the great valley that was otherwise filled with unbroken forest. He detected the clearing he was searching for and could still see the visual remnants of Kranz's spurious tree house, now so vague that they would soon disappear. The dwarf, tucked up behind the magician's saddle on the magic mantle, stirred sleepily and lifted a corner of the great cloak covering him in order to peep out.

Rimbek squirmed to see ahead, round the magician's body. He saw only a blackened valley in the pale light. To his left, a few paces off, stood one of the shadowy, fine-boned horses that always rode a few paces behind, one on either side of them. Both horses were saddled and, as they stood patiently, both sets of reins were pulled taut. Rimbek's sack of tools was still tied firmly to the saddle of the horse on the right.

'Gonzola, I'm hungry,' hissed the dwarf, poking the silent magician in the ribs.

Without a word, the magician reached under his cloak and pulled out a large, square bundle. He untied the kerchief around it and extracted a small loaf of dark brown bread, a large wedge of cheese and two boiled eggs which he passed back to Rimbek. The other loaf, wedge of cheese and boiled eggs he balanced on the pommel of the saddle, devouring the food as swiftly as he could.

'Eat quickly,' he called back to the dwarf, 'we have very little time to spare. When you finish, get a good grip and hold tightly. The last few miles will be perilous.'

Little Rimbek had just jammed the last egg into his mouth whole, when the huge black beast took off like a startled hare, whipping the cloak back and high up into the wind. Holding on for dear life, he could feel the wind rushing by but he could not hear the horse's hooves thundering on the ground. He buried his small face in the middle of the magician's back and held on with all his strength, looking neither to right nor to left. Had he done so, he would have probably panicked to see the horses soaring high above the valley floor.

Before the young dwarf had fully recovered his senses, a great thudding jolt sent him crashing into Gonzola's back. He heard the magician laugh ruefully as one of his long legs passed over the dwarf's head; he was standing on the ground, holding up one hand for his little companion.

Rimbek jumped down bravely and stood next to Gonzola, watching the other two horses moving through the trees — Rimbek jumped! It was not the trees, but the treetops. He looked beneath his feet and saw the ground far, far below. Wrapping both arms around the magician's leg, he wailed.

Gonzola laughed and patted the dwarf's head reassuringly.

'Do not worry, little friend, we shall not fall. At least, not for a while yet.'

Rimbek heard what sounded like music coming from the distance. When he looked up, the magician was concentrating on one of the horses and nodding his head. He pulled the dwarf's mantle off the black steed's rump and placed it, neatly folded, on Rimbek's shoulder. At the same instant, the sack filled with mining tools fell clattering from one of the other horses and sat there, seemingly in mid-air.

'Where are we?' Rimbek's startled voice gasped as he shouldered the heavy sack. 'How – how did we get up here – and . . .'

'We are following Astra and Flondrix. This is the imitation tree house Kranz devised to trap them. In a few moments we will be starting the final stage of our journey, travelling through the ages to the world of the Under People. Be patient, and no more questions, please.' Gonzola held up his hand as the strange music floated up from below. When Rimbek looked down, the three horses were peacefully cropping grass in a clearing far beneath his feet.

'What is that strange music I hear?' the dwarf asked, his natural curiosity not easily discouraged. Gonzola held up his hand for silence again and listened to the distant music.

'I am communicating with our invisible friends from Elvanhome. They are called Yana and Themur and you will meet them shortly,' Gonzola informed him. 'Now stand still and no more questions, Rimbek. Do you see that star, the very bright one that changes colour from blue to magenta, then to yellow and back to blue?' The dwarf followed the direction of Gonzola's long index finger and nodded, watching the star as it changed colour.

'Well,' the magician continued, 'it will be silver soon. When you see that happen, close your eyes and keep them tightly shut until I tell you to open them. But all the time you do, keep your face in the direction of that star. It is called Topar, and you are to concentrate on it with all your might, until you can actually feel its light and warmth deep inside your forehead. Is that clear?' Again, the dwarf nodded, though still quite dumbfounded.

As the star began to turn silver, Rimbek shut his eyes and held the magician's hand as tightly as he could. He felt the star glowing and soon his head was filled with an exhilarating warmth, as though the star were coming closer and closer, blazing like the sun itself.

Inside his head a strange voice began speaking with incredible speed, yet the little dwarf understood every word. Gonzola and he, with Yana and Themur, were going to travel through time to an astounding city filled with tall buildings. Everything would seem strange there, unlike anything the dwarf knew or imagined. Such voyages always started with a downward plunge into a void. But very soon he would lose all sense of up or down. When they arrived, they would all look different and be dressed differently. They would be standing in front of what was called a security officer's desk. His new name would be Louis Ragona and it would say so on his identity card. He was not to be frightened for everything would be indelibly impressed on his memory; every detail he needed to know to appear normal in that strange world would be fed into his mind during the fantastic voyage . . . the voice accelerated until it was a blur and the dwarf felt himself floating, suspended in mid-air.

Enveloped in the trance Gonzola had induced, Rimbek was unaware of the intensifying light surrounding the tree tops; the platform, the walls, the entire steel replica of Glortan's tree house became firm and visually real. The mystical bodies of Yana and Themur materialized and power from Topar flowed through them and into Gonzola's body, mounting in strength until the magician felt all his weariness drop from him like an old garment. Rimbek had all he could do to hold his eyes closed when he felt a strange hand grasp his free one. The current of energy then passed into his own body and it was a surge of power like nothing he had ever known before.

'All right, you can open your eyes for a few seconds now, Rimbek,' the magician said softly.

The dwarf's eyes flew open and he was facing two of the tallest and most wondrously formed men he had ever seen. One was holding Gonzola's hand, the other gripping his own. When the two of them joined hands, the surge of power made him feel he was rising up to dizzying heights. Their eyes twinkled like amethysts in Topar's brilliant light and long golden hair fell to their shoulders, shedding sparks of silver all about. They must be Elves! Suddenly he realized the Elves were naked . . . and . . . they had no schlongs!

The two Elves smiled and he heard a musical voice in his ear. 'Do not worry about that or anything else, little friend. Just close your eyes again and hold fast. Our journey across the ages is about to begin.'

As soon as Rimbek closed his eyes, the room began to sink, dropping faster and faster until he lost all sense of direction. He felt as though he were turning in free space, going up and down at the same time, dropping through a void and drifting beyond space or any known factor he could imagine. Facts, figures and details of strange information began to fill his mind with blinding speed. Then, it all seemed to whisper to an end, like a dream fading in the first light of dawn.

*

Rimbek's stomach nearly turned upside down when he looked at the blue trousers and shirt, the heavy-duty shoes on his feet. These were the first things he saw when he opened his eyes. A voice boomed at him and he strained to look up over the edge of a large desk.

'Are you Louis Ragona?' the security officer demanded. Behind the desk stood two marine guards, on alert with machine pistols at the ready.

Rimbek automatically reached into his shirt pocket and pulled out a magnetized, plastic identity card. The security officer grabbed it and fed it into a small machine. A green light flashed and the card was ejected.

'I am Dr Roland Warner,' a voice behind Rimbek announced. Rimbek looked around to see Gonzola, clean-shaven with trim white hair, dressed in a dark blue suit. Next to him stood two men in light blue velvet suits, long blond hair and wide-brimmed hats ... Yana and Themur! The dwarf's mouth started to fall open and he clamped it shut quickly, putting an annoyed scowl on his face.

'I'm the solid fuel expert Dr Kranz is expecting,' Gonzola continued. 'We're assigned to Laboratory A on the one hundred and sixty-fifth floor. These two,' he yanked a thumb towards Yana and Themur, 'are Ian Reine and David Queensway, my mathematician and computer expert. The midget is our rocket engine technician.'

As Gonzola spoke, he and the two men in light blue suits threw their identity cards on the desk. All three

208

cards went through the screening machine, flashed green and flew out.

'This is the only authorized exit or entrance to the Advanced Technology Building. Anyone trying to get in or out of this building by any other door is shot on sight. Is that clear?' the security man asked, passing their cards to them. 'Pin these on and keep them in sight at all times. Anyone without an identity card in sight can be shot without questioning.'

The four hurried past the desk and stopped in front of an automatic lift; the door opened and they filed in quickly, the doors hissing closed behind them. Gonzola put his forefinger to his lips and pushed the top button.

'Where are we?' whispered Rimbek, looking down at his strange clothes.

'We're in the city of the Under People,' Gonzola whispered back 'and this building is Kranz's head-quarters. Concentrate! Everything you need to know is programmed into your memory. As far as Kranz is concerned, we are here to work on a complex problem in rocket fuel logistics. When the time comes, we will do our *real* job. You'll get your special instructions then.'

'I'm sorry,' Rimbek whimpered, 'I forgot for a moment. Everything feels so strange here.'

'Wait till you look for that mad, mad schlong of yours,' giggled one of the blond men. He unzipped his trousers and flashed a delicate, exquisitely formed penis with a long, tapering foreskin.

'Put that away,' hissed the other blond, 'there's a dirty old man in the lift.'

'Why are they acting like that?' pleaded Rimbek, his terrified hands roving over his waist, searching for the coils that were no longer there.

'Because we all have to play our parts thoroughly and precisely,' Gonzola explained patiently, watching the flashing floor lights on the panel overhead. 'That's how people act here. If we exhibit any tendency that would seem abnormal, Kranz will unmask us immediately. If he received any advance warning, he won't be looking for me in a group. That, I hope, is what will buy us the time we need. Now hush . . . on your toes and keep your mind clear.'

The lift came to a smooth halt and they stepped out smartly. Unerringly, Gonzola herded them to a small laboratory at the end of the corridor. The door opposite was bolted and securely guarded by electronic alarm devices. The four trooped into the laboratory and began operations immediately. The two Elves, as David and Ian, tackled a small computer; with an imperious air Dr Roland Warner took over the desk and little Louis Ragona started tinkering with a model solid fuel rocket engine bolted down on a steel table.

Fifteen minutes went by without one word being spoken. Suddenly, the door was flung open and a languorous girl with dark red hair and a very short skirt stepped into the room. Her eyes flashed from one to another of the four men. She kicked the door shut with her black-booted foot and sauntered over to the steel table. Little Louis Ragona looked up at her and cringed. Smiling, she leaned over him and unbuttoned her tight blouse. Two large, splendid breasts spilled out, grazing his face. He uttered a cry of horror and ran across the room, leaping up into Roland Warner's lap. Dr Warner put an arm around him and covered his small crotch protectively with one hand.

The girl shrugged her shoulders and walked up behind David and Ian. She stood there waiting for one of them to turn round. As neither did, she snaked her hand out, reached between David's legs and clutched his penis with a firm grip. He shrieked and jumped, running behind Ian and wrapping his arms around him. Once more the girl shrugged and walked back to the door, buttoning up her blouse. She never looked round again, just opened the door and sauntered out. The dwarf jumped off the magician's lap and ran to the door, kicking it closed with great fury.

'Very good,' murmured the magician. 'One wrong move ... but I think we passed the second test beautifully. Back to work, gentlemen, Kranz himself will be here shortly.'

Before the next disturbance occurred, the two Elves, with the fantastic esoteric means at their disposal, had worked their way through the entire area computer system, reaching the main banks and adjusting a number of vital statistics and formula factors so that the full system was attuned to the new information that had been fed into it through their own energized impulses.

Voices across the hall could be heard as the door there shut sharply, locks grinding and whirring into place. Two seconds later their own door opened and Kranz side-stepped into the room, leaving the way for another man to enter.

'The President and Commander-in-Chief,' barked Kranz.

The four men leaped to their feet and stood to attention.

'Relax, men,' the President ordered paternally. 'What goes on *here*, Kranz?'

'This is a very special team I ordered in to work out the final fuel problems. As I mentioned, Mr President, it's going to be a tough grind. I want to make sure there are no miscalculations.'

'Are you sure it will all work out on time?' the President asked.

'Yes, sir. I expect to have that other formula we've worked on so long in the next few days. Maybe sooner.'

The President marched out of the room without another word. Kranz followed him to the door, then turned round.

'I'll be back after the blast to talk to you men. Meantime, carry on the good work.' The door closed, swallowing Kranz's words in the corridor. Gonzola listened carefully as the inaudible voices diminished.

'Chooch, as Sordo would say,' mumbled the magician, 'test number three passed with honours.' He looked at the others. 'All right, we have exactly ten minutes till the explosion.'

'What explosion?' the dwarf piped up in panic.

'You received that information too, you are merely getting over-excited,' Gonzola admonished him. 'Every day the great bombs land here and they land in the enemy country across the dead black sea. Everything is atomized. Then everything reassembles again, exactly as it was before the explosion. The whole process takes one hour. That, by the way, is when we get our most effective work done.'

'But what happens to us?' pleaded the dwarf.

'Will you be calm, sweetie?' David hissed. He turned to the magician. 'Kranz lied, you know. Most of the Tritertium 333 formula is already in the system. Construction on the element is probably almost complete. We barely got the false adjustments in there on time.'

'I thought as much,' Gonzola nodded. 'Any moment now, he will have picked Barlocks's mind clean. We'll have to get Rimbek down inside the rocket today to check out the whole device. When they do insert the new elemental material into the warhead, all the sensor adjustments will have to be changed. That simply has to be by tomorrow. You two will take our little friend down into the silo. I'll remain on the empty plain to inform the children. Remember, out of the total hour, we have a nett working time of forty minutes. No more.'

'Did you say everything melts away, even the people, everything but us? Is it like dying?' the dwarf asked piteously.

'Yes, I'm afraid so,' the magician admitted. 'We four and the children remain in our normal state, feeling only the heat and wind. And the rocket remains intact too.'

'But they feel it — the people. It kills them, doesn't it?' The dwarf came closer and leaned on Gonzola's knee.

'Yes, little friend, they die horribly each and every day, century after century. It has to be so. To save the rest of the Cosmos from atomic devastation, they had to be trapped in this day forever. At the far ends of the earth, on the original day, some few did survive. With the help of their people — ' Gonzola nodded towards the two Elves — 'those survivors founded the world we know.'

The dwarf jumped back. 'Help! I have a terrible burning, a burning right in here,' he yelped, pointing to the buttons on his blue work trousers.

'Quick, men, lift him up to the sink. He's not used to the new equipment yet,' Gonzola ordered, rising himself to help.

The Elves popped the dwarf up on the sink, fishing his penis out rapidly. It was short, thick and purple. A sudden burst of urine splashed out.

'Rather nice in a horrible sort of way, don't you think?' David asked Ian.

'Oh, I don't know. Terribly dark, isn't it?' Ian answered. They each slipped an arm round Rimbek and both of them grabbed the penis as it jumped with one gush after another.

'Stop it, stop it!' howled the dwarf.

'That's what it's for, silly,' the two said in unison, moving their hands faster and faster, drawing the foreskin far back from the bulbous brown tip.

The door burst open and Kranz stuck his head in, nodded once towards the sink and winked at Gonzola.

'Great team you've got there, Warner. No time now, have to see you after the blast. Only four minutes left.'

The head disappeared and they heard the door across the corridor opening, then being bolted securely again.

'Test number four, passed with flying colours,' murmured the magician. 'Very good, boys.'

XVII

In the Teeth of the Holocaust

The soundless wind vacuums drew unthinkable heat closer to Gonzola, Astra and Flondrix as they waited on the devastated plain where the city had stood a few minutes earlier. Everything else had been pulverized into dust that whirled and eddied, settled for a few seconds only to rise again on the next tidal wave of scorching air. When their building melted, the six figures had floated down to the dust choked, bleak landscape. As they settled, Yana, Themur and Rimbek had raced off for the hidden silo, racing against the precious forty minutes they had in which to make all the needed calculations.

The children had been startled to see and feel the dreadful reality of the holocaust — the first time they had not been in a deep coma of forgetfulness during this shattering hour. Although they had never seen Gonzola before, they sensed his identity as he gathered them to himself protectively.

*

As Gonzola watched the misty figures in the distance locate the silo and disappear below the ground, he explained Kranz's demonic plot to the bewildered children. He told them about the dreadful machine buried in the ground, its course already set for Topar, its warhead loaded with what Kranz believed would be Tritertium 333. If it should ever arrive with that ultimate element, it would be the end of the Cosmos as they knew it, the end of all that was Elvan. Even the Ancient Ones would have to withdraw, leaving the great Ra-Chand Force to fall into Kranz's evil hands; it too would be converted into a malignant force of destruction. With the help of the dwarf and the two from Elvanhome, Gonzola was converting the element back to 332 and surreptitiously changing every recorded bit of information to delude Kranz. Dropping the power of the force down one grade would make it possible for Elvanlord to destroy the dreaded vehicle in mid-course without harm to the Cosmos. But he would have only ten seconds in which to render the machine harmless. Just now, he told them, Yana, Themur and Rimbek were gathering all the vital mechanical information they needed. Tomorrow, Rimbek alone would have to enter the warhead and make the physical changes. Only he could withstand the terrifying force long enough to do so.

With Rimbek on his shoulders, Yana came swiftly towards the three waiting figures, Themur following quickly behind. Astra smiled brightly in greeting.

'Elvanlord can do it, can he not?' she asked the two Elves. They nodded and turned their faces sadly.

'Kranz has taken one terrible precaution against that,' Gonzola whispered into the dying winds. 'He plans to send you two on that dreaded voyage. He was not sure what Elvanlord could do, so he is taking no chances.'

Flondrix and Astra spoke at once, asking why they could not leave with the others when they returned to their own world. The magician shook his head unhappily and nodded to Yana.

'If we do that, Kranz will know we were here. He will discover everything we have done. It will start all over again. Next time, we may not be able to stop him.'

'But next time, he won't have us,' Astra insisted.

'He should not have had you this time,' Gonzola reminded her.

A long silence followed. Rimbek hung his head dejectedly and wanted to cry. Yana and Themur looked out over the plain in great misery. Gonzola turned his head away so he would not have to see the eyes of the children looking long and painfully into each other's.

'Gonzola,' Astra called, 'we have decided. We must go. We are ready. It can be no other way.' She turned to Yana and Themur. 'You must promise us that Elvanlord will not spare us. He cannot, it is unthinkable.' She drew Flondrix to her and they held each other with all the courage in their hearts.

'Are you sure of that?' the magician asked. 'If there is one small question, one tiny doubt, you must say so now. If Kranz senses anything like that in your innermost thoughts, we will all be exposed and the only chance we have of preventing this catastrophe will be ruined.'

The look of fierce pride in Flondrix's eyes, the sheer disdain written on his face at such a suggestion, was all the answer any of them needed. Gonzola blinked once and turned to the dwarf.

'Well, mighty workman, what is the news?'

'You were right, Gonzola, there is one adjustment I can make which will not alert the computers. At the same time, the sensors can be set as warning signals for Elvanhome. I will tell you this, that stuff is fantastically powerful.'

'Yes,' the magician said eagerly, 'but will your mantle do the trick for safe dispersal?'

'I believe so. We've handled something like it in our mountains. One degree down elementally and the mantle will work. But I hate to think what my brothers will say when they find out it is gone.'

'Do you think Kranz will be ready tomorrow?' Themur asked, winking knowingly at Rimbek.

As they were busily talking, Rimbek bent down to the ground to sort some of the tools in his sack. Seeing Astra and Flondrix fully engaged with one another, the wily dwarf reached up quickly and plucked one silver-tipped golden hair from each pubis. The children jumped, but when they looked round, the dwarf was closing up the sack with his back to them.

'. . . So, as I expect by now that the tempests in the Dark King's castle have reached their climax,' Gonzola concluded, 'tomorrow will surely be the day. Hurry, positions everyone, we have no time to lose.'

Astra and Flondrix found the exact spots in the dust where they had been when the explosion subsided. The magician, Yana and Themur and the dwarf found their places; the two Elves bending over together, the dwarf leaning down with a tool in his hand and the magician standing apart, looking off in the distance. Soon they started to lift off the ground and move up towards the sky. As they did, the first shadowy aspect of a great city, forming itself atom by atom, began appearing mistily. The six figures seemed like solid dots in the hazy atmosphere.

A few minutes later, Astra and Flondrix were back in their cages, high up in the skyscraper. Across the corridor, the other four were working feverishly in their laboratory.

XVIII

King Barlocks
Plumbs the Heights and the Depths

The Dark King stretched out on the large new bed in his completely refurnished chamber. New curtains, new chairs, tapestry wall hangings and bright red drapes gave the place a festive air, quite different from the old sombre fittings that had become rather tatty over the years. In fact, a woman's touch could be detected in practically everything, including the curtained cubicle in a corner near the bed. It contained a wash-stand, a rather elementary bidet and a commode.

The king looked over towards the drawn curtains of the cubicle, his attention attracted by sounds of splashing. Every now and then, parts of a woman's figure could be seen momentarily pressed against the curtain. As the occupant leaned over sharply, the clear outline of a lovely pair of buttocks was impressed on the thin material. The king whipped a hand under his long night-shirt and began massaging his penis with ardour and deep concentration.

'Are you at it again?' a voice reached him from behind the curtain. He pulled his hand out as if it had been scalded. He frowned for a moment, annoyed with his cowardly reaction. He pulled the night-shirt up past his ribs and exposed the semi-turgid object which lolled about in a quarter circle, the tip just grazing the skin of his abdomen. With a defiant look imprinted on his face, he made a round sweeping gesture, gathering the large tool up tenderly and masterfully in his hand.

'Do you ever think of anything else?' the voice called to him, clearly tinged with a mixture of mischief and sarcasm.

'How do I know what you are doing in there?' he yelled back. 'Ever since you had that stupid thing installed, with a foot pump that sprays water up you, I think you take your pleasures behind that curtain.'

'We were not talking about me, we were talking about you,' the soft musical voice came back with perfect feminine logic. 'If you think you are missing something in here, you are always welcome to try it out.' There was a short pause. 'Incidentally, do you ever wash that thing, or do you think I run a tongue in cheek laundry service? Perhaps I should say, a "schlong" in cheek laundry service.'

'Will you stop using those foul dwarfish words,' the king ordered. 'Considering your dratted high royal background, such language sounds exceedingly vulgar.'

A ringing laugh taunted him. 'Considering the foul and unspeakable things his royal majesty commands me to do for him, it is amazing how an odd word here and there ruffles his feathers.' More splashing sounds were heard, then the friction of a towel. 'My dear,' the voice continued, 'if I came to bed with an uncleansed cleft, you would call it outrageous names and say it sickened you like tainted fish.'

'What outrageous names have I ever called it?' he roared, pausing in his stroke.

'Oh . . .' the sound of water swishing around in her mouth choked off the voice . . . 'what was it? Yes, a bewhiskered oyster, that was it.'

'I never said that,' the king shouted, 'don't you ever get *anything* right? It's a bearded clam — *that's* what I said!'

'If I take the time needed to do the job properly,' the voice went on, ignoring his shouts, 'if I make a garden of roses for you to feast upon, you cast all sorts of aspersions on this perfectly logical device I had the blacksmith build. There is simply no pleasing you, Barley.'

'Don't call me Barley!' he howled.

'Very strange,' the voice murmured. 'You can lie there manipulating your great thing, but I must not call you endearing names. You would try any woman's patience.' There was a short pause, followed by an insinuating, humming sound. 'Speaking of trying patient women, I think I shall go straight downstairs and crawl into bed with one of the chambermaids.'

'Don't you dare!' warned the king.

The splendid presence of Glortina moved through the aperture in the curtains. Naked, she strolled slowly across the room, dragging a large mauve towel behind her on the newly carpeted stone floor. She dropped the towel regally and reached up into a fine mahogany wardrobe to withdraw a chiffon night-dress in pure white with purple hem, collar and cuffs. She drew it on and tied the wide band of purple tightly about her waist. Even in mortal guise she was the most beautiful of creatures. One would hardly notice the deeper gold of her hair or the fact that there were no fiery tips on her maidenhairs.

Barlocks drew his breath in and released his hold on the throbbing member, his gaze riveted on the full breasts which pulsated as she breathed; his feverish eyes darted to the soft pubic area which undulated invitingly as she crossed to her toilet table to brush her hair.

221

'I could come no hands, just looking at you,' he hissed through clenched teeth. She ignored the flattering remark, her attention still focused on the last imperious shout.

'Why should I not go down to one of the chambermaids?' she asked herself in the mirror with a musing expression. 'Granted, not too clean, not too sweet, but there would be no complaints. A kiss in the cleft anywhere at random — just *any*where — would send impassioned moans reaching for the sky. But with *him*?' She raised her eyes significantly and tossed her hair to one side, changing the direction of the brush strokes. 'Instructions, instructions, instructions,' she confided to her image, then changed the tone of her voice, imitating the king's petulant waspishness. 'No, no, not like that. Just a little more to the right side. Yikes! Watch that tooth. That dratted tooth should be filed down, I've told you a thousand times . . . no, no, you are going to fast! What the drat are you rushing for? Easy, easy . . . now get down there further, get it all in . . . get it all, don't you spit out one drop, drat you, or I'll strangle you!'

A peal of bright laughter filled the room. She turned and looked at his purpling face. 'You know, my dear,' she said aloud, 'you should never threaten to strangle a woman while you are in the act of choking her. Very bad manners indeed.'

'Will you come over here?' Barlocks breathed menacingly.

'Of course, light of my life, but not until I have done my one hundred strokes. With my brush, that is. I imagine you have done yours already, have you not?' she asked archly.

Seeing his face contorting dangerously, she put down the brush and moved to the edge of the bed, smiling down at him. She reached out one of her slender, lovely hands and patted his monster lightly, watching it shudder. With two fingers and her delicate thumb, she pulled the foreskin up, drawing it over the swollen glans, then released it suddenly.

'No more dratted games!' he choked. 'I want you and I want you now.' He clutched her arm and pulled her towards him. 'I have longed for you, dreamed of you, suffered the tortures of the damned for you all these years and you hold me at arm's length now? I've waited long enough. Ever since lunch!'

From across the great gap of time, Kranz's mind reached out for hers, his will binding hers with promises of power beyond all known power. Power supreme over the whole Cosmos, hers to share when her enemies were defeated, when those who had deserted her and left her to this ignoble fate had been vanquished. For one tiny instant, another voice reached her, a voice way back in her memory of previous being. It asked her what she was doing, what she had become . . . was she then the fabled nemesis of her people . . . but the voice was gone and Kranz's will fastened on hers again.

Glortina's face became pinched, fixed with a hungry, desperate look, an animal look, half cunning, half greedy, but more than all those. It was the look that crosses a human face when all other orientation is lost in the lust for power and revenge. With hardly a discernible change of line or shadow, that lovely face became distorted, as though its normal glow had taken on an evil aeruginous cast.

'No more games?' she purred. 'Then we have to start concentrating, don't we? You have to let your mind go back across the aeons to the source of your race memory. You must concentrate on Tritertium 333. On that very last three. There is one little segment left, remember? Well, find it! Find it and bring it forth as you let your mind go completely, submitting yourself to all the incredible pleasures I shall give you. Pleasures of sexual magic that will drive you winging beyond the beyond. Concentrate!'

Barlocks felt himself slipping, his mind no longer his own, caught in the grasp of something so powerful his senses reeled with awe and terror. As the last vestige of control was sliding from his grasp, his eyes looked into hers, pleading.

'Why?' he rasped, his voice hardly audible. 'Why are you doing this, you of all people?'

Ignoring his plea, her head plunged down and the whole of his swollen shaft disappeared inside her mouth. A great and ghostly organ chord resonated in the chamber, filling his ears and sending unbearable vibrations through his bones. He felt his mind shatter into millions of fragments, tossed by strange winds, as the overwhelming and almost unendurable pleasure took hold of him totally. Behind his eyes, as though reflected on a great screen, the complex formula segment of Tritertium 333 appeared; as it came into sharp focus, he began to scream with utter abandon.

*

Across the unspeakable gap of time, Kranz heard the scream and sat bolt upright on his laboratory table, his legs crossed and tucked beneath him, his face a mask of deep concentration. His eyes were pulled far back into his head and he was oblivious to the night and the stars outside the windows of the building that towered to the sky. The complex formula appearing behind Barlocks's eyes reached him; the hand clutching the pen began racing over a pad on the table, strange glyphs and mystical symbols, complex mathematical equations appearing on the paper with incredible speed. The smallest smile lingered in the corner of Kranz's mouth . . . a smile of victory.

224

Seated in their cages, the grim and defiant faces of Astra and Flondrix looked out at him through the steel mesh with deep loathing.

In the laboratory across the corridor, Rimbek snored serenely on the steel table next to the model rocket engine. Yana and Themur, who had been bent over laboratory equipment for hours, held up two small test tubes which became illuminated by the light of stars in the darkened room.

Gonzola gazed up at the test tubes from behind his desk, his eyes asking the unspoken question. The two Elves nodded affirmatively. From the two delicate hairs, plucked surreptitiously by Rimbek from Astra and Flondrix, they had made a perfect cloning essence. When tomorrow's work was done, two exact replicas of the children would be locked in Kranz's cages.

The old magician nodded his thanks and smiled grimly. He was deeply disturbed because he would have to deceive the children, but it was the only way. They would all be returning to Glortan together, but if they had given the captives any indication of that plan today, Kranz would surely have detected their excited anticipation. They would also have had to tell the children about the replicas they would create from the two hairs. The magician knew only too well how strong the doppelgänger syndrome could be. Astra and Flondrix would feel so emotionally attached to their duplicates the misery would be almost unbearable for them.

Gonzola sighed and leaned back in his chair. Yes, the children would fall into a deep trance during the journey back across time. It would give the rest of them an opportunity to ease the pain for Astra and Flondrix, a pain that would be profound and agonizing for their exact doubles who would perish in Kranz's foul space machine.

XIX

Ever Tighter
the Skeins of Fate

❀❀❀❀❀❀❀

Five minutes before the blast the next day, Kranz stopped at Dr Warner's laboratory to congratulate the boys on the splendid technical job they had done. Apologizing for the fact that he would not see them after the blast, he left with all Warner's calculations.

Fevered activity broke out again as soon as his footsteps had crossed the corridor and the doors there had been bolted. Yana had the two test tubes in his hand and he secreted them, carefully wrapped, in Rimbek's tool sack while Themur strapped the mantle on the dwarf's shoulders. Gonzola busily stuffed slips of paper in his pockets. He turned and looked at the Elves. They nodded assent. Rimbek's head bounced up and down affirmatively. They all closed their eyes as the horrendous sound and incredible heat struck the building.

In the settling dust on the empty plain, Gonzola seemed to be everywhere at once. For a few moments he was below in the silo, leaving only when the dwarf prepared to enter the nose cone of the great machine. Yana and Themur were just as busy, one running off as the other returned to keep the children company.

When the precious forty minutes were almost over, Gonzola returned to the children, but his eyes were riveted to the spot where Rimbek must emerge at any moment. The great cloud billowed higher and higher over their heads, the tidal winds diminishing until at last there was total silence.

Rimbek's head appeared above ground, followed by his squat body. The magician signalled furiously and the dwarf ran as fast as he could, kicking up great quantities of dust as he raced towards them. His little legs pumping like pistons, he was wishing he had his proper schlong so he could do the corkscrew spring-leap.

'The rest of Rimbek's tools are over there,' Gonzola said rather off-handedly to Yana, 'would you pick them up?'

Yana moved over to the sack and bent down, apparently arranging things. Next to the tools were the two sets of footprints originally made by Astra and Flondrix. No one saw him empty the contents of one test tube into Flondrix's prints, the contents of the other into Astra's. He popped the empty tubes into the sack and picked it up, rejoining the group just as Rimbek puffed up.

Gonzola grabbed Rimbek's hand as soon as the tools were tossed over his shoulder. The two tall Elves grabbed the children's hands and moved them closer. A second later, all hands were joined and both Flondrix and Astra looked round the circle in astonishment. Then Astra's eyes saddened.

'This is good-bye, then,' she sobbed, pressing close to Flondrix. 'We'd better stand in our proper places.'

'Just a few seconds more,' breathed Gonzola. 'Let's all close our eyes for those few seconds and give our deepest thanks, one to another, in our hearts.'

Before the children could guess what was happening,

the shadowy steel walls had formed and the dreadful downward time plunge had started. They shrieked and tried to break away, but the bonds of energy that held them all together were too strong. Down into the abysmal void of time they hurtled, their voices lost to all ken.

*

In the clearing of the quiet valley in the great forest, the imitation tree house Kranz had wrought to capture the children formed itself against the sky. Gonzola's great black horse looked up and neighed. The other two horses turned, looked at their companion, then raised their heads towards the tree tops. Unlike ordinary horses, they neither balked nor panicked. A few muscles twitched and they stood their ground.

Gonzola and Rimbek were the first two to slide down the long silken rope from the tree tops. They were followed by Yana and Themur, each carrying an inert form across his shoulders. Rimbek fussed and looked miserable, kicking at the ground near the horses; he felt as though he had been an accomplice in a foul plot. Gonzola stood next to him, his arm over his shoulders, trying to console him. Dwarfs, he knew, are usually a bit crafty and not quite so high-minded. He hoped Rimbek would be able to cope with his normal life in the White Mountains after so much exposure to Elvan sensitivity.

Astra and Flondrix were in deep comas, the result of their exposure to Kranz's emanations and the journey they had just made. They had had none of the refortifying the others had undergone, and this was impossible to accomplish in the short interval before leaving the blasted city. It would be some hours before they recovered.

When the two tall Elves joined them, Gonzola

asked them to take the children on their horses. While they were still unconscious, Yana and Themur must reach their minds and explain what had happened and why. The children would be terribly upset about the replicas left in their places, but they would have to learn to accept this; they had to know that even Elvanlord might have blanched at destroying the real Flondrix and Astra.

Nodding, the two silent and deeply concerned Elves mounted their horses with the children in their arms. Gonzola swung his long leg over the saddle and leaned over to lift Rimbek up behind him. The horses moved up the side of the valley in a long, easy lope.

When they were about two hundred yards along the path, the horses halted and Gonzola reached under his cloak to withdraw a short, thick bar of a strange metal that gleamed with sullen foreboding in the bright sunlight. He held it out at arm's length and Yana leaned back, extending his arm until his fingertips touched the end of the bar. Themur turned and extended his hand to touch Yana's shoulder. The bar of glowing metal began to throw off showers of sparks. The effect was so eerie and disturbing that Rimbek hid his face in the folds of the magician's cloak. When the metal turned white, Gonzola drew his arm back and threw the bar in a high arc, the trajectory bringing it down, spinning end over end until it struck the now shadowy platform in the trees below. There was a blinding flash and the platform vanished.

'Well, that is the end of that,' the magician murmured. He turned his head and gazed at Yana. 'You are certain that Kranz will not be able to detect your resetting of his time channel?'

'When he comes to us, he will arrive at Glortan's real tree house, I assure you,' the Elf smiled.

'Comes to us?' squeaked the dwarf. 'Is he really?'

He coughed once, feeling his skin crawl. 'What – what will he do?'

'He's coming to fight the final battle of the worlds,' Gonzola answered, no small amount of colour draining from his tired face. 'And that is a battle none of us in the entire Cosmos can afford to lose,' he added, half to himself.

Before Rimbek could ask his next question, the black horse shot forward and the other two fell in behind. Mile after mile melted behind them as Gonzola watched the sun sink; he wanted to get those children back to Glortan as fast as he could.

XX

Bright Expectations
and Dark Premonitions

Gonzola laid out cheese, crisp apples, boiled eggs and a number of slices of brown bread on the stones surrounding their campfire. With small forked twigs, Rimbek busied himself toasting the bread over the coals; Gonzola rose, stretched his arms and legs and walked over to the saddles, gazing down at the children sleeping. Their tired young bodies were covered in leaves where they lay, wrapped in each other's arms, in the accommodating hollow between the roots of an enormous white birch tree. The magician leaned over and pulled a small flask of rich red wine from one of the seemingly bottomless saddle bags.

Two sips of ordinary wine would never have driven the tiredness from his bones so swiftly. When he stored the flask, twenty years fell from his face and stature. He smiled, wondering what those two from Elvanhome had put into the wine. Through narrowed eyes, he watched the last streaks of pink being absorbed in the intensifying blues and purples of the western sky behind the camp. One strong shaft of orange light still held the uppermost pinnacle of the elusive White

231

Mountains to the south-east. They had been riding hard all day, following the outer edge of the enchanted forest as it unrolled before them in a north-easterly direction. Tomorrow, they would turn due east and pound across the long, long trail that cut through the forest south of the Dark King's Realm. At the end of that trail was the Sacred Glade. So far, so good; but the old man knew he would not breathe easily until that Glade surrounded them all.

Rimbek whistled softly to himself as he turned the bread to toast on the other side. His infectious good spirits eddied through the cosy little clearing. In the distance, a small brook, tumbling over stones, answered the dwarf's soft whistle. He turned to beckon the magician when the toast was done.

Yana and Themur moved silently across the carpet of the forest, their appearance already considerably less solid-looking than it had been when they mounted their horses that morning. Yana carried a small pot of water which he placed on the edge of one of the stones so that it would warm rapidly over the fire. Themur searched in his saddle bags for a very small flask and a bag of luminous cloth, tied with a drawstring of plaited silver threads.

Returning to the fire, Gonzola watched Themur pour four drops of liquid from the flask into the pot. Next, he extracted four small, round yellow-brown balls from the cloth pouch and dropped them into the pot. Yana watched the brew carefully, registering every degree of temperature rise with his eyes. As Themur returned to his saddle, Gonzola called after him.

'Are you quite sure you didn't take the wrong yellow ball from that pouch?'

The tall Elf smiled and turned. His figure seemed only dimly limned against the darkening sky. He placed his hand on his chest, moving it up until,

against the back of his hand, a smaller pouch materialized. He squeezed the pouch so that Gonzola would
know there was one spherical shape inside.

'That is with me night and day. And there it will
stay until . . .'

'Until!' Gonzola broke in emphatically, holding up
a warning hand. The Elf smiled in acknowledgement
and returned to the fire when he had stored the flask
and larger pouch.

Finally, Yana lifted the pot and nodded to Themur.
They crossed to the sleeping children and removed all
the leaves. They fed each a mouthful of the brew and
quickly rubbed handfuls of it over every part of their
bodies. A warm glow soon radiated from Flondrix and
Astra. They smiled with happy, new strength in their
sleep. Astra drew Flondrix's head closer, to cradle it
more comfortably on her shoulder. The tall Elves
covered them over with leaves again and the children
slept on. When they returned to the fire, they each
had a mouthful of the brew and rubbed the remainder
over their bodies.

His eyes wide with wonder, Rimbek stuffed the
last egg into his mouth and chewed happily.

'Is that all they are going to eat?' he whispered to
Gonzola.

'That's all they need,' the old man answered simply.
When Rimbek looked up again, the two figures, which
had seemed so solid after the application of the broth
in the pot, were beginning to fade once more.
Rimbek's mouth was half opened in protest when
Yana announced that he and Themur would drift off
now until the morning. They wished the magician and
the dwarf a pleasant and easy night. The Elves would
be resting, but they would also be alert.

'They *are* disappearing . . . vanishing. Look!'
moaned the dwarf, suddenly missing them very much.

'They are under that tree, one on either side of the children, protecting them. Now finish your supper,' Gonzola ordered. He sniffed the air, shook his head and reached inside his cloak. Into the fire he pitched a pinch of red powder; the fire died down, glowered a few seconds and belched up a ghastly cloud of dark grey smoke. In moments, a terrible stench pervaded the small clearing and rapidly worked its way through the woods on all sides. A moan of disgust sounded from the area under the birch tree. Three more moans followed.

'Ugh!' choked Rimbek. 'What did you do *that* for? There was such a beautiful smell from the Elves' stuff — whatever it was they drank and bathed in.'

'Precisely,' agreed the magician grimly. 'Any sensitive nose with a bit of craft behind it would have no trouble knowing there were Elves in the vicinity. For ten miles about — north, south, east, west, to say nothing of straight up or straight down.'

As he spoke, a very faint green light shone from the fire. It flickered this way and that, like a ferret's nose, searching a scent. The magician's face blanched; he rolled over on the ground, wrapping Rimbek in his cloak as he did so. He was careful to cover the dwarf's mouth with one hand so he could not call out. They remained rolled up in the great cloak for quite a few minutes. When the magician pulled back a fold of the cloth to peer out, the greenish flame was gone. He sat up, holding Rimbek close to him, still wrapped in the cloak.

'Why did you do that? What did you see?' Rimbek whispered, his body caught in the greatest shiver of ugly premonition he had ever known. The feeling clung to him, no matter how he tried to shake it off. It was a terrible sensation, like hundreds of cold worms crawling over his body. Nervously, he tightened his coils round his waist and adjusted the barbed tip in the golden screw.

'You never answer *one* tiny question,' the dwarf complained, digging his elbow into the magician's ribs.

'The Beast Beneath is down there somewhere; he's sniffing about. I do not know if he has discovered our presence yet,' the wizard answered.

'But he can't get loose, what can he do to us?' Rimbek pointed in the direction of the birch tree. 'Bumbree is locked up securely, isn't she?'

Gonzola smiled and hugged the dwarf closer. He was like a curious child. One answer produced four new questions. Yes, Bumbree was locked up securely . . . now. Kranz was not and neither was Sordo. Daemon-Baalim's bonds seemed weaker already. With enough help . . . well, who could say the Beast Beneath would not break free? That would have to be a worry for the others, Rimbek had enough to do. The magician impressed upon him that it was of the greatest importance that he head for the White Mountains in the morning with great speed. He had to convince everyone there that they had searched far and wide, but had failed totally. They had never been able to find the children. Especially, he had to convince Sordo of this. If *he* got one inkling that this was not true, Kranz would find out soon enough, whether Sordo wanted him to or not.

Inside the small black box made of lead and Antertium 99 secreted in the dwarf's tool sack was enough of the element sample he had taken from the nose cone of Kranz's great rocket; enough for Rimbek to develop properly in the very bowels of the mountain. The fate of everyone depended upon him. He must go to sleep now so that he would be sure to arrive at the White Mountains before the magician and the Elves

235

arrived at the Sacred Glade. When the time came, Gonzola would send for him.

'How will you send for me? How will I know when the time comes?' Rimbek persevered.

'Tonight, while you sleep, Yana, Themur and I will teach you to thought-read. You will be able to receive messages from great distances this way. While we are at it, we will also teach you what you have to do with the contents of that black box. Everything must be ready on time. Now, will you go to sleep?'

'Tell me one more thing, please,' the dwarf coaxed. 'Why are Yana and Themur always becoming invisible?'

The magician laughed and shook his head. If you are visible, it takes great quantities of energy to become invisible, he explained. Since, in this world, those from Elvanhome appear invisible, they have to use up energy to be visible. Of course, then the dwarf wanted to know if they were visible back in Elvanhome. When the magician told him they were, he wanted to know if it then took energy for them to become invisible in Elvanhome. In Elvanhome, the magician went on tirelessly, there would be no reason. No Elf would ever do that. It would be deceitful. Elves don't hide from Elves.

'Never? Not even one Elf? Is there never such a thing as a bad Elf? Once in awhile, we get a bad dwarf.'

'No, there is no such thing,' Gonzola assured him. Inside his mind, however, another thought was forming. A thought he did not like to harbour. The one unpredictable card that could be played against them. Like the enigmatic card with a man hanging upside down.

'What are you waiting for?' the magician demanded, opening his cloak. 'Get up there and go to sleep. Right now!'

'Oh, all right. But I hate to leave you in the morning. Will – will Astra be – will she be all better?' There was a hint of moisture in Rimbek's eyes.

'Yes, Rimbek. We all love Astra. Show it by doing your part. A mighty important part it is, I assure you. Off you go.'

Reluctantly, his feet dragging, Rimbek approached the large tree just behind them. One great branch hung over the campsite and he measured it with his eyes. He pulled in his buttocks and uncoiled in a trice, heaving the sharp, steely tip of his schlong up over the limb. Straight up he sprang, landing squarely on the broad branch. Coiled again in a jiffy, he curled up comfortably against the trunk.

Gonzola moved back and braced himself against the tree, drawing his great cloak more tightly about him. He picked up his broad black travelling hat from the ground and jammed it down on his head, the brim lowered to his eyes. Those eyes smouldered as he watched the fire, attuning his thought pattern to those of the two Elves.

Concentrating intensely, he felt the first of Yana's thoughts come to him. Yana had been aware of the magician's thoughts when Rimbek had asked if there was never a bad Elf. Since the earliest days of Elvanhome, long before the time of men, it had been known that one day there would be a wayward Elf. Somewhere in the eternal stream of creation, one bad particle lay dormant. When it did surface, the stream would be cleansed forever and the evolution of the Elves would be completed. Yana's thought was in the form of a question. With all the difficulties ahead of them, did the magician have a premonition that this event was upon them? The magician could not hold back his answer. It was: yes. The ether was clear again as the Elves began tuning their sensitive thought projections to the dwarf in the tree. Gonzola heard a movement above.

'No thumping up there,' he growled to the branch above.

'You are as bad as my father and three brothers!' the hurt voice of Rimbek came back to him.

'See?' chortled the magician. 'You will be just as well off at home.'

*

Rimbek stood on the low ridge as the sun rose, watching the horses grow smaller and smaller as they moved down towards the plain below. They were skirting the enchanted forest, for the moment heading towards the far distant mountains to the north, the very same mountains Flondrix, as the innocent shepherd Igorin, had roamed with his sheep as a boy.

The dwarf knew that Gonzola and the Elves would turn into the forest in about one hour, changing course for the last time to head due east. They would rest and let the horses graze before they started the last long lap of the journey. There would be no further stops once they entered the thick wood. He looked behind him at the rising sun glinting on the spires of the White Mountains. If he started now and kept a good pace, he would be in Schtoonk's Schtronghold well before his friends approached the Sacred Glade.

With one last longing look at the figures diminishing on the landscape, he turned again and ran down the side of the ridge to the now deserted and lonely campsite. He scolded himself and told himself to stop acting like a deserted waif. With one last sweeping look about the quiet clearing, he took his platforms from the pocket inside his goatskin waistcoat and uncoiled. When he had the platforms in their proper places and well tightened, he did a few straight up and down spring-

238

leaps to make sure he had not lost his skill. Satisfied, he bounced off the platforms and reached down to pick up his sack of tools. As he raised it off the ground, the sack wriggled slightly and from somewhere below, he heard a noise, very muffled indeed, but much like an annoyed cat whose tail has been stepped on. Something popped menacingly in the dead fire and then he felt the earth tremble. The movement made the dwarf think that something was moving away . . . away towards the plain! Rimbek stood frozen in stark horror as seconds ticked away. He felt the premonition of the night before returning. He trembled indecisively, looking towards the rising sun, then back towards the ridge he had descended a few minutes earlier.

Rimbek stamped his foot, threw the heavy sack up and put his arms through the carrying straps, settling the load on his back and shoulders. He bounded on to the platform and, with his first great spring-leap, shot into the trees, heading north. Keeping the fringe of the forest in sight, he bounded erratically as he sped dizzyingly through the trees, missing them by mere fractions of an inch. All the while a fierce argument bubbled inside his head. Gonzola would be furious. The Elves would burn him with looks of scorn. Astra would refuse to talk to him. No, they would never have to know. He would hide, he would watch them until they remounted and thundered into the forest. Once they were on that last leg of the journey, he would feel better. A couple of hours would be lost, yes. He was willing to travel that much harder, deny himself rest or refreshment, if only he could be sure they started through the enchanted forest safely. He didn't know why, but he felt sure they would be safer once they entered the wood.

A voice inside his head asked him just what one small dwarf could do if his friends were in trouble.

Brushing that aside, at least he knew he would be with his friends if anything untoward happened.

Before the horses arrived at the terminus of the path which ran eastward through the heart of the enchanted forest, Rimbek was sitting just behind the outermost trees, a little to one side of the path, leaning against a towering oak. He watched the horses veer east to approach the path; as they drew closer, once again the strange prickling ran up and down his spine and he felt the dreadful sensation of the cold worms crawling on his skin. Then he knew for certain that something had vibrated beneath the floor of the forest, a tentative, searching movement difficult to pinpoint. Without even knowing why, he reached into the tool sack resting on the ground next to him and searched hurriedly for the small black box made of lead and Antertium 99. He placed the box on top of his head and settled back against the tree. Just as suddenly as it had begun, the restless probing beneath the ground dwindled and was gone.

While still about two hundred yards from the forest, Gonzola held up his hand and the party halted. They had almost reached the long shadows cast by the trees, the grass lush and dense on the open plain around them. The magician dismounted and turned the reins loose so the horse could graze. Yana and Themur, riding one horse, dropped lightly to the ground as Flondrix helped Astra down from the other. With sparkling eyes, Rimbek watched the four Elves clasp hands and form a circle. They began to dance over the grass, circling the grazing horses and leaping higher and higher, whirling at a furious pace. Soon, they were moving so breathlessly fast the dwarf could distinguish no more than a blur. Smiling, the magician sat down and reached inside his cloak for a couple of eggs which he downed with apparent relish.

Abruptly, the great black steed neighed so piercingly the very forest rang with the sound. He pawed the ground wildly and the other two horses reared up, screaming loud neighs of defiance. The dancers froze expectantly and Gonzola rose quickly to his feet. To the west of the group, straight ahead of Rimbek and only a hundred yards beyond where his friends stood rooted to the ground, a crashing rumble rent the ground. At a signal from the magician, the Elves became instantly invisible.

As they all watched in horror, an enormous cliff of rock shot straight up from the ground and rose giddily to a tremendous height with a cracking and shattering of stone, earth and air that nearly deafened the spectators. The rubble of countless rocks rolled across the gentle plain, making the horses rear up again, their nostrils flaring defiantly.

From inside the stone cliff, an imprisoned voice broke forth in a guttural rumble that rose to an ear-splitting crescendo, ending in a fit of maniacal laughter.

'Well,' the voice spat out, finally choking off its horrid mirth, 'the thief has arrived! The one who holds my priceless thrall, my captive slave. Revenge is sweet.'

Gonzola's hands shot out on either side of him; invisibly, the four Elves came quickly to join forces with him. The cliff trembled as they did, but it held firm.

'The once great magician makes puny jokes,' the rumbling voice smote them. 'Does he think he pits his strength against the weakened spirit once chained beneath? No, no, times are changing, proud Gonzola, times are changing and you read not well the winds of time. Now, you shall not subdue me so easily.'

The five standing before the cliff moved slowly, thrusting their bodies back and their joined hands forward until they had made of themselves the figure of a five-pointed star, the great pentacle of magic. The cliff trembled, wrenching and shaking, tearing loose the ground and vibrating wildly in the air. Yet again, save for some large slabs of rock breaking free from the upper surfaces, it held firm. The mad, riotous laughter mocked them once more, ringing across the plain.

'Keep trying, foul necromancer, keep trying. All your tricks and Elvangifts of cunning will not help you now. The winds and times are changing. Soon, I shall be free, fully free, the last restraining bonds split asunder and shredded forever. I have the forces now, I have the wills under my bidding. If you have the courage, step in here and challenge me. You will never step out again.'

'What do you want of me?' Gonzola shouted, his voice clear and defiant, but his heart grieved. He was not sure this new power of the Beast Beneath could be overcome.

'You know what I want,' the cliff growled back at him. 'I smell it. Render unto me that which is mine. Give me Bumbree!'

'And if I do not?' demanded the magician.

The dreadful laughter roared back from the cliff. 'You shall soon find out. The last time you won. But you lay there like the dead for a month or more, hardly breathing. You are older now and still mortal. I am stronger now and still eternal. I will devour you, you fool, and take back my treasure. Hurry, Gonzola, I am waiting.'

Glued to the tree, his lips contorted in grief and horror, the dwarf watched the face of his dear friend and knew he was communicating silently with the Elves. Though he could hear nothing, the method he had learnt in his sleep brought the thoughts to him. They came from everywhere at once, jumbled and difficult to sort out. It seemed the Elves were begging

Gonzola to give up the witch; they would take their chances, there must be another way to confine her. Gonzola felt the balance of power was already too fine and not necessarily in their favour ... Yana and Themur would understand that. The dwarf heard the rumbles of cruel laughter tearing through the walls of the cliff. The last thought the dwarf understood, before the rumble became a deafening roar, was Yana's. He assured Gonzola he would win, but it would mean giving all his strength. There would be little left of the magician for the days ahead ... when his help would be needed most.

When the roar did break loose, Rimbek was slammed into the tree, another enormous cliff rising only a few feet in front of him, nearly burying him in rough stones and pebbles. The small black box fell from his head and struck the rubble. As it did, the base of the cliff shrank back.

Rimbek understood everything at once. The black box! His friends were captured inside those great walls of rock. Daemon-Baalim was so close to full freedom he could bind them, virtual prisoners, with huge cliffs of stone towering over them on all sides. Could the horses be made to rise in the air as they had done once before? As if to answer that thought came the terrifying, raucous sounds of enormous birds circling the high cliffs. Great eagle vultures, twice the size of any horse. He knew the sound and he knew these gigantic birds had no fear of men, horses, magic or Elves.

Looking at the ground where the box trembled, then at the sack of tools sticking up through the pebbles, he pulled himself loose. With blinding speed he extracted the tools he needed, picked up the black box and stored it inside his waistcoat and whirled headlong into the cliff. Powdered rock shot out of the side of the cliff at an incredible rate, piling up in mounds as the harsh whirring bit dug deeper and deeper into the cliff. Rimbek did not open the box until he was well inside. Just as he caught the lid between his fingers, he breathed a fervent hope that he would still be alive when it was all over.

Tritertium 332, though not the ultimate form of the dreaded element, here began to do strange things deep inside the cliff. Everywhere stone melted and began pouring back into the ground at an astonishing rate. First the cliff crumbled, then began to evaporate into thin air. As though the entire thing were composed of wet papier mâché or melting wax, down and down it went, folding in on itself like a cake disturbed in an oven. The awful birds above screeched as they disappeared in the sky.

A terrifying howl rent the air so piercingly that the five prisoners on the plain held their ears. Inside the last remaining portion of rock, a second before it vanished, that sound did a lot to damage Rimbek's hearing for days on end.

The prisoners looked about them in amazement. Where cliffs had been, there was nothing but scorched, smoking grass. Some of the trees at the edge of the forest had been uprooted and were now leaning crazily against their neighbours. Then Gonzola's sharp eye spotted the small body sprawled at the rim of a still smouldering crevasse which was about to close. He watched the diminutive blackened figure shut a small box, stuff it inside his waistcoat and roll over on the smoking grass. The magician and the four Elves raced across the plain, followed by their horses.

As they ran, a stricken, garbled voice faintly squeaked from somewhere deep down under the dwarf: 'I'll get you, Gonzola, I'll get you yet!' Lying on the ground, at the very border of consciousness, Rimbek heard the words which were lost to those running towards him.

'Careful!' shouted Gonzola, halting the others in their tracks. He whipped off his great cloak and threw it over the dwarf, wrapping him round and round in many folds. He lifted the dwarf then and held him in his arms.

'You fool, you silly little fool,' he scolded, 'do you know how lucky you are to be alive?' Rimbek shook his head, clearing it and returning to full consciousness. He looked about, trying to recall just where he was.

'If the Beast had detected your presence in time, you'd be down there somewhere. For ever!' the magician fumed.

'Funny way to say thank you to a friend,' mumbled the dwarf, on the verge of tears.

'Absolutely right,' Astra chimed in, looking over Gonzola's shoulder. 'It must have been Rimbek who defeated that horror, but the method –' she looked at Yana and Themur quizzically – 'how did he do it?'

'I assume you closed that little black box carefully before you put it away, my friend,' the magician queried with a warning look. Rimbek nodded his head apprehensively. 'But you forgot I told you *never, never,* to open it until you got to the very base of your mountain, didn't you?'

'I didn't even think,' protested Rimbek, 'you were prisoners! What could I do? I just grabbed my tools . . . Oh!' he exclaimed, trying to struggle free of the magician's arms. 'My tools! Where are my tools?'

The tools were scattered all over the ground and Gonzola warned Yana and Themur to handle them gingerly and stow them in the sack as quickly as possible. He put Rimbek down and unwrapped him, hoping that the cloak had absorbed enough of the radiation. Kranz would quickly divine what Daemon-Baalim could not understand.

'Are you all right now?' he asked. Rimbek took a

245

few tentative steps and smiled up at the magician. Gonzola sat on his heels and hugged the dwarf warmly.

'Gonzola, I had to follow you,' Rimbek whispered. 'That premonition I had last night . . . remember when the fire turned green? It happened again today. He was under the campsite, I knew it. I knew something would happen.'

'We all owe so much to you, little friend,' Gonzola admitted with deep feeling. 'Now hear me well. You must be off like the wind. Stop only to wash well at the first river, for your experience has blackened you completely. Then straight for home, understand? As fast as you can spring-leap. Oh . . . about that missing mantle of yours. Tell them we were attacked by great eagle vultures. Sordo will believe that.'

'Will I see you soon? And — and Astra?' His voice sounded so forlorn that the four Elves gathered round and hugged and kissed him.

'You will be with us sooner than you think,' the magician promised him. He stood and called his horse. In a twinkling, they were all mounted and thundering down the path, lost almost immediately in the dense forest. Rimbek waved, looked once about the now deserted and scorched plain and got ready to spring-leap. Soon he passed the old campsite and was heading towards the White Mountains faster than he had ever travelled on his own before.

XXI

In My Lady's Chamber
A Nasty Plot Unfolds

۞۞۞۞۞۞۞

In the south-east tower of the Dark King's castle, just under the special dome which had been constructed there, was Gonzola's laboratory and observatory. A week after the journey to the Sacred Glade, the magician sat at his large table, which was cluttered with books and strange apparatus of all sorts. By the light of two large candles, he jotted notes in a small book that never left his person. He used the unknown characters of an ancient language, long forgotten by almost every inhabitant of this age of man.

He put down the pen and leaned back in the comfortable old leather chair. The children were back with Glortan and, after many long and worrisome discussions with the Elvan King, the final strategies had been agreed upon; Gonzola was to return to the Dark King's service and rest himself for the ordeal ahead. Now, already late into the night, the old man was still worrying himself with endless calculations, checking and rechecking every detail.

Looking across the room to assure himself the door was securely bolted, he put his hand under the table's surface and pressed a hidden control knob. Slowly, the platform on which table and chair stood began rising towards the ceiling. He blew out the candles and pressed another control knob. The domed ceiling opened in the centre, the two halves folding back. Table, chair and magician, in the pallid light, appeared to be suspended under the sky. With astrolabe and telescope, his nightly scanning of the sky commenced. Sheet after sheet of paper filled with figures, ciphers, glyphs and notations in the ancient characters he used. After an hour's intensive study, he leaned back and sighed. He and Glortan were still in total agreement. They knew the night Kranz would arrive, and they knew it would be the exact second the moon reached its zenith.

Yes, that they knew, that they could calculate with precision. But the few imponderables that remained vexed the old man sorely. When the shock of Daemon-Baalim's recent defeat at Rimbek's hands had worn off, how much had the Beast Beneath divined of the other 'presences' with the magician? Would Kranz read the truth there? Yana was guarding Bumbree, but what unpredictable accident might occur there? The pact between King Schtoonk and the Dark King was made; they would march against Glortan, assured of Kranz's unassailable power, but what of the will and mind of Sordo? And what of Rimbek, deep in the very roots of the White Mountains? Just one slip there . . . Gonzola sighed again and pushed the jumble of papers and instruments to one side.

Tapping his fingernails on the smooth surface of the table, he turned and stared at the pale light shimmering in the windows of the north-eastern tower. Faint shadows moved across the king's chamber. Reaching under the table, the magician made a few adjustments on hidden dials. A square panel, part of the central surface of the table, began rising on its own, secured near the front of the desk by tiny hinges and supported at the rear by slender rods. It stopped a few inches short of ninety degrees. In the recess beneath it, shallow trays of strange, luminescent fluids glowed in the dark. Gonzola reached round the erected square of shining desk surface and stuck a long forefinger into one of the shallow trays. The panel began to glow as shadows flickered across its surface. He selected another tray and stuck the forefinger of his free hand into that. Glortina's radiant, naked body appeared on the panel, as though seen hazily through the window of the chamber from immediately outside. The magician immersed both fingers more deeply in the liquids and Glortina's body filled the panel, sharp in every detail. Her lips were moving and the magician stuck one thumb into another solution. From behind the panel, Glortina's voice could be heard, softly at first, then becoming louder and clearer.

'Whatever has taken you so long, do you want to be late for your own banquet and the council of war?' Glortina stamped her exquisite foot as her face contorted with unbridled anger.

Barlocks stood just inside the chamber door, making way for an old, limping crone who entered, bowing, with piles of shimmering, gauzy cloth draped over her extended arms. Glortina whipped the cloth from the old woman's arms and shook it out, whirling it up in the air and down over her head. It fell in fold after fold over her body, becoming a breath-taking gossamer gown that trailed on the floor behind her. The crone fell to her knees and began making the last-minute adjustments on the hem in front.

Barlocks looked at the peerless vision before him and his hand unconsciously slid down the front of his hose. His other hand remained on his hip, a large velvet cap suspended from the fingers. He was attired in a

249

beautifully tailored black velvet tunic, hose and slippers, all of them emblazoned with small golden crowns, delicately embroidered.

Impetuously, Glortina pulled the dress away from the horny hands as the needle made the last stitch; she turned and viewed the result in her new, floor-length polished silver mirror. One indifferent raised eyebrow was as much approval as she could offer for the weeks of painstaking labour. The crone, still on her knees, turned to pick the last remnants of thread from the carpet. Pushing her feet into small golden sandals, Glortina spun round and gave the old woman a vicious kick, sending her sprawling across the carpet.

'Get out of here! Haven't you fussed about long enough?' she screamed.

Whimpering and jibbering, the crippled seamstress hobbled from the chamber as quickly as she could.

'Close that door — and get your hand out of there!' Glortina snarled at the startled king. He looked down, amazed to find his own hand where it was. He yanked it free and blushed.

'I thought maybe . . . if we had a few spare minutes . . .'

'Will you listen to me?' she demanded, picking up a brush from the toilet table and whipping it angrily through her hair. 'You have to be bright and alert tonight. There are a few delicate points concerning your alliance with Schtoonk the barons don't like. We must win them over. Don't you understand? We cannot afford any dissension in the ranks.'

'Glortina, darling, why don't you leave all that to . . .'

'Leave what to you?' she cut him off mockingly. 'Have you not bungled enough already? Do you think we have all the time in the world?' Glortina dropped the brush on the table with a clatter, kicking the long train behind her as she turned in front of the window. She gazed up at the moon and stars, pursing her lips. 'Little enough time, indeed,' she murmured.

'Oh, darling, you are just getting yourself upset over nothing,' Barlocks soothed, stepping up behind her and slipping his arms about her. She tore herself loose and stormed back to the mirror.

'I asked you a question earlier today,' she reminded him, 'and you still have given no answer. What are you going to do about *him*?'

'About who?' he asked, rubbing his nose.

'About *whom*!' she corrected. 'About that useless old buffoon, Gonzola. Did you actually invite him to the banquet tonight? *And* the council of war afterwards?'

'Well, naturally,' he hemmed nervously, 'everyone knows he is my most trusted adviser.'

'No, everyone does *not* know,' she turned on him, scowling. 'Some of the most powerful barons and earls suspect him of the greatest treachery. And so do I. They suspect him of trafficking with that fatuous brother of mine.'

'Glortina, that's not fair. He was Glortan's prisoner. He was held hostage for your safety here,' Barlocks wheedled, trying to put his arms about her again.

'Stop that!' she ordered, slapping his hand. 'Maybe *you* believe that story. I certainly do not. What was he up to? Do you really know?'

'My dear, he did arrange to get that dreadful curse taken off me.' His eyes roved adoringly over her. 'And he did arrange the most wonderful thing that ever happened to me . . . you.'

'Arrrgh!' she snarled, with extreme vexation. 'You are the most exasperating imbecile I have ever encountered.'

'Glortina, please don't be like this. What do you want me to do?' he begged.

'Send him away. Send him away tonight.' She stepped closer to the king and ran her fingers through the thick unruly curls on his head.

'How can I do that? He is already invited . . .'

'How can I do that?' she mimicked. 'Very easily. Send him a message . . . no, better still, send him an official, sealed document, an important mission.'

'You're confusing me,' he complained. 'What sort of mission?'

'He is to go to my brother. He is to sue for peace. He will tell my brother that you have had second thoughts, that this whole campaign is ill-conceived. Yes, and that you wish to betray the dwarfs and join forces with him,' she concluded, smiling.

'Your brother would never believe that . . . now,' Barlocks said, not quite sure why he said so. After his mind and the race memory it held had been drained, a convenient blank had been left in its place.

'Precisely,' she murmured, rubbing her tantalizing breasts against the soft velvet of his tunic. 'My brother will know him for a renegade or a raving lunatic. In either case, he will bind him so that he can do no more harm. We will all be able to breathe easier then.'

'But I can't just go to Gonzola . . .'

'Do you never listen?' she demanded. 'You send a sealed document of state. Send it with Rodney de Minge. He is tough-minded, incisive and completely ruthless. Gonzola is to be on his way within the hour.'

'How can I do a thing like that? All these years he has been . . .' the king attempted to dissuade her but she caught his head between her hands and drew him closer.

'If you will kneel down in front of me,' she coaxed, picking up a golden comb from the table next to the large mirror, 'I'll comb out your hair.' As she said this, she hiked up the hem of her dress. With a look of greedy delight, the monarch fell to his knees.

She combed his hair indolently as his face hungrily burrowed between her exposed thighs.

'And you will add to that document that he is prohibited, for reasons of state, from taking that ugly black beast from the stables. Nor can the throne spare him another horse. He will make his journey on foot. That should take him some time.'

The king's amazed eyes and pearl-soaked beard appeared. 'He doesn't need a horse. He has other ways of travelling – swifter than the wind.'

Glortina laughed until tears rolled down her cheeks. 'Barley, you are the bitter end. Do you honestly think that old fool could find his way out of a flour sack?'

'But we *need* a magician. I won't feel – well – safe without him.' The king's eyes were truly stricken as he spoke.

'Don't be such a fool! Sordo will be here in a day or two to help conclude the alliance. He is a lot more trustworthy than Gonzola ever was. We will have powerful allies too, fear not.'

'Whom?' he asked.

'*Who*,' she corrected teasingly. 'We shall talk about that when the time comes. Now, do you want me to comb your hair or don't you?' She put the comb between her teeth and grabbed his ears, pressing his face between her legs. As she combed, her nose wrinkled disdainfully at the greedy, guzzling sounds below.

*

Gonzola pulled his fingers out of the trays and the picture faded immediately. Whistling lightly, he made many hurried adjustments. As the platform descended with a barely audible hiss, the top of the table lowered, resuming its normal appearance. When the platform touched the floor, the wizard pushed all the masses of books and equipment back into their usual disorderly array.

Down the stairs and across the huge courtyard, he slipped in and out of the shadows, never alerting one of the many guards milling about. Quietly, he saddled and bridled the great black steed and whispered softly in his ear. Five minutes later he was back in the observatory, the candles flickering and bouncing bright, twinkling reflections off his deep-set eyes as he busied himself over a small knapsack. He left it standing inconspicuously in a corner, his broad black travelling hat on top of it.

Humming tunelessly, he sat in his big chair behind the table, crossing his elegant black-booted ankles on the papers scattered over the table's surface. Twenty minutes later, as he heard heavy footfalls on the tower stairs, he was deeply engrossed in an ancient tome which described some of the more unusual sexual fancies of pre-historic water sprites and woodland nymphs.

Gonzola smiled at the thunderous, splintering knock at the heavy oaken door. Baron Rodney de Minge used the pommel of his great broadsword for practically everything. Gonzola shrugged; many strapping men tend to be a bit impotent, he reflected.

'Come in, the door is unlocked,' he called out cheerfully.

De Minge entered with a scowl, crossed the room ponderously and tossed a sealed scroll onto the wizard's table. He stood there, his brows beetling, waiting for the magician to read it.

Gonzola broke the seal and pretended to read the document with great interest, nodding his head seriously as his dilated eyes flew back and forth across the lines.

When he looked up, de Minge was still standing motionless, his hands on his hips.

'My greetings to his majesty,' the sage said politely, 'and his wish shall be my command. I will be on my way in less than half an hour.' He held the document over one of the candles and kept it there until there was nothing left but a few charred flakes at the base of the candlestick.

The heavy footfalls of de Minge thundered down the stairs, the door left ajar behind him. Gonzola pursed his lips and cocked his head, waiting until the last echo died. He rose, clicked his heels and did a small jig to the corner of the room. A few minutes later, he was walking through the main portcullis, knapsack on his shoulders, his travelling hat firmly on his head and a long staff in his hand. He nodded to the guards as he strode out on the drawbridge.

'Travelling again so soon, good Master Gonzola?' inquired the captain of the guard solicitously.

'Aye, indeed,' replied the magician. 'There is never a dull moment in the king's diplomatic service.'

'What of your great steed? Do you not travel far?' the captain asked.

'Oh, I do indeed,' the seer answered blithely, 'but the king has asked me to go on foot so I might pass as an ordinary wayfarer. 'Tis not the time to bring attention to the royal emissaries.' Gonzola pointed his staff to the many campfires glowing from one end of the greensward to the other, the entire plain dotted with the tents of the gathering hosts of battle.

'Very wise,' agreed the soldier, 'if less comfortable and more wearying. None could miss the renowned magician on that singular beast. Good fortune in your travels, Master Gonzola, and a safe journey home.'

Gonzola waved cheerfully and stepped off the drawbridge on to the firm ground on the far side. He sauntered southward towards the enchanted forest, twirling his staff in the air and whistling lightly. The captain watched his tall figure recede, lose itself, to be picked up by one of the campfires as he passed. Slowly, the creaking and clanking chains drew the bridge up until the soldier had to look to one side to see the now tiny figure pass one of the last fires. Suddenly, he heard a terrible crash of wood and metal behind him and the shouts of the grooms. Crash! Boom! Then a scream. Before he could more than jump to safety, the thundering of hooves caught him up and he saw, from the corner of his eye, the sparks flying over the cobbles beside him.

Up went the terrible black beast, straight up the drawbridge and over the high end, soaring out into the air like a bird in flight. The captain ran to the side of the bridge, now halted in mid-lift, and looked out. Men were scattering in every direction as the huge animal leaped over one tent after the other, strewing the panicking soldiers into sprawling heaps. The horse headed straight towards the mountains in the west. Later, the captain had to swear to this before the king and that terrible woman of his and the statement had to be corroborated by his two guardsmen who had been cranking up the drawbridge when the horse broke loose.

When the magician reached the forest, he turned east and walked along its border for a while, still whistling a rather tuneless, monotonous air. When his keen ear caught the distant rumble of hoofbeats in the forest, he entered the wood and, when he was well into the trees, his whistle became sharper, louder and clearer. In less than two minutes, the mighty horse was under him and they galloped off through the night.

XXII

With Heart in Mouth
Rimbek takes his Leave

Rimbek sat uncomfortably and ill at ease at the very edge of the nesting shelf; Kneko, his bride, had gone off to have dinner with her mother and he had been left to watch the egg. It had grown quite a bit since the wedding and there were some highly suggestive rumours circulating about the fact that it was larger than all the rest, though Rimbek was the smallest of the four brothers. Even the twins, who had been hatched from one egg themselves, were bigger than he.

He closed his eyes and immediately he seemed fast asleep. No, that wasn't true – he pinched himself to make sure – but he was certainly having vivid dreams. He saw Gonzola's face clearly, smiling at him and beckoning him. The picture changed and he saw himself in a deep and secret spot in the bowels of the mountain, a spot he alone knew about. He was moving a heavy slab of Antertium 99 from the front of a concealed crypt. He reached in and extracted a small black box. The picture changed again. With the tool sack over his shoulders and the black box securely buttoned into his inside pocket, he was fitting the wooden pieces

257

to his uncoiled schlong, making ready for a long, spring-leaping journey.

'You are supposed to lie close to the egg and keep it warm, you ninny. What good do you think you're doing like that?'

His eyes popped open to see Kneko climbing up into the nest in an ungainly manner, weighed down by her huge meal. He was about to chide her for that when he remembered she was eating for two.

'Sorry, darling, I guess I just haven't got the knack yet,' he apologized.

'Stop off at mother's on your way to work, I'm sure there is enough food for you,' she said, wriggling herself into a more comfortable position. 'Oh, and don't forget to be back here on time to relieve me for my late snack.' She held up her downy face for his dutiful kiss and then concentrated her entire attention on the lovely brown egg.

Rimbek had not taken two dozen steps from his mother-in-law's kitchen when the sound of a multitude of running feet bore down on him. He stood there with the savoury pie, cheese, boiled eggs, buttered bread, cake and a small flask of mead neatly wrapped in a large kerchief and watched fifty dwarfs come racing round the bend ahead, barrelling straight towards him, his brother Dimbek in the lead.

'Hurry along,' they all shouted, 'the king has called us up for mobilization. All healthy males below two hundred. Pack up your things and come to the armoury. We'll be marching out before dusk.'

'Where . . . what . . . huh?' Rimbek could hardly gather his wits. He still felt halfway inside some strange form of sleep. Dimbek stopped for a moment to slap some sense into him.

'We have an alliance with the Dark King. He has gathered all his forces from as far as the Enderlands and we will march together to overthrow the Elves, once and for all. Hurry, I expect to see you in the armoury within the hour.' With that, Dimbek raced off after the receding footfalls which had already rounded the next bend in the tunnel.

Rimbek leaned against the smooth wall, wiping his forehead in stunned amazement. He put the kerchief down on the floor and picked it up again, shaking his head. Something . . . something . . . 'That's it!' he said aloud. Those strange, dream-like pictures he had seen in the nesting room. Gonzola had sent for him!

At least twenty times over the next two hours Rimbek wished he had been able to slip under the old magic mantle. All the way down to the crypt and back, every corner he rounded he ran smack into another group of cheering 'soldiers' who were strapping themselves into breast-plates or swinging swords and heavy maces or battle-axes round their heads with more enthusiasm than skill. Rimbek suddenly realized how conspicuous and suspect he looked in nothing but his normal waistcoat, with a sack of tools and a kerchief full of food in his hands. Hardly a proper military figure, he warned himself.

Coming round the last turning before the great eastern portals, he found a helmet, a breastplate and a small spear lying on the ground. Before he could wonder who dropped them he heard hundreds of thundering footfalls approaching from behind. Slipping into a niche in the wall, he donned the armour and helmet and hid his tools behind him. A few fearful thoughts shivered through his mind as the shouting and yelling mob drew closer; he shut his eyes and told himself to stop trembling.

The mass of bodies crowded tighter and tighter at the end of the tunnel, pressing up to the niche and flowing back. On the third wave, Rimbek slipped into the midst of the crowd unnoticed and started shouting as loudly and boldly as the rest. When the portals opened, all the dwarfs streamed out into the afternoon sunlight, sergeants, lieutenants and captains shouting for order and trying desperately to make a disciplined formation out of the exuberant chaos.

Moving slyly from group to group, Rimbek soon made his way to the edge of the forest. He slipped behind a tree as one of the sergeants began drilling the last group he had joined. When they started marching across the broad grassland, he made good his escape into the depths of the forest. A few minutes later, he was making mighty corkscrew spring-leaps through the trees, still wearing the armour, the spear sticking up through the top of his tool sack.

*

As Rimbek went bounding through the forest, far off in the Dark King's Realm, the emissary, Sordo, sat on his horse to one side of Barlocks and stole covert glances at the brilliant Glortina on the king's opposite side. The plateau on which they had reined in their mounts commanded an excellent view of the castle, plain and greensward below them, with Ungar's vale and the mountains behind them to the west.

Glortina sat her horse majestically in a fine suit of silver-plated armour the king had commissioned specially for her. Except for the long golden hair wafted about her by the breeze, she looked every inch a warrior. Barlocks had considerable scruples about her joining him in this venture, Sordo mused, but she would not be left behind. A woman's body, he thought, but there was something far from woman-like inside that head.

Barlocks stood up in his stirrups and signalled down to the commanders in the field. Horses began swinging in a long arc, a cavalry charge followed by yeomen on foot with long bows at the ready, and the pikemen bringing up the rear. Before Barlocks was firmly seated again to appraise the mock skirmish, Glortina was flying down the hill, her horse's mane and her own lustrous hair streaming in the wind. She was bent on tongue-lashing one of the barons for his uneven ranks and the disorder of the stragglers.

'She makes an impressive field commander, this bold and fiery queen of yours, sire,' Sordo observed.

'I am the supreme commander here,' barked the king angrily, 'and don't you forget it, you dwarf-lover!'

'Of course, your majesty, no one was questioning that,' apologized Sordo.

The dwarfs' magician scratched under his beard. This nettlesome monarch and the prickly dwarf king would clash disastrously, he feared. And when Schtoonk discovers there is a woman in the field? he asked himself. It would be no small feat to get them marching together as a coordinated force.

When the regal Glortina came galloping back up the hillside, Sordo's hand rested on the serpent's head and the ruby apple where his wide belt joined. A tingling went up through his arm and his temples ached with the battle of terrible forces which raged inside his head.

Kranz had assured the wily magician his plot could not fail. The destruction of Topar would in turn destroy Elvanhome, breaking the link with the Elvan forces here. Gone would be their great magical powers and they would fall before the armies of Schtoonk and Barlocks like weakened, confused children. But each time Sordo touched that belt of his, terrifying doubts arose. How about that woman? Was it reasonable that she should voluntarily give up her rightful place as the Elvan King's sister? For Barlocks? Sordo flicked a stealthy glance in their direction. There was a legend, some sort of legend buried deep in the annals of Elvan Lore. What was it again . . .?

XXIII

Glortan Prepares

()()()()()()()

The brilliant full moon appeared above the trees as Gonzola paced up and down Glortan's domed observatory, watching the Elvan craftsmen at their work. Rimbek, his hands clasped behind his back, followed faithfully at the magician's heels. Save for the magician, the dwarf and the half dozen Elves working diligently on a tall, sturdy tower, the entire area was deserted.

The tower rose up from the ground below, just touching the rim of the open observatory. Elvan workers stepped off the dome's ridge and climbed up and down the smooth surface, polishing and sealing the thick plates of lead and Antertium 99 which formed the tower's outer shell. A small platform atop the tower was exactly nine feet above the observatory dome when closed. In the light of the rising moon, it could be seen that the tower itself was precisely north of the domed tree house.

One of the Elves leaped lightly down to the observatory and approached the pacing magician.

'Shall we try our little friend out now?' he asked the magician politely.

'All right, Rimbek, hop up there and start practising,' Gonzola directed.

The Elf picked Rimbek up and tossed him to his

companion above. The second Elf reached up and opened a small door in the tower's smooth surface, popping the dwarf inside.

In a count of ten seconds, Rimbek went through the motions of opening a black box, setting it down in the centre of the compartment, throwing the door open and a rope out (which was attached to a rung at the back of the enclosure), sliding down the rope quickly with his eyes closed and falling to the floor, his face buried in his arms.

Gonzola made him go through the rehearsal fifteen times before he was satisfied that the timing was right. The first few times the Elves had to catch the dwarf's hurtling figure since the door, which automatically clanged shut, severed the rope as it did so. The last two attempts, Rimbek was within inches of the floor when the door snapped shut. While the dwarf was brushing his knees for the last time, Gonzola noticed the increasing glow on the eastern wall of the observatory.

Glortan appeared in the room carrying a large coffer in his hands. He walked to the dais where now only two thrones stood and placed the weighty container on the pedestal next to the brazier. His face was grim and drawn as he stepped back to contemplate it; he bowed his head for a minute or more, deep in thought. He turned and smiled wanly.

'Rimbek did his job well in the mountains,' he assured the magician. 'Now I have done the rest. Inside the coffer, in that little black box, rests the mightiest and most terrible speck in the universe. If anything goes wrong, that universe is doomed.'

There was an ominous silence in the great domed room. At a signal from the king, two of the Elves on the dome's ridge above lifted a ladder and placed the base on the floor of the chamber, the top resting against the tower just below the small open door.

The king reached down and rested his hands on the dwarf's shoulders. He told Rimbek they would have to leave him now, since he alone among them could withstand exposure to the speck of Tritertium 333. He had his instructions and the king hoped he had memorized them well. He was to take the black box up inside the tower with him and sit on it. When the final moment came, the inside of the tower would be glowing so brightly he might easily believe the moon had fallen through the platform. The king and Gonzola would reach his mind with a thought at the precise moment of action; he would hear the word: 'Now!' He would open the box, exit and slide down the rope as he had been instructed. The success of their entire scheme was now in his hands.

'Most important of all, little friend, you are not to open your eyes. If you but glance at what will be happening in this room, you will be turned to stone. There is nothing our powers can do to prevent that,' the king warned him.

Gonzola flexed his knees and embraced Rimbek warmly. One by one, the Elves on the rim above bounded down to the catwalks below and disappeared. When Glortan and Gonzola left, Rimbek found himself alone in the silent room, facing the coffer which waited for him with its deadly treasure.

*

Two hours later, Glortan and Gonzola were speeding towards the western entrance to the Sacred Glade. Astra, in a flood of tears, was helping Yana to ease Flondrix down from Themur's shoulder. A deep, ugly gash had been torn in the boy's hip. Glortan knelt next to Flondrix and placed his hand over the wound. His eye gauged the line of the arrow's flight and he knew that had it not been deflected, it would have hit the exact spot in an Elvan spine that would bring death — the centre of the Io-Chand.

Grim-faced, the king and the magician listened to the story, told almost simultaneously by the two from Elvanhome and Glortan's distraught daughter. Since they had told the boy who his mother and father were, he had been brooding. When news of the Dark King's encampment reached them, Flondrix had slipped away, the other three in hot pursuit. He had reached there seconds before them, running towards Barlocks and Glortina, shouting 'Mother!' 'Father!' He told them to put down their arms and seek peace. Barlocks, delirious, had rushed towards the boy, but Glortina grabbed an archer's bow and quiver; with blinding speed she had sent two arrows into the air, the first knocking the armour-clad king to the ground, the second grazing the boy's hip as Themur grabbed him, throwing him over one shoulder and invisibly fleeing the camp. As they ran, they could hear Glortina's enraged, animal shrieks, ordering soldiers to shoot them down; the poor soldiers, bewildered, looked frantically about for what their eyes could no longer see.

The long premonition of Glortan and Gonzola became a gruesome reality as the two looked into each other's eyes. Glortina must be the Fallen One the Elves had always known would appear one day.

When Glortan removed his hand, the wound had closed over and was healing with visible rapidity. They helped the dazed Flondrix to his feet and he limped about, finding each step easier than the last. Astra held him tightly to her then and begged him never to be so foolish again.

'Let us get Flondrix back to safety, your majesty,' Gonzola warned, 'for we have not heard the end of this yet. I warrant you, this will not be the last attempt on his life. This fell turn of events will make overwhelming demands on us all.' He pointed to the moon, already wending its inexorable way to the zenith.

*

In the Dark King's camp, not too many miles west of the Sacred Glade, Ungar stirred the large cauldron of steaming venison stew and watched the men file past the rough serving board with their mess bowls at the ready. Other women served them and responded to their coarse suggestions and innuendoes with snorts of mock disapproval. When one soldier ran up with the news about the queen and the strange Elf who had called her mother, it took Ungar only seconds to realize who the boy was and the significance of what had happened. She turned the ladle over to one of the other women and slipped into the shadows.

It was no trouble to find one of the camp women upended beneath the trees. Mounted on her, her skirts flung up over her head, was a drunken yeoman with stout buttocks heaving and pounding. Ignoring his happy grunts and wheezes, Ungar slipped the quiver of arrows from the low branch where they hung and lifted his long bow from the ground. A few minutes later she was well hidden to one side of the king's tent, waiting for the treacherous queen to appear, an arrow nocked on the bowstring.

One of the king's captains approached the tent at a run, panting heavily. The king and Sordo came out to see the distressed soldier fall to his knees. The queen was gone, he reported, she had taken the bow and arrows of one of his men and fled into the woods. When they had pursued her, she had shot the legs from under two of the men, threatening to leave them all on the ground.

Barlocks lost control and became hysterical. Sordo tried to calm him, reminding him that his men had to be mustered within the half hour for the march to the Sacred Glade. The Dwarf King was already on the march and it was vital that all their forces be gathered for the attack when the moon reached its zenith. Sordo called for his horse and took his leave, now in a desperate hurry to rejoin the dwarfs.

Ungar did not wait to hear the end of that exchange. She moved back through the shadows and was soon running down the path to the Sacred Glade with a lightness and speed incredible for a woman her size. The miles evaporated effortlessly behind her, as though nothing could tax the stamina toughened by years in the mountains.

So swiftly did she move that a figure sprawled across the path was behind her leaping feet before she could stop. Turning back, she found a tall Elf breathing his last, a long arrow sticking out of his back, near the base of his spine. The twigs and small branches scattered in the path told her he had been high in the trees when struck down. A long bow and a quiver of arrows had been tossed to one side of the path near him.

'Who are you?' a weak whisper asked her.

'I am Ungar,' she replied simply, kneeling, 'the foster mother of the boy the queen has wounded. She goes now to the Sacred Glade to kill — to kill — my son.'

'She took my bow and all but one of my arrows. That last one lies on the ground beneath me,' the Elf gasped painfully. 'Take it to the Elvan King and Gonzola and tell them how you found me. Say to them that Sylvor is stricken and will die. Say that the mother who would kill her son is the Fallen One. They must know quickly, before it is too late. Tell them her own Elvan power is returning . . .'

If there was something left unsaid, Ungar did not know. The last few sounds that came from the dying Elf were unlike any words she had ever heard before.

With careful reverence, she moved his light body to the side of the path and picked up the arrow. For some moments she stared at its barbed tip and then down at Sylvor, whose eyes had closed. Grim-faced, Ungar turned and raced towards the Sacred Glade, her heart pounding with dismay for the son she called Igorin.

*

Gonzola paced back and forth along the western border of the Sacred Glade, peering down the path towards the far distant clanging of Barlocks's army on the move. Abruptly, he spun about and faced south, listening for the equally distant sounds of the marching dwarfs. For at least the hundredth time that night he scanned the heavens, carefully marking the positions of the moon and the stars, his eyes quickly swivelling back to the path and the northern perimeters of the Glade.

At any moment now Topar's brightness would increase, doubling and trebling as the forces there built up to intercept the deadly destruction aimed at it by Kranz. Had Kranz discovered the fuel calculations had been falsely recircuited? he wondered. According to Kranz's meticulous planning, Topar would shatter across the sky mere minutes after the moon reached its zenith. Actually, the great rocket would be precisely halfway there, for ten whole seconds vulnerable to its own destruction by the counter-forces of Elvanlord. The Cosmos, as they knew it, rested on those ten vital seconds.

Glortina, unclothed and as close to her true Elvan self as she could get with the aid of Kranz's powers, saw the magician's troubled figure and slipped off silently through the screening trees. She circled the Glade and worked her way to a point behind the great tree house. She saw the tower and its platform and guessed immediately that Kranz was to arrive there, not in the west. He was already on his way; she bit her lip and thought about that. Daemon-Baalim was to have spirited him to the Sacred Glade, but had that flat-headed beast ever been on time for anything? Perhaps better this way, but what else had Glortan and that fool Gonzola tampered with? She could not penetrate the secret of the tower, but she did know Flondrix was here in the Sacred Glade, not out in the space vehicle as Kranz believed. Yes, and as Elvanlord believed too. If Elvanlord guessed otherwise . . . Suddenly she knew!

Selecting the perfect tree, Glortina went straight up the trunk like a weightless cat, Sylvor's bow and quiver slung over her naked shoulder. She halted at a point behind a straight, stout branch which overlooked the dome and the tower. Hugging the tree close to her, she bent every bit of her limited powers on the task of becoming invisible. The trance would be deep, so deep she would be unaware of what would be taking place. At the right moment, she would have but seconds to run to the end of the branch and send one arrow on a true course. Yes, she knew. There was but one way Glortan could convince Elvanlord that Flondrix and his precious Astra were really here. The message of Chandrala! would beam itself instantaneously from the observatory to Elvanhome. Flondrix must die before he entered the 'singing rings'. She would have but a few precious seconds to snap out of the trance and let fly the fatal arrow.

Gonzola did not move, but he knew the once imponderable balance in the enemy's favour was now a reality. Glortina was already loose in their midst. His shaggy head had begun turning slowly, homing in on the source of the disturbing vibrations, when he heard rapid footsteps coming towards him. He sped swiftly down the path to intercept them.

Leaning wearily against a tree, Ungar panted heavily, her heart pounding as though it would burst through her ribs. On Gonzola's open hand balanced Sylvor's Elvan arrow.

'Are you sure he said the Fallen One?' he whispered hoarsely in the big woman's ear, the words falling painfully from his lips. She nodded once.

The magician looked down at the slender, cleverly fashioned shaft and then his eyes moved up to the woman's stricken face. He read each nuance of pain and foreboding. It was not merely the long race through the forest which made her heart pound so. Once more he looked down at the arrow, hefting it in his hand; but what he weighed and balanced in his mind was something more momentous. Without a whimper of regret she would lay down her life that the boy might live. No doubt about that, he told himself. This is love. And only love can cleanse evil.

He told Ungar not to move until he returned; it would be fatal for her to set one foot inside the Sacred Glade. Again, her only answer was an obedient nod. Behind the unblinking eyes he perceived an ocean of grief.

Gonzola moved back to the fringe of the Glade, blending blackly within the shadows of the huge trees. Taking his first bearing on the closed observatory dome, his eye followed a line to the platform atop the tower. Measurements and equations moved through his mind with the speed of a computer. When every angle had been checked and cross-checked, his gaze rested at last on one stout branch, the one Glortina had selected. The limb jutted out towards the platform, stopping abruptly five feet to the rear and fifteen feet above it. The end of the broad branch would afford a full view of the interior of the observatory – as would the platform – the moment the dome was fully opened.

Slipping back through the trees, the magician's mind raced this way and that. She would never have taken this desperate risk if . . . if she had known just a bit sooner that Flondrix was here . . . if Kranz was already on his way and she could no longer warn him . . . if – if – if! The word rang through his mind like a stuttered oath.

When he arrived at Ungar's side, he reached into the inner depths of his cloak and withdrew a small silver pentacle suspended from a matching chain. He slipped it over her head and hung it round her sun-darkened neck. Warning her that she must not remove the pendant for as long as she remained in the Sacred Glade, he guided her silently to a tree which gave her cover and offered an unobstructed view of the platform and the overhanging branch.

He pointed to the branch and told her that sights would be seen and sounds would be heard that would drive most mortals insane. If she took her eye off that branch for one second . . . she nodded impatiently, her gaze fixed irrevocably on the broad bough above the platform. Sinking to one knee, she braced her body against the tree and nocked Sylvor's arrow on the bowstring. Yes, she remembered the precise spot where the arrow had entered Sylvor's body. Yes, she understood that her arrow must speed forth just before the other bowstring was fully drawn; not an eye blink before, not an eye blink later. And if she missed . . .

'I will not miss,' she hissed, 'is he not my child?'

Gonzola blended into the trees once more, circling towards the south. There was not an Elvan archer in sight; they were all moving silently through the tree tops before the two advancing armies.

'Sordo must arrive on time,' he muttered to himself, 'not too early, not too late.' Once more his mind was fully occupied with exhaustive calculations as Topar's swollen, blazing orb rivalled the moonglow spilling over the Sacred Glade.

XXIV

The Grim Battle
Is Joined

◍◍◍◍◍◍◍

Elvan lights sparkled in the trees, burning brighter and brighter by the second, the coruscating play running up and down the trunks and out across the branches until every leaf glowed with an intense iridescence. Tiny motes of the fire rolled across the white grass of the Sacred Glade, making the purple tops of the clover burn brilliantly. The entire Glade was ringed and filled with a light that seemed stronger than even the sun of midday could manage. The moon paled as it touched upon its zenith.

Glortan and Aureen sat upon their thrones in the centre of the Glade, the staunch army of Elvan archers fanning out in circles of hundreds upon hundreds, bows at the ready. The Elvan King and Queen kept their eyes fixed upon the platform atop the tower; they ignored the sounds of trumpets and shouts, the clamour of the armies of Schtoonk and Barlocks surrounding the clearing. These armies were blocked by a huge force field they could not pass; an invisible wall as impenetrable as steel. But they were also rooted to the ground by the awesome splendour unfolding before them.

A hush fell over the gathered hosts as the moon

entered its zenith. The great disc paled as Topar's light blazed more brightly. Suddenly the stillness was broken by a low moaning sound that sighed through the trees. The eerie noise mounted until it seemed all the winds of the world had been released at once. Men and dwarfs covered their ears as the baleful sound sent uncontrollable, morbid shivers through them. The tower began to glow, first a dull red tinge that heightened in the shrieking winds until it became orange, then yellow, bursting into a blinding white fire that crackled as it shook the tower, making it shudder violently.

Inside the tower, the incredible heat buffeted Rimbek unmercifully. He felt his coils jump and whiplash about his waist, creating a thump-madness greater than he had ever known. It became so unendurable, the barbed tip worked its way free of the golden screw in his navel; despite his own stern commands to himself, he lost control. Before he knew what was happening, his heel was on top of the tip, thumping madly as the heat from the black box under his bottom increased.

A crash so horrendous reverberated through the forest that the trees moaned in response, their trunks and limbs groaning and grinding, afflicted by a torture greater than they could bear. As the sound subsided, the plaintive cries of dwarfs and men tormented the air. Showering sparks over the dome and down on to the grass below, a large shimmering box of steel appeared over the platform of the tower. In the blink of an eyelid, it disintegrated to reveal a shadowy figure materializing in the quivering incandescence.

Hands on hips, an aura of blue flame surrounding his body, stood the sneering Kranz. In the middle of the emblem on his tunic, the great eye glowered ominously.

Glortan reached over and took the Elvan Queen's hand in his own. The light surrounding the two thrones became so bright even the Elves closest to them could see nothing but the fierce aura of fire. An evil mocking laugh was hurled from the platform, ringing through the trees and rebounding back across the Glade.

'You may start counting the seconds now, Glortan. Look up! Watch the end of Topar and Elvanhome. Witness the flight of your precious Ancient Ones to beyond the Unknown.'

As Kranz spoke, he held his hand aloft and pointed significantly towards the moon. Lowering his finger, he aimed it until the light of Topar seemed to rest brightly on his nail.

'Sordo, step forth and blend your will with mine. Daemon-Baalim, I summon you forth to freedom now. Sordo, release me!' he commanded.

On the south-western edge of the Glade, Sordo stepped through the invisible wall unscathed and raised his hand. Before he could open his mouth, Gonzola was at his side; he pressed Sordo's free hand forcibly over the serpent's head and the ruby apple on the tongue-tied magician's belt.

A deafening animal bellow broke from Kranz's lips. So great was the shattering howl of pain that men and dwarfs cowered on the ground, covering their heads with their arms to escape the hideous noise.

'Sordo,' the voice quivered in wrath, 'my finger points to Topar. Watch it and repent. In but a few moments, all who deny me will perish. Act now, or you are doomed with the rest.'

Gonzola's calm voice rose up from below the tower. In a few well-chosen words, he told Kranz how his plans had been foiled. It was Kranz who should watch, for now he would see his foul dream atomized across the skies as Elvanlord obliterated the great spacecraft.

Another dreadful howl smote the forest. 'You liar! You meddlesome old stooge! Your two beloved Elves are in that rocket and Elvanlord knows it well. You will never convince him otherwise.'

'He will be convinced. So will you. Right now.' Gonzola raised his hand.

As the great dome rolled back, from behind the Elvan ring of fire, Glortan's voice tolled across the Glade with the bright clean sound of a great bell.

'You watch and watch well, Kranz. You are about to see the last thing you will ever see. Watch, you fiend, I command it!'

Kranz's head swivelled to the illuminated interior of the observatory; once fixed there, he could not shift his gaze again.

Lying on the golden couch elevated on its dais, Flondrix held his hands high so Astra's slender arches fitted into each palm. His silver tip and the vermilion, crowning each magnificent, towering spire, blazed brightly in the light of Topar. The great star quivered and a wide corona surrounded it. Flondrix breathed deeply and dropped his hands. At that precise instant, the inner voices of Glortan and Gonzola sent the unspoken word 'NOW!' hurtling against the door of the tower.

As Astra plunged down, doubly impaled on the twin spires, Rimbek shot through the door and slid down the rope, burying his head in his arms as he hit the observatory floor. The door clanged to above him, yanking his rump upin to the air. The barbed tip of his schlong was caught fast, fusing itself with the near molten metal. He whimpered once, but never looked up. With all his might, he began forcing his bottom down.

The unspoken word 'NOW!' reached Glortina, electrifying her consciousness. She slipped round the tree trunk, holding every vestige of invisibility as long as she could. When she reached the end of the branch,

275

a deadly arrow already nocked on the bowstring, she saw Kranz frozen on his perch, hands level with his head, the fingers curled like claws. He seemed poised to leap down into the observatory to tear the lovers apart. He had looked, the fool had looked, she told herself. He had seen what no mortal eyes may witness. Petrifying as he stood, his colour was changing to a ghastly granite gray. It must be reversed!

Lips drawn back in a snarl of fury, Glortina's knuckles whitened as the bowstring reached her cheek, her whole form becoming fully visible. Just before the arrow left the bow, its fell tip aimed at Flondrix's spine, the long bow of Ungar twanged and that arrow found its mark, piercing Glortina's spine at the Io-Chand centre. Disbelief etched painfully across her face, she tottered, watching her own deflected arrow skim crazily to one side to enter the back of Kranz's neck. His mouth opened wide but no scream came.

Glortina plunged down to land on Kranz's pierced neck, her legs spread wide and her arms flung back, one last baleful cry trailing behind her. She impaled herself cruelly on the shaft of the arrow, the stiffened figure of Kranz rocking with the impact. Feeling the arrow's feathers thrust inside her, she struggled to pull back. Below, on the floor of the observatory, Rimbek made one final, mighty downward heave of his buttocks. His schlong snapped off, snaking away from his body like an elastic whip to circle Kranz's neck and Glortina's hips. The momentum of the flailing schlong tore the molten barbed tip free of the tower door, the two ends making one more whiplash before tying themselves into a bow at Kranz's throat.

And down came Astra, sinking swiftly in indescribable bliss, her breath held and every nerve vibrating, urging forth the last iota of purposeful strength in the two radiant bodies. Just before her senses and her inner being passed out into the gulf of the heavens beyond the beyond, she was certain at last that her beloved would enter the 'singing rings'. Elvanlord would know!

In the last instant before the granite suffused his neck and head, Kranz strained his eyes towards the sacred star of the Elves. Shedding a brilliant light across the sky, Topar vied with the moon. Scattered in space before the great star was an ever-widening stream of aching white light, eddying in thin ribbons across the heavens. In his last despairing moment, Kranz knew Gonzola had spoken the truth.

A dismal rumble rose up from the earth, rocking and shaking the tower until it teetered dizzily. Having lost his way twice, Daemon-Baalim raced towards his promised freedom, late even for that fateful appointment. Up through the platform, skewering each of Kranz's feet, a pair of horrible black horns appeared. The platform shuddered once more as a flat head clanged into the bottom of it. The compressed molten metal hissed, rising up through the platform to coat the silent figures above in a bronze-like carapace. Then all was still. No roar of betrayal or last moan issued from the Beast Beneath.

*

Gonzola, Yana and Themur stood below the tower and gazed up at the gruesome spectacle, a tinge of wearied sadness marring their victory. Preoccupied, almost as an afterthought, Yana balanced the amber globe in his hand and measured the distance to Kranz's open mouth. As his arm came back, Gonzola stayed the throw. There was nothing more to fear from Bumbree. Yana dropped the sphere on the ground and touched it with his toe.

The amber ball sparkled and glowed as cracks opened; the small prison finally shattered in the grass to release the tiny snake. Then with a puff of smoke and the stench of rotten eggs, Bumbree, in all her unthinkable ugliness, stood before them, her three great dugs heaving with malevolence. She spun on her great ham-like shanks and yelled when she saw the two figures glowing dully on top of the tower. When she saw the bronzed horns jutting up through Kranz's feet, a dreadful howl broke from her slobbering lips and she ran towards the ruddy tower.

'My darling, I'm here, I'm here!' she shouted. 'Daemon-Baalim, darling, come out, I give you all my powers, you are free. Come out and destroy them all!'

Bumbree reached out to touch the tower and a bolt of tremendous force struck her, knocking her ten feet back to land clumsily and unceremoniously on her fat, pimple-ridden bottom. She looked about her balefully, her uncomprehending face pouting and quivering in utter frustration. Gonzola snapped his fingers and pointed meaningfully towards the western fringe of the Glade. With a hurt and puzzled whine, Bumbree clambered to her feet and lumbered out of sight, her ungainly rump swaying awkwardly as she ran.

Pale Elvan fire flickered and surrounded the thrones in the centre of the Glade when Gonzola joined Yana and Themur there. In the quiet sky above, the out-bound trails of light trembled and altered course slightly. For a very few seconds, the remnants of Kranz's shattered power formed into mystical characters of High Elvish. Five pairs of knowing eyes focused on the brief, significant display. When the phenomenon disappeared, the four Elves and the magician looked to one another, sharing the full meaning in their inter-linked thoughts.

The message had read: HAIL FLONDRIX ... AND THE NEW AGE OF MAN.

XXV

Serenity Reigns
in the
Sacred Glade

Scattered in wailing dis-
order, ranks broken and all discipline lost, the terrified
hosts of men and dwarfs fled through the trees,
anxious to put as much distance between the Glade
and themselves as possible: men pounding to be free
of the enchanted forest, dwarfs spring-leaping madly to
gain the sanctuary of the White Mountains.

Gradually, the clamour diminished, leaving a sooth-
ing silence in the mystical clearing. As the moon
dropped towards the western rim of trees, only the
keenest ear would detect the susurrus as the lightest of
pre-dawn breezes played with the leaves high above.

Inside the great tree house, under the closed dome,
Astra and Flondrix sat cross-legged on the dais and
gazed up at the two thrones. With eyes closed, Glortan
and Aureen were emptying their hearts of sadness as
the last moment approached. The two children smiled
dutifully, trying desperately to hide their tears and
save the king and queen the burden of their grief.

Flondrix had listened attentively as Glortan told him
the import of the New Age of Man. As Flondrix

Elvanman, his would be the last reign of guardianship here. He would make peace with Barlocks and succeed him as King of Men with Astra at his side. The evolution of the Elves was complete, the great evolution of man begun. At dawn or soon after, when the fell tower had lost the last of its rufescence and had turned an ashen grey, the Elves would carry it far off to the Cave of the Silent Stones. Therein it would be left and sealed, in a place known only to their people. In the New Age of Man, there would be no need of such things.

A faint tinkling sound echoed through the room as Yana and Themur appeared, one on each side of the thrones. Lustrous Elvan lights played about the foot of the regal seats, mounting up the four bodies, irradiating them with breath-taking beauty. Astra gasped and Flondrix opened his mouth, about to call out, to beg that they would tell him about his mother before they left. Without opening her eyes or moving her lips, Aureen told him their dear and most honoured friend, Gonzola, would do all that when they were gone. From the mind of Glortan, he received the message that he was to listen well to all the old sage had to say; he would now be Flondrix's true and faithful teacher.

Not a cry, not a sound of farewell was heard as Themur reached out to take Aureen's hand, Yana taking the king's. The king and queen joined hands and the great dome rolled back. As the Elvan lights glowed and burned more brightly, the four bodies dimmed, fading from view. When the thrones were dark and empty, a magnificent chord of music resounded across the sky.

Fighting his own tears in the carved chair covered in warm, comforting gossamer material, Gonzola felt the dwarf's body tremble against his knee. Rimbek was crying unashamedly, his face buried in the magician's cloak. With paternal tenderness, he patted the small head.

'Children,' he called out hoarsely, 'you may sit upon the thrones now. You might as well start getting used to them.'

Astra and Flondrix rose slowly and walked towards the magician. They joined hands and shared a brief glance.

'We would prefer a walk in the Sacred Glade now,' Astra announced. 'Perhaps we can visualize them on the Path to Elvanhome.'

''Twill only make your sadness grow,' Gonzola advised, 'but a walk would benefit us all.' He rose and helped Rimbek to his feet. Astra reached down and took one of the dwarf's hands, helping him manoeuvre the delicate vine catwalks.

Following behind, Gonzola told Flondrix the pre-ordained legend of the Fallen One. When he had finished, he opined that once again, in their Infinite Wisdom, the Ancient Ones had timed it so. They had all survived an ordeal too dreadful to imagine and now, as the Elvan son of the Fallen One and the king of men, Flondrix would unite the best of each world and guide man through a difficult period of evolution. When Gonzola reached the part concerning Glortina's end, Flondrix wept openly. Gently, the magician reminded him about the two arrows aimed at him — and how each had come within a hair's breadth of taking his life.

As they neared the western path, Astra winked down at the dwarf and held a warning finger to her lips. Before them a large misshapen figure knelt on the ground, crying uncontrollably into the trunk of a tree. They stopped and waited for the magician and Flondrix. Flondrix placed a hand on the magician's shoulder.

'Who saved my life?' he asked, his voice breaking.

Before the magician could answer, they were all stunned to see a dishevelled man leap out of the shadows near the path, brandishing a huge sword over his head.

'You! It *is* you, you foul piece of sheep dung! You killed her, you shot that cursed arrow. One of my soldiers saw you do it. Now die!'

Flondrix hurtled forward like a streak of lightning. As he struck the man's back, he knew who the wretched, sobbing creature on the ground was. His heart nearly snapped in his chest. How little thought he had ever given to the only *real* mother he had ever known!

Man and boy tumbled over and over in the grass, the sword scything off into the underbrush.

'My liege, would you murder your own son too?' Gonzola called out.

The king peered closely in the fading light of the moon. It was! It was his lost son!

'No, not you, my son,' he groaned, embracing Flondrix. 'That wretch killed your mother. Let me get my hands . . .'

Flondrix heaved the king to his feet and Gonzola held the monarch's arms, pinning him to his own chest. Covering the distance in one bound, Flondrix lifted the weeping woman to her feet and threw his arms about her. They stood there for a long while, hugging and kissing each other. Gonzola released Barlocks and he staggered a pace forward, his mouth hanging open in amazement. With an arm round her shoulders, Flondrix led Ungar back to the Dark King.

'You were mistaken, father,' the boy stated simply. '*This* is my mother, the only real mother I have ever known. And you would have slain her for saving my life.'

Bewildered, the king looked from one to the other. Flondrix and Astra linked arms with Ungar and strode back to the tree house. When the king's puzzled eyes sought Gonzola's, the old magician gave Barlocks a severe lecture, one that had been coming to him for seventeen years. When the lecture was over, the Dark King buried his head on the magician's shoulder and wept like a child. He did not raise his head until he heard Flondrix call out: 'Father!'

Barlocks blinked his eyes and his jaw dropped. He did not recognize the stunning woman who stood between Flondrix and Astra. There was something familiar about her, it was true; she was not all that young, but from head to foot she exuded a tremendous charm and warmth. Her body was clad in a golden dress and she wore small golden slippers on her feet. Slim, yet extremely robust and strong-looking, her hair flowed over her shoulders and brilliant stones sparkled in it. Most important of all, her mouth was full and inviting as she laughed at his bewilderment. From her eyes shone the most intense good humour and genuine friendliness he had ever seen.

'Who — who is this?' he stammered at last.

'Well, my lord,' said Flondrix mischievously, 'since this is my mother and you are my father, I think you must have been married to the wrong woman, don't you?'

'King Barlocks,' Astra announced sweetly, 'this is Ungar Elvangift, my mother-in-law. If you ask her nicely, I am sure she would accept your proposal. It is within our power to bind you together. Well . . . what say you?'

The king stood rooted to the ground, quite speechless. Recovering finally, he bowed and held out his hand. Ungar took it and moved lightly to him, to be swept up in his arms with a good-natured smile. Gone was the old brooding solemnity, all her dour looks. Her face shone brightly as he kissed her over and over. Her laughter tinkled gaily through the Sacred Glade.

'There are rooms ready for everyone,' Astra told them with an unmistakable gleam in her eye. 'Our people will make you welcome and see to all your needs.'

'Do you have a very quiet one for our young friend here?' Gonzola asked, placing an affectionate hand on Rimbek's shoulder. 'He has to spend a day or two in deep meditation until he regrows his — well, you know what I mean . . .'

'I'm in no hurry,' Rimbek protested. 'All in good time, don't rush me.'

'How will you get back to the White Mountains?' Gonzola demanded, smiling a bit ruefully. Just as he suspected, young Rimbek was becoming very Elvish in his outlook.

'I can walk. Why do you want to get rid of me so soon?' The dwarf looked so hurt and miserable Astra knelt down and put her arms around him.

'You can stay as long as you want. You are our friend and you are always welcome among us. Remember that, dear Rimbek,' she told him. Astra stood up, gave Gonzola a stern glance and skipped over to Flondrix's side. Taking his hand in hers, she looked meaningfully towards the forest.

'And where are you two going?' asked Gonzola, raising his eyebrows like a disapproving father.

'Oh, just off for a romp, the dawn will soon be here,' she answered lightly.

Without another word, the children walked a few paces away from the group. As the four others watched them go, Astra turned into a radiant doe and raced for the wood. Flondrix, as a wild woodland faun, was bounding off in hot pursuit, his magnificent endowment plunging before him.

'I do not think that is very seemly,' said the shocked Ungar. 'My son, for all the world, going off like a mad goat.'

'That's my boy,' said Barlocks, taking her hand and leading her towards the great tree house.

Rimbek turned to look up at the magician, on the point of asking a question, when a thunderous crash sounded in the trees to the west. A moment later, Bumbree hurtled into the clearing, two flaming branches in her hands. With a menacing growl, she waved the huge brands at Gonzola.

'In the sacred name of Daemon-Baalim, I bring the dreaded curse of the witches down upon you, foul magician, and consign you to the Ultimate Horror!' With these words, she crossed the branches and charged at Gonzola.

The old magician laughed, shaking his head. Ignoring the advancing witch, he leaned over and told Rimbek to spit as hard as he could in the direction of the threatening blaze. The little dwarf leaned back, rolled his tongue in his mouth and blasted an immense fan of spittle towards the advancing flames. Bumbree came to a halt, looking dismally at the sizzling branches. The fire had gone out instantly.

'Go back to your stinking cottage, Bumbree, it is all over. The Beast Beneath is no more and that is the end of your salacious, mixed-up magic. Begone, before I lose my patience and turn my little friend loose on you.' Gonzola snapped his fingers and Bumbree dropped the smoking pieces of wood. Bawling like a chastened child, she stumbled away, shambling grotesquely towards the sanctuary of the forest.

'Have pity on her,' whispered Rimbek, the words out of his mouth before he was aware of the thought behind them.

With a careless wave of his hand, the magician

responded to the dwarf's compassionate plea. The Bumbree they knew disappeared and in her place stood a rather buxom and voluptuous woman with but two breasts, albeit enormous ones. Well-formed, with flaxen hair and an almost pretty face, Bumbree looked down in surprise. She turned once or twice, trying to admire herself, preening and simpering all the time. With a coy giggle, she pranced off into the forest, humming to herself in a very pleased manner.

Awe-struck, Rimbek looked up at the magician. 'What are you going to do now?' he asked.

'Hmmmmn,' rumbled Gonzola reflectively. 'I think I shall take a cold plunge in the river, go for a long walk and then . . . come back and have another cold plunge.'

'Chooch! I think I'll join you,' said the dwarf.